CHRISTMAS WITH THE PRINCE

BY
MICHELLE CELMER

AND

RESERVED FOR THE TYCOON

BY
CHARLENE SANDS

MILLS &
BOON

"Liv," he called softly, but she didn't budge.

Apparently she was more tired than she'd realized. He found a spare blanket in the closet, and walked back to the bed to cover her. For reasons he couldn't begin to understand, he felt compelled to just look at her.

She's not your type, he reminded himself.

If he was going to be honest with himself, his "type" had plenty to offer physically, but intellectually, he was usually left feeling bored and unfulfilled. Maybe it was time for a change of pace.

Seducing a woman like Liv might be just what he needed to spice things up.

CHRISTMAS WITH THE PRINCE

BY

MICHELLE CELMER

All the characters in this book have no existence outside the imagination of the author, and have no relation whatsoever to anyone bearing the same name or names. They are not even distantly inspired by any individual known or unknown to the author, and all the incidents are pure invention.

Published in Great Britain 2010
Harlequin Mills & Boon Limited,
Eton House, 18-24 Paradise Road, Richmond, Surrey TW9 1SR

© Michelle Celmer 2009

ISBN: 978 0 263 88189 9

51-1210

Harlequin Mills & Boon policy is to use papers that are natural, renewable and recyclable products and made from wood grown in sustainable forests. The logging and manufacturing processes conform to the legal environmental regulations of the country of origin.

Printed and bound in Spain
by Litografía Rosés S.A., Barcelona

Bestselling author **Michelle Celmer** lives in southeastern Michigan with her husband, their three children, two dogs and two cats. When she's not writing or busy being a mom, you can find her in the garden or curled up with a romance novel. And if you twist her arm real hard you can usually persuade her into a day of power shopping. Michelle loves to hear from readers. Visit her website at www.michellecelmer.com, or write her at PO Box 300, Clawson, MI 48017, USA.

To my mom,
Who has been not only my teacher, my confidante,
and my most dedicated fan, but one of my best friends.
Love you!

Dear Reader,

Welcome to the next installment of my ROYAL SEDUCTIONS series. I can hardly believe we're already on book six, the story of Prince Aaron Felix Gastel Alexander and genetic botanist Olivia Montgomery. A royal heir and an orphan abandoned at the age of three.

Can you say, opposites attract?

These two were definitely a handful! How do you take two independent, headstrong people and make them bend to your creative will? The truth is, you don't. As a writer, all you can really do is sit back and let them lead you on their journey. And with Aaron and Liv, there was never a dull moment. Especially when these two very different people suddenly realized maybe they weren't so different after all. And when all is said and done, family isn't about bloodlines and pedigrees and fitting in, but instead the people you hold most dear in your heart.

Don't forget to look for the next book in the ROYAL SEDUCTIONS series, the story of Princess Louisa and millionaire mogul Garrett Sutherland.

Best,

Michelle

One

Olivia Montgomery was attractive for a scientist.

Attractive in a brainy, geeky sort of way. From a distance, at least. And not at all what Prince Aaron had expected.

He watched her gaze up at the castle from his office window, a look of awe on her heart-shaped face, her bow mouth formed into a perfect *O* beneath eyes as large as dinner plates.

He supposed it wasn't every day that a woman was asked to uproot her entire life, stay at a royal castle for an indeterminable period and use her vast knowledge to save an entire country from potential absolute financial devastation.

Of course, from what he'd read of their new guest, her life to date had been anything but typical. Most kids didn't graduate from high school at fifteen, receive their Ph.D. at twenty-two and earn a reputation as a pioneer in the field of botanical genetics at twenty-four. He would swear she didn't look a day over eighteen, due in part to the long, blondish-brown hair she wore pulled back in a ponytail and the backpack she carried slung over one shoulder.

He watched as Derek, his personal assistant, led her into the castle, then he took a seat at his desk to wait for them, feeling uncharacteristically anxious. He had been assured that in the field of genetic botany, she was the best. Meaning she could very well be their last hope.

Specialist after specialist had been unable to diagnose or effectively treat the blight plaguing their crops. A disease that had begun in the east fields, and spread to affect not only a good portion of the royal family's land, but had recently been reported in surrounding farms, as well. Unchecked, the effects could be financially devastating to their agriculturally based economy.

His family—hell, the entire country—was counting on him to find a way to fix it.

Talk about pressure. He used to believe that his older brother, Christian, the crown prince, had it rough, carrying the burden of one day taking over as ruler, and the responsibility of marrying and producing a royal heir. But to Aaron's surprise, after a slightly rocky start, Chris seemed to be embracing his new title as husband.

For Aaron, the thought of tying himself down to one woman for the rest of his life gave him cold chills. Not that he didn't love women. He just loved lots of different women. And when the novelty of one wore thin, he liked having the option of moving on to something new. Although, now that Chris was blissfully married off, their mother, the queen, had taken an active and unsettling interest in Aaron's love life. He never knew there were so many eligible young women with royal blood, and his mother seemed hell-bent on setting him up with every single one of them.

She would figure out eventually that all the meddling in the world wouldn't bring him any closer to the altar. At least, he hoped she would. She could instead focus on marrying off his twin sisters, Anne and Louisa.

Several minutes passed before there was a rap at Aaron's office door. Undoubtedly Derek had been explaining policy for meeting members of the royal family to their guest. What she should and shouldn't do or say. It could be a bit overwhelming. Especially for someone who had never been in the presence of royalty before.

"Come in," he called.

The door opened and Derek appeared, followed

closely by Miss Montgomery. Aaron rose from his chair to greet her, noticing right away her height. He was just over six feet tall, and in flat-heeled, conservative loafers she stood nearly eye level. It was difficult to see her figure under the loose khaki pants and baggy, cable-knit sweater, although she gave the impression of being quite slim. *Too* slim, even. All sharp and angular.

Missing was the lab coat, pocket protector and cola-bottle glasses one might expect from a scientist. She wore no makeup or jewelry, and was for all accounts quite plain, yet she was undeniably female. Attractive in a simple way. Cute and girlish. Although at twenty-five, she was definitely a woman.

"Your Highness," Derek said, "May I introduce Miss Olivia Montgomery, of the United States." He turned to Miss Montgomery. "Miss Montgomery, may I present Prince Aaron Felix Gastel Alexander of Thomas Isle."

Miss Montgomery stuck her hand out to shake his, then, realizing her error, snatched it back and dipped into an awkward, slightly wobbly curtsy instead, her cheeks coloring an enchanting shade of pink. "It's an honor to be here, sir—I mean, Your Highness."

Her voice was softer than he'd expected. Low and breathy, and dare he say a little sexy. He'd always found an American accent undeniably appealing.

"The honor is mine," he said, reaching out for a shake. She hesitated a second, then accepted his hand. Her hands were slender and fine-boned, with long fingers that wrapped around his with a surprisingly firm grip. Her skin was warm and soft, her nails short but neatly filed.

She gazed at him with eyes an intriguing shade—not quite brown, and not quite green—and so large and inquisitive they seemed to take up half her face. Everything about her was a little overexaggerated and…unexpected.

But she couldn't be any less his type. He preferred his women small and soft in all the right places, and the more beautiful the better. Not particularly smart, either, because frankly, he wasn't in it for the conversation. The fewer brains, the less likely he was to become attached. As long as she could navigate a golf course or squash court, or rock a pair of cross-country skis. Sailing experience was a plus, as well, and if she could climb a rock wall, he would be in sheer heaven.

Somehow he didn't see Miss Montgomery as the athletic type.

"I'll be in my office if you need me, sir," Derek told him, then slipped out of the room, closing the door behind him. As it snapped shut, he could swear he saw Miss Montgomery flinch.

He gestured to the chair opposite his desk. "Miss Montgomery, make yourself comfortable."

She set her backpack on the floor beside her and sat awkwardly on the very edge of the cushion. She folded her hands in her lap, then unfolded them. Then she tucked them around the sides of her thighs and under her legs. She looked very *un*comfortable.

"I apologize for being so late," she said.

He perched on the corner of his desk. "I hear you hit some bad weather on the way over."

She nodded. "It was a bumpy flight. And I'm not real crazy about flying to begin with. In fact, I might look into taking a ship home."

"Can I offer you a drink, Miss Montgomery?"

"No, thank you. And please, call me Liv. Everyone does."

"All right, Liv. And because we'll be spending quite some time together, you should call me Aaron."

She hesitated, then asked, "Is that...allowed?"

He grinned. "I assure you, it's perfectly acceptable."

She nodded, her head a little wobbly on the end of a very long and slender neck. She had the kind of throat made for stroking and nibbling. But somehow he didn't see her as the nibbling type. She had shy and repressed written all over her. No doubt, he could teach her a thing or two. Not that he intended to. Or even possessed the desire.

Well, maybe just a little, but purely out of curiosity.

"My family apologizes that they couldn't be here to greet you," he told her. "They're in England to see my father's cardiologist. They'll be back Friday."

"I look forward to meeting them," she said, although she sounded more wary than enthusiastic.

She had no reason to be apprehensive. In the history of his father's reign as king, her visit might very well be the most anticipated and appreciated. Not that she was offering her services for free. They had agreed to make a handsome donation to fund her research. Personally she hadn't asked for anything more than room and board. No special amenities, or even a personal maid to tend to her care.

"I'm told that you looked at the disease samples we sent you," he said.

She nodded, not so wobbly this time. "I did. As well as the data from the other specialists."

"And what conclusion have you drawn?"

"You have yourself a very unusual, very resistant strain of disease that I've never seen before. And trust me when I say I've pretty much seen them all."

"Your references are quite impressive. I've been assured that if anyone can diagnose the problem, it's you."

"There is no *if*." She looked him directly in the eye and said firmly, "It's simply a matter of *when*."

Her confidence, and the forceful tone with which she spoke, nearly knocked him backward.

Well, he hadn't seen that coming. It was almost as though someone flipped a switch inside of her and a completely different woman emerged. She sat a little straighter and her voice sounded stronger. Just like that, he gained an entirely new level of respect for her.

"Have you thought about my suggestion to stop all agricultural exports?" she asked.

That was *all* he'd been thinking about. "Even the unaffected crops?"

"I'm afraid so."

"Is that really necessary?"

"For all we know, it could be lying dormant in the soil of areas that *appear* unaffected. And until we know what this thing is, we don't want it to get off the island."

He knew she was right, but the financial repercussions would sting. "That means we have only until the next season, less than five months, to identify the disease and find an environmentally friendly cure."

Environmentally friendly so that they could maintain their reputation as a totally organic, green island. Millions had been spent to radically alter the way every farmer grew his crops. It was what set them apart from other distributors and made them a valuable commodity.

"Can it be done in that time frame?" he asked.

"The truth is, I don't know. These things can take time."

It wasn't what he wanted to hear, but he appreciated her honesty. He'd wanted her to fly in, have the problem solved in a week or two, then be on her way, making him look like a hero in not only his family, but also his country's eyes.

So much for that delusion of grandeur.

"Once I get set up in the lab and have a few days to study the rest of the data, I may be able to give you some sort of time frame," she said.

"We have a student from the university on standby, should you need an assistant."

"I'll need someone to take samples, but in the lab I prefer to work alone. You have all the equipment I need?"

"Everything on your list." He rose to his feet. "I can show you to your room and give you time to settle in."

She stood, as well, smoothing the front of her slacks with her palms. He couldn't help wondering what she was hiding behind that bulky sweater. Were those breasts he saw? And hips? Maybe she wasn't as sharp and angular as he'd first thought.

"If you don't mind," she said, "I'd rather get right to work."

He gestured to the door. "Of course. I'll take you right to the lab."

She certainly didn't waste any time, did she? And he was relieved to know that she seemed determined to help.

The sooner they cured this blight, the sooner they could all breathe easy again.

Two

Liv followed her host through the castle, heart thumping like mad, praying she didn't do something stupid like trip over her own feet and fall flat on her face.

Prince Aaron was, by far, the most beautiful man she had ever laid eyes on. His hair so dark and soft-looking, his eyes a striking, mesmerizing shade of green, his full lips always turned up in a sexy smile.

He had the deep and smoky voice of a radio DJ and a body to die for. A muscular backside under dark tailored slacks. Wide shoulders and bulging pecs encased in midnight-blue cashmere. As she followed him through the castle she felt hypnotized by the fluid grace with which he moved.

He was…perfect. An eleven on a scale of one to

ten. And the antithesis of the scientists and geeks she was used to keeping company with. Like William, her fiancé—or at least he would be her fiancé if she decided to accept the proposal of marriage he had stunned her with just last night in the lab.

Fifteen years her senior and her mentor since college, Will wasn't especially handsome, and he was more studious than sexy, but he was kind and sweet and generous. The truth was, his proposal had come so far out of left field that it had nearly given her whiplash. They had never so much as kissed, other than a friendly peck on the cheek on holidays or special occasions. But she respected him immensely and loved him as a friend. So she had promised to give his proposal serious thought while she was away. Even though, when he'd kissed her goodbye at the airport—a real kiss with lips and tongue—she hadn't exactly seen fireworks. But sexual attraction was overrated and fleeting at best. They had respect and a deep sense of friendship.

Although she couldn't help wondering if she would be settling.

Yeah, right. Like she had a mob of other men pounding down her door. She couldn't even recall the last time she'd been on a date. And sex, well, it had been so long she wasn't sure she even remembered how. Not that it had been smoking hot anyhow. The one man she'd slept with in college had been a budding nuclear physicist, and more concerned with mathematical equations than figuring out sexual complexities. She bet Prince Aaron knew his way around a woman's body.

Right, Liv, and I suppose the prince is going to show you.

The thought was so ridiculous she nearly laughed out loud. What would a gorgeous, sexy prince see in a nerdy, totally *unsexy* woman like her?

"So, what do you think of our island?" Aaron asked as they descended the stairs together.

"What I've seen of it is beautiful. And the castle isn't at all what I expected."

"What did you expect?"

"Honestly, I thought it would be kind of dark and dank." In reality, it was light and airy and beautifully decorated. And so enormous! A person could get hopelessly lost wandering the long, carpeted halls. She could hardly believe she would be spending weeks, maybe even months, there. "I expected stone walls and suits of armor in the halls."

The prince chuckled, a deep, throaty sound. "We're a bit more modern than that. You'll find the guest rooms have all the amenities and distinction you would expect from a five-star hotel."

Not that she would know the difference, seeing as how she'd never been in anything more luxurious than a Days Inn.

"Although…" He paused and looked over at her. "The only feasible place for the lab, short of building a new facility on the grounds, was the basement."

She shrugged. It wouldn't be the first time she'd worked in a basement lab. "That's fine with me."

"It used to be a dungeon."

Her interest piqued. "Seriously?"

He nodded. "Very dark and dank at one time, complete with chains on the wall and torture devices."

She gazed at him skeptically. "You're joking, right?"

"Completely serious. It's been updated since then of course. We use it for food and dry storage, and the wine cellar. The laundry facilities are down there, as well. I think you'll be impressed with the lab. Not dark or dank at all."

Because the majority of her time would be spent staring in a microscope or at a computer screen, what the lab looked like didn't matter all that much to her. As long as it was functional.

He led her through an enormous kitchen bustling with activity and rich with the scents of fresh baked bread and scintillating spices. Her stomach rumbled and she tried to recall the last time she'd eaten. She'd been way too nervous to eat the meal offered on the plane.

There would be time for food later.

Aaron stopped in front of a large wood door that she assumed led to the basement. "There's a separate employee entrance that the laundry staff use. It leads outside, to the back of the castle. But as a guest, you'll use the family entrance."

"Okay."

He reached for the handle but didn't open the door. "There is one thing I should probably warn you about."

Warn her? That didn't sound good. "Yes?"

"As I said, the basement has been updated."

"But…?"

"It did used to be a dungeon."

She wasn't getting his point. "Okay."

"A lot of people died down there."

Was she going to trip over bodies on her way to the lab or something? "Recently?"

He laughed. "No, of course not."

Then she wasn't seeing the problem. "So…?"

"That bothers some people. And the staff is convinced it's haunted."

Liv looked at him as though he'd gone completely off his rocker.

"I take it you don't believe in ghosts," Aaron said.

"The existence of spirits, or an afterlife, have never been proven scientifically."

He should have expected as much from a scientist. "Well, then, I guess you have nothing to fear."

"Do you?" she asked.

"Believe in ghosts?" Truthfully, he'd never felt so much as a cold draft down there, but people had sworn to hearing disembodied voices and seeing ghostly emanations. There were some members of the staff who refused to even set foot on the stairs. Also there was an unusually high turnover rate among the laundry workers. But he was convinced that it was more likely overactive imaginations than anything otherworldly. "I guess you could say I try to keep an open mind."

He opened the door and gestured her down. The stairwell was narrow and steep, the wood steps creaky under their feet as they descended.

"It is a little spooky," she admitted.

At the bottom was a series of passageways that led to several different wings. The walls down here were still fashioned out of stone and mortar, although well lit, ventilated and clean.

"Storage and the wine cellar are that way," he said, pointing to the passages on the left. "Laundry is straight ahead down the center passage, and the lab is this way."

He led her to the right, around a corner to a shiny metal door with a thick glass window that to him looked completely out of place with its surroundings. He punched in his security code to unlock it, pulled it open and hit the light switch. The instant the lights flickered on he heard a soft gasp behind him, and turned to see Liv looking in wide-eyed awe at all the equipment they'd gotten on loan from various facilities on the island and mainland. The way one might view priceless art. Or a natural disaster.

She brushed past him into the room. "This is perfect," she said in that soft, breathy voice, running her hands along pieces of equipment whose purpose he couldn't begin to imagine. Slow and tender, as if she were stroking a lover's flesh.

Damn. He could get turned on watching her do that, imagining those hands roaming over him.

If she were his type at all, which she wasn't. Besides, he wasn't lacking for female companionship.

"It's small," he said.

"No, it's perfect." She turned to him and smiled, a dreamy look on her face. "I wish my lab back home were this complete."

He was surprised that it wasn't. "I was under the impression that you were doing some groundbreaking research."

"Yes, but funding is an issue no matter what kind of work you're doing. Especially when you're an independent, like me."

"There must be someone willing to fund your research."

"Many, but there's *way* too much bureaucracy in the private sector. I prefer to do things my way."

"Then our donation should go far."

She nodded eagerly. "The truth is, a few more weeks and I might have been homeless. You called in the nick of time."

She crossed the room to the metal shipping containers that had preceded her arrival by several days. "I see my things made it safely."

"Do you need help unpacking?"

She vigorously shook her head. "There are sensitive materials and equipment in here. I'd rather do it myself."

That seemed like an awful lot of work for one person. "The offer for the assistant is still good. I can have someone here Friday morning."

She looked at her watch, her face scrunching with confusion. "And what's today? The time change from the U.S. has me totally screwed up."

"It's Tuesday. Five o'clock."

"P.M.?"

"Yes. In fact, dinner is at seven."

She nodded, but still looked slightly confused.

"Out of curiosity, when was the last time you slept?"

She scrunched her face again, studied her watch for a second, then shrugged and said, "I'm not sure. Twenty hours at least. Probably more."

"You must be exhausted."

"I'm used to it. I keep long hours in the lab."

Twenty hours was an awfully long time, even for a workaholic, and he'd traveled often enough to know what jet lag could do to a person. Especially someone unaccustomed to long plane trips. "Maybe before you tackle unpacking the lab you should at least take a nap."

"I'm fine, really. Although, I guess I wouldn't mind a quick change of clothes."

"Why don't I show you to your room."

She looked longingly at all of the shiny new equipment, then nodded and said, "All right."

He switched off the lights and shut the door, hearing it lock automatically behind him.

"Will I get my own code?" she asked.

"Of course. You'll have full access to whatever and wherever you need."

He led Liv back through the kitchen and up the stairs to the third floor, to the guest rooms. She looked a bit lost when they finally reached her door.

"The castle is so big and confusing," she said.

"It's not so bad once you learn your way around."

"I don't exactly have a great sense of direction. Don't be surprised if you find me aimlessly wandering the halls."

"I'll have Derek print you up a map." He opened her door and gestured her in.

"It's beautiful," she said in that soft, breathy voice. "So pretty."

Far too feminine and fluffy for his taste, with its flowered walls and frilly drapes, but their female guests seemed to appreciate it. Although he never would have pegged Liv as the girly-girl type. She was just too…analytical. Too practical. On the surface anyhow.

"The bathroom and closet are that way," he said, gesturing to the door across the room. But Liv's attention was on the bed.

"It looks so comfortable." She crossed the room to it and ran one hand over the flowered duvet. "So soft."

She was a tactile sort of woman. Always stroking

and touching things. And he couldn't help but wonder how those hands would feel touching him.

"Why don't you take it for a spin," he said. "The lab can wait."

"Oh, I shouldn't," she protested, but she was already kicking off her shoes and crawling on top of the covers. She settled back against the pillows and sighed blissfully. Her eyes slipped closed. "Oh, this is heavenly."

He hadn't actually meant right that second. The average guest would have waited until he'd left the room, not flop down into bed right in front of him. But he could see that there was nothing average about Olivia Montgomery.

At least she hadn't undressed first. Not that he wasn't curious to see what she was hiding under those clothes. He was beginning to think there was much more to Liv than she let show.

"You'll find your bags in the closet. Are you sure you wouldn't like a maid to unpack for you?"

"I can do it," she said, her voice soft and sleepy.

"If you change your mind, let me know. Other than that, you should have everything you need. There are fresh towels and linens in the bathroom. As well as toiletries. If you need anything else, day or night, just pick up the phone. The kitchen is always open. You're also welcome to use the exercise room or game room, day or night. We want you to feel completely comfortable here."

He walked to the window and pushed the curtain aside, letting in a shaft of late-afternoon sunshine. "You have quite a lovely view of the ocean and the gardens from here. Although there isn't much to see in the gardens this time of year. We could take a walk out there tomorrow."

Or not, he thought, when she didn't answer him. Then he heard a soft rumbling sound from the vicinity of the bed.

She had turned on her side and lay all curled up in a ball, hugging the pillow. He walked over to the bed and realized that she was sound asleep.

"Liv," he called softly, but she didn't budge. Apparently she was more tired than she'd realized.

He found a spare blanket in the closet, noticing her luggage while he was in there, and the conspicuously small amount of it. Just two average-size bags that had seen better days. The typical female guest, especially one there for an extended stay, brought a whole slew of bags.

He reminded himself once again that Liv was not the typical royal guest. And, he was a little surprised to realize, he liked that about her. It might very well be a refreshing change.

He walked back to the bed and covered her with the blanket, then, for reasons he couldn't begin to understand, felt compelled to just look at her for a moment. The angles of her face softened when she slept, making her appear young and vulnerable.

She's not your type, he reminded himself.

If he was going to be honest with himself, his "type" had plenty to offer physically, but intellectually, he was usually left feeling bored and unfulfilled. Maybe it was time for a change of pace.

Seducing a woman like Liv might be just what he needed to spice things up.

Three

It was official. Liv was lost.

She stood in an unfamiliar hallway on what she was pretty sure was the second floor, looking for the staircase that would lead her down to the kitchen. She'd been up and down two separate sets of stairs already this morning, and had wandered through a dozen different hallways. Either there were two identical paintings of the same stodgy-looking old man in a military uniform, or she'd been in this particular hallway more than once.

She looked up one end to the other, hopelessly turned around, wondering which direction she should take. She felt limp with hunger, and the backpack full of books and papers hung like a dead weight off one shoulder. If she didn't eat soon, her blood sugar was going to dip into the critical zone.

She did a very scientific, eenie-meenie-minie-moe, then went left around the corner and plowed face-first into a petite, red-haired maid carrying a pile of clean linens. The force of the collision knocked her off balance and the linens fell to the carpet.

"Oh my gosh! I'm so sorry!" Liv crouched down to pick them up. "I wasn't watching where I was going."

"It's no problem, miss," the maid said in a charming Irish brogue, kneeling down to help. "You must be our scientist from the States. Miss Montgomery?"

Liv piled the last slightly disheveled sheet in her arms and they both stood. "Yes, I am."

The maid looked her up and down. "Well, you don't much look like a scientist."

"Yeah, I hear that a lot." And she was always tempted to ask what she did look like, but she was a little afraid of the answer she might get.

"I'm Elise," the maid said. "If you need anything at all, I'm the one to be asking."

"Could you tell me where to find the kitchen? I'm starving."

"Of course, miss. Follow this hallway down and make a left. The stairs will be on your right, about halfway down the hall. Take them down one flight, then turn right. The kitchen is just down the way."

"A left and two rights. Got it."

Elise smiled. "Enjoy your stay, miss."

She disappeared in the direction Liv had just come from. Liv followed her directions and actually found the kitchen, running into—although not literally this time—Prince Aaron's assistant just outside the door.

"Off to work already?" he asked.

"Looking for food actually. I missed dinner last night."

"Why don't you join the prince in the family dining room."

"Okay." She could spend another twenty minutes or so looking for the dining room, and possibly collapse from hunger, or ask for directions. "Could you show me where it is?"

He smiled and gestured in the opposite direction from the kitchen. "Right this way."

It was just around the corner. A surprisingly small but luxurious space with French doors overlooking the grounds. A thick blanket of leaves in brilliant red, orange and yellow carpeted the expansive lawn and the sky was a striking shade of pink as the sun rose above the horizon.

At one end of a long, rectangular cherry table, leaning casually in a chair with a newspaper propped beside him, sat Prince Aaron. He looked up when they entered the room, then rose to his feet.

"Well, good morning," he said with a smile, and her stomach suddenly bound up into a nervous knot.

"Shall I take your bag?" Derek asked her.

Liv shook her head. That backpack had all of her research. She never trusted it to anyone else. "I've got it, thanks."

"Well, then, enjoy your breakfast," Derek said, leaving her alone with the prince. Just the two of them.

Only then did it occur to her that she might have been better off eating alone. What would they say to each other? What could they possibly have in common? A prince and an orphan?

The prince, on the other hand, looked completely at ease. In jeans and a flannel shirt he was dressed much more casually than the day before. He looked so...*normal.* Almost out of place in the elegant room.

He pulled out the chair beside his own. "Have a seat."

As she sat, she found herself enveloped in the subtle, spicy scent of his aftershave. She tried to recall if William, her possibly-soon-to-be fiancé, wore aftershave or cologne. If he had, she'd never noticed.

The prince's fingers brushed the backs of her shoulders as he eased her chair in and she nearly jolted against the sudden and intense zing of awareness.

He was *touching* her.

Get a grip, Liv. It wasn't like he was coming on to her. He was being *polite* and she was acting like a schoolgirl with a crush. Even when she *was* a schoolgirl she had never acted this way. She'd been above the temptation that had gotten so many other girls from high school in trouble. Or as her last foster mom, Marsha, used to put it, *in the family way.*

Then the prince placed both hands on her shoulders and her breath caught in her lungs.

His hands felt big and solid and warm. You are not going to blush, she told herself, but already she could feel a rush of color searing her cheeks, which only multiplied her embarrassment.

It was nothing more than a friendly gesture, and here she was having a hot flash. Could this be any more humiliating?

"Do you prefer coffee or tea?" he asked.

"Coffee, please," she said, but it came out high and squeaky.

He leaned past her to reach for the carafe on the table, and as he did, the back of her head bumped the wall of his chest. She was sure it was just her imagination, but she swore she felt his body heat, heard the steady thump of his heart beating. Her own heart was hammering so hard that it felt as though it would beat its way out of her chest.

Shouldn't a servant be doing that? she wondered as he poured her a cup and slid it in front of her. Then he *finally* backed away and returned to his chair, resuming the same casual, relaxed stance—and she took her first full breath since she'd sat down.

"Would you care for breakfast?" he asked.

"Please," she said, though her throat was so tight,

she could barely get air to pass through, much less food. But if she didn't eat something soon, she would go into hypoglycemic shock. She just hoped she didn't humiliate herself further. She was so used to eating at her desk in the lab, or in a rush over the kitchen sink, she was a little rusty when it came to the rules of etiquette. What if she used the wrong fork, or chewed with her mouth open?

He rang a bell, and within seconds a man dressed in characteristic butler apparel seemed to materialize from thin air.

"Breakfast for our guest, Geoffrey," he said.

Geoffrey nodded and slipped away as stealthily as he'd emerged.

Liv folded her hands in her lap and, because most of her time was spent huddled over her laptop or a microscope, reminded herself to sit up straight.

"I trust you slept well," the prince said.

She nodded. "I woke at seven thinking it was last night, then I looked outside and noticed that the sun was on the wrong side of the horizon."

"I guess you were more tired than you thought."

"I guess so. But I'm anxious to get down to the lab. You said I'll get a password for the door?"

"Yes, in fact…" He pulled a slip of paper from his shirt pocket and handed it to her. As she took it, she felt lingering traces of heat from his body and her cheeks flushed deeper red.

She unfolded the paper and looked at the code—

a simple seven-digit number—then handed it back to him.

"Don't you want to memorize it?" he asked.

"I just did."

His eyes widened with surprise, and he folded the paper and put it back in his pocket. "Your ID badge will be ready this morning. You'll want to wear it all the time, so you're not stopped by security. It will grant you full access to the castle, with the exception of the royal family's quarters of course, and any of our agricultural facilities or fields."

"You mentioned something about a map of the castle," she said, too embarrassed to admit that she'd actually gotten lost on her way to breakfast.

"Of course. I'll have Derek print one up for you."

"Thank you."

"So," Prince Aaron said, lounging back in his chair and folding his hands in his lap. "Tell me about yourself. About your family."

"Oh, I don't have any family."

Confusion wrinkled his brow. "Everyone has family."

"I'm an orphan. I was raised in the New York foster care system."

His expression sobered. "I'm sorry, I didn't know."

She shrugged. "No reason to be sorry. It's not your fault."

"Do you mind my asking what happened to your parents?"

It's not like her past was some big secret. She had always embraced who she was, and where she came from. "No, I don't mind. My mom died a long time ago. She was a drug addict. Social services took me away from her when I was three."

"What about your father?"

"I don't have one."

At the subtle lift of his brow, she realized how odd that sounded, like she was the product of a virgin birth or something. When the more likely scenario was that her mother had been turning tricks for drug money, and whoever the man was, he probably had no idea he'd fathered a child. And probably wouldn't care if he did know.

She told the prince, "Of course *someone* was my father. He just wasn't listed on my birth certificate."

"No grandparents? Aunts or uncles?"

She shrugged again. "Maybe. Somewhere. No one ever came forward to claim me."

"Have you ever tried to find them?"

"I figure if they didn't want me back then, they wouldn't want me now, either."

He frowned, as though he found the idea disturbing.

"It's really not a big deal," she assured him. "I mean, it's just the way it's always been. I learned to fend for myself."

"But you did have a foster family."

"Families," she corrected. "I had twelve of them."

His eyes widened. "Twelve? Why so many?"

"I was…difficult."

A grin ticked at the corner of his mouth. *"Difficult?"*

"I was very independent." And maybe a little arrogant. None of her foster parents seemed to appreciate a child who was smarter than them and not afraid to say so, and one who had little interest in following their *rules*. "I was emancipated when I was fifteen."

"You were on your own at *fifteen?*"

She nodded. "Right after I graduated from high school."

He frowned and shook his head, as if it was a difficult concept for him to grasp. "Forgive me for asking, but how does an orphan become a botanical geneticist?"

"A *lot* of hard work. I had some awesome teachers who really encouraged me in high school. Then I got college scholarships and grants. And I had a mentor." One she might actually be marrying, but she left that part out. And that was a big *might*. William had never given her this breathless, squishy-kneed feeling when he touched her. She never felt much of anything beyond comfortable companionship.

But wasn't that more important than sexual attraction? Although if she really wanted to marry William, would she be spending so much time talking herself into it?

The butler reappeared with a plate that was all but

overflowing with food. Plump sausages and eggs over easy, waffles topped with cream and fresh fruit and flaky croissants with a dish of fresh jam. The scents had her stomach rumbling and her mouth watering. "It looks delicious. Thank you."

He nodded and left. Not a very talkative fellow.

"Aren't you eating?" she asked Prince Aaron.

"I already ate, but please, go ahead. You must be famished."

Starving. And oddly enough, the prince had managed to put her totally at ease, just as he'd done the night before. He was just so laid-back and casual. So…*nice.* Unlike most men, he didn't seem to be put off or intimidated by her intelligence. And when he asked a question, he wasn't just asking to be polite. He really listened, his eyes never straying from hers while she spoke. She wasn't used to talking about herself, but he seemed genuinely interested in learning more about her. Unlike the scientists and scholars who were usually too wrapped up in their research to show any interest in learning about who she was as a person.

It was a nice change of pace.

The prince's cell phone rang and he unclipped it from his belt to look at the display. Concern flashed across his face. "I'm sorry. I have to take this," he said, rising to his feet. "Please excuse me."

She watched him walk briskly from the room and realized she was actually sorry to see him go. She couldn't recall the last time she'd had a conversation with a man who hadn't revolved in some way around her research, or funding. Not even William engaged in social dialogue very often. It was nice to just talk to someone for a change. Someone who really listened.

Or maybe spending time with the prince was a bad idea. She'd been here less than a day and already she was nursing a pretty serious crush.

Four

"Any news?" Aaron asked when he answered his brother's call.

"We have results back from Father's heart function test," Christian told him.

Aaron's own heart seemed to seize in his chest. Their father, the king, had been hooked to a portable heart pump four months ago after the last of a series of damaging attacks. The procedure was still in the experimental stages and carried risks, but the doctors were hopeful that it would give his heart a chance to heal from years of heart disease damage.

It was their last hope.

Aaron had wanted to accompany his family to

England, but his father had insisted he stay behind to greet Miss Montgomery. *For the good of the country,* he'd said. Knowing he'd been right, Aaron hadn't argued.

Duty first, that was their motto.

"Has there been any improvement?" Aaron asked his brother, not sure if he was ready to hear the answer.

"He's gone from twenty percent heart capacity to thirty-five percent."

"So it's working?"

"Even better than they expected. The doctors are cautiously optimistic."

"That's fantastic!" Aaron felt as though every muscle in his body simultaneously sighed with relief. As a child he had been labeled the easygoing one. Nothing ever bothered Aaron, his parents liked to brag. He was like Teflon. Trouble hit the surface, then slid off without sticking. But he wasn't nearly as impervious to stress as everyone liked to believe. He internalized everything, let it eat away at him. Especially lately, with not only their father's health, but also the diseased crops, and the mysterious, threatening e-mails that had been sporadically showing up in his and his siblings' in-boxes from a fellow who referred to himself, of all things, as the Gingerbread Man. He had not only harassed them through e-mail, but also managed to breach security and trespass on the castle grounds, slipping in and out like a ghost despite added security.

There had been times lately when Aaron felt he was days away from a mandatory trip to the rubber room.

But his father's health was now one concern he could safely, if only temporarily, put aside.

"How much longer do they think he'll be on the pump?" he asked his brother.

"At least another four months. Although probably longer. They'll retest him in the spring."

Aaron had been hoping sooner. On the pump he was susceptible to blood clots and strokes and in rare cases, life-threatening infections. "How is he doing?"

"They had to remove the pump to test his heart and there were minor complications when they reinserted it. Something about scar tissue. He's fine now, but he's still in recovery. They want to keep him here an extra few days. Probably middle of next week. Just to be safe."

As much as Aaron wanted to see his father home, the hospital was the best place for him now. "Is Mother staying with him?"

"Of course. She hasn't left his side. Melissa, the girls and I will be returning Friday as planned."

The girls being Louisa and Anne, their twin sisters, and Melissa, Chris's wife of only four months. In fact, it was on their wedding night that the king had the attack that necessitated the immediate intervention of the heart pump. Though it was in no way Chris and Melissa's fault, they still felt responsible for his sudden downturn.

"Now that Father is improving, maybe it's time you and Melissa rescheduled your honeymoon," Aaron told him.

"Not until he's off the pump altogether," Chris insisted, which didn't surprise Aaron. Chris had always been the responsible sibling. Of course, as crown prince, slacking off had never been an option. But while some people may have resented having their entire life dictated for them, Chris embraced his position. If he felt restricted by his duties, he never said so.

Aaron wished he could say the same.

"Did Miss Montgomery arrive safely?" Chris asked.

"She did. Although her flight was delayed by weather."

"What was your first impression of her?"

He almost told his brother that she was very cute. And despite what she'd told him, he couldn't imagine her as ever being difficult. She was so quiet and unassuming. But he didn't think that was the sort of *impression* Chris was asking for. "She seems very capable."

"Her references all checked out? Her background investigation was clean?"

Did he honestly think Aaron would have hired her otherwise? But he bit back the snarky comment on the tip of his tongue. Until their father was well, Chris was in charge, and that position deserved the same respect Aaron would have shown the king.

"Squeaky-clean," Aaron assured his brother. "And after meeting her, I feel confident she'll find a cure."

"Everyone will be relieved to hear that. I think we should—" There was commotion in the background, then Aaron heard his sister-in-law's voice, followed by a short, muted conversation, as though his brother had put a hand over the phone.

"Is everything okay, Chris?"

"Yes, sorry," Chris said, coming back on the line. "I have to go. They're wheeling Father back to his room. I'll call you later."

"Send everyone my love," Aaron told him, then disconnected, wishing he could be there with his family. But someone needed to stay behind and hold the fort.

He hooked his phone on his belt and walked back to the dining room. Liv was still there eating her breakfast. She had wiped out everything but half of a croissant, which she was slathering with jam. He didn't think he'd ever seen a woman polish off such a hearty meal. Especially a woman so slim and fit.

For a minute he just stood there watching her. She had dressed in jeans and a sweater and wore her hair pulled back into a ponytail again. He couldn't help grinning when he recalled the way she seized up as he put his hands on her shoulders, and the deep blush in her cheeks. He knew he wasn't exactly playing fair, and it was wrong to toy with her, but he'd never met a woman who wore her emotions so blatantly on her sleeve. There was little doubt that she was attracted to him.

She looked up, saw him standing there and smiled. A sweet, genuine smile that encompassed her entire face. She wasn't what he would consider beautiful or stunning, but she had a wholesome, natural prettiness about her that he found undeniably appealing.

"Sorry about that," he told her, walking to the table.

"S'okay," she said with a shrug, polishing off the last of her croissant and chasing it down with a swallow of coffee. "I think that was the most delicious breakfast I've ever eaten."

"I'll pass your compliments on to the chef." Instead of sitting down, he rested his arms on the back of his chair. "I'm sorry to say you won't be meeting my parents until next week."

Her smile vanished. "Oh. Is everything all right?"

"My father's doctors want to keep him a few days longer. Just in case."

"It's his heart?" she asked, and at his questioning look, added, "When I was offered the position, I looked up your family on the Internet. A ton of stuff came back about your father's health."

He should have figured as much. The king's health had been big news after he collapsed at Chris's wedding reception. But other than to say he had a heart "problem," no specific information had been disclosed about his condition.

"He has advanced heart disease," Aaron told her.

Concern creased her brow. "If you don't mind my asking, what's the prognosis?"

"Actually, he's in an experimental program and we're hopeful that he'll make a full recovery."

"He's getting a transplant?"

"He has a rare blood type. The odds of finding a donor are astronomical." He explained the portable heart pump and how it would take over all heart function so the tissue would have time to heal. "He's very fortunate. Less than a dozen people worldwide are part of the study."

"Heart disease is genetic. I'll bet you and your siblings are very health-conscious."

"Probably not as much as we should be, but the queen sees to it that we eat a proper diet. You know how mothers are." Only after the words were out did he realize that no, she probably didn't know, because she'd never had a real mother. He felt a slash of guilt for the thoughtless comment. But if it bothered her, she didn't let it show.

She dabbed her lips with her napkin, then set it on the table beside her plate. Glancing at the watch on her slender wrist, she said, "I should get down to the lab. I have a lot of unpacking to do."

He stepped behind her to pull her chair out, and could swear he saw her tense the slightest bit when his fingers brushed her shoulders. She rose to her feet and edged swiftly out of his reach.

He suppressed a smile. "You're sure you don't need help unpacking?"

She shook her head. "No, thank you."

"Well, then, lunch is at one."

"Oh, I don't eat lunch. I'm usually too busy."

"All right, then, dinner is at seven sharp. You do eat dinner?"

She smiled. "On occasion, yes."

He returned the smile. "Then I'll see you at seven."

She walked to the door, then stopped for a second, looking one way, then the other, as though she wasn't sure which direction to take.

"Left," he reminded her.

She turned to him and smiled. "Thanks."

"I'll remind Derek to get you that map."

"Thank you." She stood there another second, and he thought she might say something else, then she shook her head and disappeared from view.

The woman was a puzzle. Thoughtful and confident one minute, then shy and awkward the next. And he realized, not for the first time, that she was one puzzle he'd like to solve.

After a long morning in the fields and an afternoon in the largest of their greenhouse facilities, Aaron looked forward to a quiet dinner and an evening spent with their guest. Even though normally he would arrange some sort of physical, recreational activity like squash or tennis or even just a walk in the gardens, he was more interested in just talking to Liv. Learning more about her life, her past. She was the first woman in a long time whom he'd found both attractive and intellectually stimulating. And after a few drinks to loosen her up a bit, who knew where the conversation might lead.

He changed from his work clothes and stopped by her room on his way downstairs to escort her to the dining room, but she wasn't there. Expecting her to already be at the table waiting for him, he headed down, but found all of the chairs empty.

Geoffrey stepped in from the pantry.

"Have you seen Miss Montgomery?" Aaron asked.

"As far as I know she's still in the lab, Your Highness."

Aaron looked at his watch. It was already two minutes past seven. Maybe she'd lost track of the time. "Will you wait to serve the first course?"

Geoffrey gave him a stiff nod. "Of course, Your Highness."

A servant of the royal family as long as Aaron could remember, Geoffrey prided himself on keeping them on a strict and efficient schedule. Tardiness was not appreciated or tolerated.

"I'll go get her," Aaron said. He headed through the kitchen, savoring the tantalizing scent of spicy grilled chicken and peppers, and down the stairs to the lab. Through the door window he could see Liv, sitting in front of a laptop computer, typing furiously, papers scattered around her.

He punched in his code and the door swung open,

but as he stepped into the room, Liv didn't so much as glance his way.

Her sweater was draped over the back of her chair and she wore a simple, white, long-sleeved T-shirt with the sleeves pushed up to her elbows. Her ponytail had drooped over the course of the day and hung slightly askew down her back.

"It's past seven," he said softly, so as not to startle her, but got no response. "Liv?" he said, a little louder his time, and still she didn't acknowledge that he was there.

"Olivia," he said, louder this time, and she jolted in her chair, head whipping around. For a second she looked completely lost, as though she had no clue where she was, or who *he* was.

She blinked several times, then awareness slid slowly across her face. "Sorry, did you say something?"

"It's past seven."

She stared at him blankly.

"Dinner," he reminded her.

"Oh…right." She looked down at her watch, then up to her computer screen. "I guess I lost track of time."

"Are you ready?"

She glanced up at him distractedly. "Ready?"

"For *dinner.*"

"Oh, right. Sorry."

He gestured to the door. "After you."

"Oh…I think I'll pass."

"Pass?"

"Yeah. I'm right in the middle of something."

"Aren't you hungry?"

She shrugged. "I'll pop into the kitchen later and grab something."

"I can have a plate sent down for you," he said, even though he knew Geoffrey wouldn't be happy about it.

"That would be great, thanks," she said. "By the way, were you down here earlier?"

He shook his head. "I've been in the field all day."

"Does anyone else know the code for the door?"

"No, why?"

"A while ago I looked over and the door was ajar."

"Maybe you didn't close it all the way."

"I'm pretty sure I did."

"I'll have maintenance take a look at it."

"Thanks," she said, her eyes already straying back to the computer screen, fingers poised over the keys.

Geoffrey wouldn't consider it proper etiquette for a guest of the royal family to refuse a dinner invitation and then dine alone at a desk, but even he couldn't argue that Liv was not the typical royal guest.

She could eat in the bathtub for all Aaron cared, as long as she found a cure for the diseased crops.

"I'll have Geoffrey bring something right down."

She nodded vaguely, her attention back on her computer. He opened his mouth to say something else, but realized it would be a waste of breath. Liv was a million miles away, completely engrossed in whatever she was doing.

Doing her job, he reminded himself. They hadn't flown her in and paid good money so that she could spend her time amusing him.

He wondered if this was a foreshadow of what her time here would amount to. And if it was, it was going to be a challenge to seduce a woman who was never around.

Five

Liv studied the data that had been compiled so far regarding the diseased crops and compared the characteristics with other documented cases from all over the world. There were similarities, but no definitive matches yet. She wouldn't know for sure until she compared live samples from other parts of the world, which she would have to order and have shipped with expedited delivery.

She yawned and stretched, thinking maybe it was time for a short break, and heard the door click open.

She dropped her arms and turned to see Prince Aaron walking toward her. At least this time there was actually someone there. Despite a thorough check from a maintenance man, she'd found the door open several times, and once she could swear she'd seen someone peering at her through the window.

"Dinner not to your liking?" he asked.

Dinner? She vaguely remembered Geoffery coming by a while ago.

She followed the direction of his gaze to the table beside her desk and realized a plate had been left for her. Come to think of it, she was a little hungry. "Oh, I'm sure it's delicious. I was just wrapped up in what I was working on."

"I guess you were. You haven't slept, have you?"

"Slept?" She looked at her watch. "It's only ten."

"Ten *a.m.*," he said. "You've been down here all night."

"Have I?" It wouldn't be the first time she'd been so engrossed in her work that she forgot to sleep. Being in a lab with no windows probably didn't help. Unless she looked at her computer clock, which she rarely did, it was difficult to keep track of the time, to know if it was day or night. She'd been known to work for days on end, taking catnaps on her desk, and emerge from the lab with no idea what day it was, or the last time she'd eaten.

And now that she'd stopped working long enough to think about it, she realized that her neck ached and her eyes burned with exhaustion. A good sign that it was time for a break.

"When we hired you, we didn't expect you to

work 24/7," he said, but the playful smile said he was just teasing her.

"It's just the way I work." She reached back to knead the ache that was now spreading from her neck into the slope of her shoulders.

"Neck ache?" he asked, and she nodded. "I'm not surprised. Although gripping the muscles like that is only going to make it hurt more."

"It's stiff," she said.

He expelled an exasperated sigh and shook his head. "Why don't you let me do that."

Him?

She didn't think he was serious…until he stepped behind her chair. He was actually going to do it. He was going to rub her neck. He pushed her hands out of the way, then draped her ponytail over her left shoulder.

"Really," she said. "You don't have to—"

The words died in her throat as his hands settled on her shoulders.

The warmth of his skin began to seep through the cotton of her shirt and her cheeks exploded with heat. And as if that wasn't mortifyingly embarrassing and awkward enough, he slipped his fingers underneath the collar of her shirt. She sucked in a surprised breath as his hands touched her bare skin.

"The trick to relax the muscle," he told her, "is not to pinch the tension out, but to instead apply even pressure."

Yeah, right. Like there was any way she was going

to be able to relax now, with his hands touching her. His skin against her skin.

He pressed his thumbs into the muscle at the base of her neck and, against her will, a sigh of pleasure slipped from her lips. He slid his thumbs slowly upward, applying steady pressure. When he reached the base of her skull, he repeated the motion, until she felt the muscles going limp and soft.

"Feel good?" he asked.

"Mmm." Good didn't even begin to describe the way he was making her feel. Her head lolled forward and her eyes drifted shut.

"It would be better with oil," he said. "Unfortunately I don't have any handy."

The sudden image of Prince Aaron rubbing massage oil onto her naked body flashed through her brain.

Oh, no. Don't even go there, Liv. This was not a sexual come-on. He was just being polite. Although at that moment she would give anything to know what it would feel like. His oily hands sliding across her bare skin…

As if that would ever happen.

He sank his thumbs into the crevice beside her shoulder blades and a gust of breath hissed through her teeth.

"You have a knot here," he said, gently working it loose with his thumbs.

"You're really good at this," she said. "Did you take a class or something?"

"Human anatomy."

"Why would a prince in an agriculturally based field need a human anatomy class?"

"It might surprise you to learn that there was a time when I was seriously considering medical school."

Actually that didn't surprise her at all. She had the feeling there was a lot more to Prince Aaron than he let people see. "What changed your mind?" she asked.

"My family changed it for me. They needed me in the family business, so I majored in agriculture instead. End of story."

Somehow she doubted it was that simple. There was a tense quality to his voice that belied his true feelings.

"I guess that's the benefit of not having parents," she said. "No one to tell you what to do."

"I guess" was all he said, and she had the distinct impression she'd broached a subject he preferred not to explore. He gave her shoulders one last squeeze, then backed away and asked, "Feel better?"

"Much," she said, turning toward him. "Thank you."

"Sure," he said, but the usual, cheery smile was absent from his face. In fact, he looked almost…sad. Then she realized the inference in what she'd just said. His father was *dying,* his only hope a risky experimental procedure, and here she was suggesting that not having parents was a good thing.

Here he was being nice to her, and she was probably making him feel terrible.

Way to go, Liv. Open mouth, insert foot.

"Aaron, what I said just then, about not having parents—"

"Forget it," he said with a shrug.

In other words, *drop it*.

The lack of sleep, especially after that relaxing massage, was obviously taking its toll on her. She was saying stupid and inappropriate things to a man she knew practically nothing about. A virtual stranger.

A stranger who had the authority to fire her on a whim if it suited him.

"You should get some rest," he said.

He was right. She was long overdue for a power nap. "Now, if I can just find my way back to my room," she joked.

"Didn't Derek bring you a map?"

She looked down at her desk, papers strewn everywhere. "It's here. Somewhere."

He smiled and gestured to the door. "Come on, I'll walk you up."

"Thank you." She slipped her laptop in her backpack and slung it over her shoulder, grabbing the plate of uneaten food on her way out.

Even though he was silent, the tension between them seemed to ease as she followed the prince out of the lab and up the stairs. She left the plate in the kitchen and received a distinct look of disapproval from the butler.

"Sorry," she said lamely, and he answered with a stiff nod. That on top of what she'd said to the prince filled her with a nagging sense of guilt as they walked up to her room. She was obviously way out of her league here. This was going to take a lot of getting used to.

When they reached her door, she turned to him and said, "Thanks for walking me up."

He smiled. "My pleasure. Get some rest."

He started to turn away.

"Aaron, wait!"

He stopped and turned back to her.

"Before you go, I wanted to apologize."

His brow furrowed. "For what?"

"What I said in the lab."

"It's okay."

"No, it isn't. It was really…thoughtless. And I'm sorry if I made you feel bad."

"Liv, don't worry about it."

"I mean, I basically suggested you would be better off without parents, which, considering your father's health, was totally insensitive of me. My verbal filter must be on the fritz."

He leaned casually against the doorjamb, a look of amused curiosity on his face. "Verbal filter?"

"Yeah. People's thoughts go through, and the really dumb and inappropriate stuff gets tossed out before they can become words. Lack of sleep must have mine working at minimum capacity. I know it's a pretty lame excuse. But I'm really, *really* sorry. I'm just an employee. I have no right asking you personal questions or talking about your family, anyway."

For several long, excruciating seconds he just looked at her, and she began to worry that maybe he really was thinking about firing her. Then he asked, "Will you have dinner with me tonight?"

Huh?

She insulted him, and he invited her to share dinner with him? She might have thought he was extending a formal invitation just to be polite, but he looked sincere. Like he really *wanted* to have dinner with her.

"Um, sure," she said, more than a touch puzzled.

"Seven sharp."

"Okay."

"I'll warn you that Geoffrey loathes tardiness."

"I'll be on time," she assured him.

He flashed her one last smile, then walked away.

She stepped into her room and shut the door, still not exactly sure what just happened, but way too tired to try to sort it out. She would think about it later, after she'd had some sleep.

As inviting as the bed looked, the draw of a steaming shower was too appealing to resist. The sensation of the hot water jetting against her skin was almost as enjoyable as Aaron's neck massage had been. After her shower she curled up under the covers, planning to sleep an hour or two before heading back down to the lab.

She let her tired, burning eyes drift shut, and when she opened them again to check the clock on the bedside table, it was six forty-five.

* * *

Liv had been so wracked with guilt when Aaron walked her to her room this morning, she hadn't been paying attention to how they got there. And of course her handy map was in the lab, buried under her research. Which was why, four minutes before she was supposed to be in the dinning room, she was frantically wandering the halls, looking for a familiar landmark. The castle was just so big and quiet. If only she would run into someone who could help. She was going to be late, and she had the feeling she was already in hot water with Geoffrey the butler.

She rounded a corner and ran—literally—into someone.

Plowed into was more like it. But this time it wasn't a petite maid. This time it was a hulk of man, built like a tank, who stood at least a foot taller than her own five-foot-ten-inch frame. If he hadn't caught her by the arms, the force of the collision probably would have knocked her on her butt.

He righted and swiftly released her.

"Sorry," she apologized, wondering how many more royal employees she would collide with while she was here. "It was my fault. I wasn't looking where I was going."

"Miss Montgomery, I presume?" he said in a slightly annoyed tone, looking, of all places, at her chest. Then she looked down and realized she'd forgotten to pin on her ID badge. She pulled it from the outer pocket of her backpack and handed it to him. "Yeah, sorry."

His badge identified him as Flynn, and she couldn't help thinking that he looked more like a *Bruno* or a *Bruiser.*

He looked at the photo on her badge, then back at her, one brow raised slightly higher than the other. He didn't say, *You don't look like a scientist,* but she could tell he was thinking it.

He handed it back to her. "You should wear this at all times."

"I know. I forgot." She hooked it on her sweater, managing not to skewer her skin as she had yesterday. "Maybe you can help me. I'm trying to get to the dining room," she told him. "I've lost my way."

"Would you like me to show you the way?"

She sighed with relief. "That would be wonderful. I'm about three minutes from being late for dinner, and I'm already in the doghouse with Geoffrey."

"We can't have that," he said, gesturing in the direction she'd just come from. "This way, miss."

This time she paid attention as he led her downstairs to the dining room and she was pretty sure that she would be able to find her way back to her room. But she would keep the map with her at all times, just in case.

Prince Aaron was sitting in the dining room waiting for her, nursing a drink, when they walked in.

"I found her, Your Highness," Flynn told him.

"Thank you, Flynn," the prince said.

He nodded and left, and Liv realized it was no accident that she'd encountered him in the hallway.

"How did you know I would get lost?" she asked him.

He grinned. "Call it a hunch."

He rose from his chair and pulled out the adjacent chair for her, and as she sat, his fingers brushed the backs of her shoulders. Was he doing it on purpose? And if so, why did he feel the need to touch her all the time? Did he get some morbid kick out of making her nervous?

The only other time she'd had an experience with a touchy-feely person was back in graduate school. Professor Green had had a serious case of inappropriately wandering hands that, on a scale of one to ten, had an ick factor of fifteen. All of his female students fell victim to his occasional groping.

But unlike her professor, when Aaron touched her, she *liked* the way it felt. The shiver of awareness and swift zing of sexual attraction. She just wished she knew what it meant.

He eased her chair in and sat back down, lounging casually, drink in hand. "Would you like a drink? A glass of wine?"

"No, thank you. I have to stay sharp."

"What for?"

"Work."

He frowned. "You're working tonight?"

"Of course."

"But by the time we finish dinner, it will be after eight o'clock."

She shrugged. "So?"

"So, I have an idea. Why don't you take a night off?"

"Take a night off?"

"Instead of locking yourself in the lab, why don't you spend the evening with me?"

Six

The confused look on Liv's face was as amusing as it was endearing. She was as far from his type as a woman could be, yet Aaron wanted inside her head, wanted to know what made her tick.

Geoffrey appeared with the first course of their dinner, a mouthwatering lobster bisque. He knew this because he'd managed to sneak a taste before the chef had chased him out of the kitchen.

"How about that drink?" he asked Liv.

"Just water, please. Bottled, if you have it."

Geoffrey nodded and left to fetch it.

"You never answered my question," he said.

She fidgeted with her napkin. "I'm here to work, Your Highness."

"Aaron," he reminded her. "And you just worked a twenty-four-hour shift. Everyone needs a break every now and then."

"I had a break. I slept all day."

He could see he was getting nowhere, so he tried a different angle: the guilt card. He frowned and said, "Is the idea of spending time with me really so repulsive?"

Her eyes widened and she vigorously shook her head. "No! Of course not! I didn't mean to imply…" She frowned and bit her lip.

He could see that she was this close to giving in, so he made the decision for her. "It's settled, then. You'll spend the evening with me."

She looked hesitant, but seemed to realize that she had little choice in the matter. "I guess one night off wouldn't kill me."

"Excellent. What do you do for fun?"

She stared blankly.

"You do have fun occasionally, right?"

"When I'm not working I read a lot to catch up on the latest scientific discoveries and theories."

He shot her a skeptical look.

"That's fun."

"I'm talking social interaction. Being with other human beings."

He got a blank look from Liv.

"What about sports?" he asked.

She shrugged. "I'm not exactly athletic."

A person would never know it by her figure. She

looked very fit. He knew women who spent hours in the gym to look like Liv, and would kill to have a figure like that naturally.

"Do you go to movies?" he asked. "Watch television?"

"I don't get to the movies very often, and I don't own a television."

This time his eyes widened. "How can you not own a television?"

"What's the point? I'm never home to watch it."

"Music? Theater?"

She shook her head.

"There must be *something* you like to do besides work and read about work."

She thought about it for a moment, chewing her lip in concentration, then she finally said, "There is *one* thing I've always wanted to try."

"What's that?"

"Billiards."

Her answer surprised him. "Seriously?"

She nodded. "It's actually very scientific."

He grinned. "Well, then, you're in luck. We have a billiards table in the game room, and I happen to be an excellent teacher."

Ten minutes into her first billiards lesson, Liv began to suspect that choosing this particular game had been a bad idea. Right about the time that Aaron handed her a cue and then proceeded to stand behind her, leaning her over the edge of the table, his body pressed to hers, and demonstrating the appropriate way to hold it.

Hard as she tried to concentrate on his instructions, as he took her through several practice shots, she kept getting distracted by the feel of his wide, muscular chest against her back. His big, bulky arms guiding her. His body heat penetrating her clothes and warming her skin. And oh, did he smell good. Whatever aftershave or cologne he'd used that morning had long since faded and his natural, unique scent enveloped her.

It's just chemical, she reminded herself. And wholly one-sided. He wasn't holding her like this for pleasure, or as some sort of come-on. He was giving her a billiards lesson. Granted, she'd never had one before, but it stood to reason this was the way one would do it. Although the feel of him guiding the cue, sliding it back and forth between her thumb and forefinger, was ridiculously erotic.

If he did have some other sort of lesson on his mind, one that had nothing to do with billiards, she was so far out of her league that she couldn't even see her own league from here. Although, she had to admit, the view here was awfully nice.

"Have you got that?" Aaron asked.

She realized all this time he'd been explaining the game to her and she had completely zoned out. Which was absolutely unlike her. She turned her head toward him and he was so close her cheek collided with his chin. She could feel his breath shifting the wisps of hair that had escaped her ponytail.

She jerked her head back to look at the table, swallowing back a nervous giggle. Then she did something that she hardly ever did, at least, not since she was a rebellious teen. She *lied* and said, "I think I've got it."

He stepped back, racked up the balls, then said, "Okay, give it a try."

She lined the cue up to the white ball, just the way he'd shown her, but she was so nervous that when she took the shot she hit the green instead, leaving a chalky line on the surface. She cringed and said, "Sorry."

"It's okay," he assured her. "Try it again, but this time get a little closer to the ball. Like this." He demonstrated the motion with his own cue, then backed away.

She leaned back over, following his actions, and this time she managed to hit the ball, but the force only moved it about six inches to the left, completely missing the other balls, before it rolled to a stop. "Ugh."

"No, that was good," he assured her. "You just need to work on your aim and put a little weight behind it. Don't be afraid to give it a good whack."

"I'll try."

He set the cue ball back in place and she leaned over, lining it up, and this time she really whacked it. A little too hard, because the ball went airborne, banking to the left, right off the table. She cringed as it landed with a sharp crack on the tile floor. "Sorry!"

"It's okay," he said with a good-natured chuckle, rounding the table to fetch the ball. "Maybe not quite so hard next time."

She frowned. "I'm terrible at this."

"You just started. It takes practice."

That was part of the problem. She didn't have *time* to practice. Which was exactly why she was hesitant to try new things. Her motto had always been, If you can't be the best at something, why bother?

"Watch me," he said.

She stepped aside to give him room. He bent over and lined up the shot, but instead of keeping her eyes on his cue, where they were supposed to be, she found herself drawn to the perfect curve of his backside. His slacks hugged him just right.

She heard a loud crack, and lifted her gaze to see the balls scattering all over the table.

"Just like that," he said, and she nodded, despite the fact that, like before, she hadn't been paying attention. He backed up and gestured to the table. "Why don't you knock a few around. Work on your aim."

Despite her awkwardness, somehow Aaron always managed to make her feel less…inept. And after some practice and a couple of false starts, she was actually getting the hang of it. She even managed to keep all the balls on the table where they belonged and sink a few in the pockets. When they played a few actual games, she didn't do too badly, although she had the sneaking suspicion he was deliberately going easy on her.

After a while, despite having slept most of the day, she started yawning.

"Maybe we should call it a night," he said.

"What time is it?"

"Half past twelve."

"Already!" She had no idea they'd been playing that long.

"Past your bedtime?" he teased.

"Hardly." As if on cue, she yawned again, so deeply moisture filled her eyes. "I don't know why I'm so sleepy."

"Probably jet lag. It'll just take a few days for your system to adjust. Why don't you go to bed and get a good night's sleep, then start fresh in the morning."

As eager as she was to get back down to the lab, he was probably right. Besides, she really needed samples and her assistant wouldn't be here until the next morning. Maybe she could take some time to catch up on a bit of reading.

"I think maybe I will," she told him.

He took her cue and hung it, and his own, on a wall rack. "Maybe we can try this again, tomorrow night."

"Maybe," she said, and the weird thing was that she really wanted to. She was having fun. Maybe *too* much fun. She had a job to do here. That disease wasn't going to cure itself. It had been hours since she'd even thought about her research, and that wasn't at all like her.

"I'll walk you to your room," Aaron said.

"I think I can find my way." They were some-where on the third floor, and if she took the nearest steps down one floor she was pretty sure she would be near the hallway her room was on.

"A gentleman always walks his date to the door," he said with a grin. "And if nothing else, I am *always* a gentleman."

Date? Surely he was using that word in the loosest of terms, because she and Aaron were definitely not *dating*. Not in the literal sense. He meant it casually, like when people said they had a *lunch date* with a friend. Or a *dinner date* with a work associate.

She picked up her backpack from where she'd left it by the door, slung it over her shoulder and followed him out into the hall and down the stairs. She wanted to remember how to get there, should she ever decide to come back and practice alone every now and then.

"By the way, do you play poker?" he asked as they walked side by side down the hall toward her room.

"Not in a long time."

"My brother, sister and I play every Friday night. You should join us."

"I don't know…"

"Come on, it'll be fun. I promise, it's much easier than billiards."

She wondered if that would be considered proper. The hired help playing cards with the family. Of course, since she'd arrived, he'd treated her more like a guest than an employee.

"If you claim you have to work," he said sternly, "I'll change the door code and lock you out of the lab."

She couldn't tell if he was just teasing her, or if he would really do it. And who knows, it might be fun. "They won't mind?"

"My brother and sister? Of course not. We always invite palace guests to join in."

"But I'm not technically a guest," she said as they stopped in front of her door. "I work for you."

He was silent for a moment as he seemed to digest her words, looking puzzled. Finally he said, "You don't have the slightest clue how valuable you are, do you?"

His words stunned her. Her? Valuable?

"What you've been through. What you've *over-come*…" He shook his head. "It makes me feel very insignificant."

"I make you feel that way?" she asked, flattening a hand to her chest. *"Me?"*

"Why is that so hard to believe?"

"You're royalty. Compared to you, I'm nobody."

"Why would you think you're nobody?"

"Because…I am. What have I ever done?"

"You've done a hell of a lot more than I ever have. And think of all that you still have the chance to do."

She could hardly believe that Aaron, a *prince,* could possibly hold someone like her in such high esteem. What was he seeing that no one else did?

"I'm sure you've done things, too," she said.

He shook his head. "All of my life I've had things

handed to me. I've never had to work for *anything*. And look at the adversity you've overcome to get where you are."

She shrugged. "I just did what I had to do."

"And that's my point exactly. Most people would have given up. Your determination, your *ambition*, is astounding. And the thing I like most is that you don't put on airs. You don't try to be something that you're not." He took a step closer and his expression was so earnest, so honest, her breath caught. "I've never met a woman so confident. So comfortable in her own skin."

Confident? Was he serious? She was constantly second-guessing herself, questioning her own significance. Her worth.

"You're intelligent and interesting and kind," he said. "And fun. And I'm betting that you don't have a clue how beautiful you are."

Did the guy need glasses? She was so…plain. So unremarkable. "You think I'm beautiful?"

"I don't think you are. I *know* you are. And you wouldn't believe how much I've wanted to…" He sighed and shook his head. "Never mind."

She was dying to know what he was thinking, and at the same time scared to death of what it might be. But her insatiable curiosity got the best of her.

Before she could stop herself she asked, "You wanted to do what?"

For a long, excruciating moment he just looked at

her and her heart hammered relentlessly in anticipation. Finally he grinned that sexy simmering smile and told her, "I wanted do this." Then he wrapped a hand around the back of her neck, pulled her to him and kissed her.

This was not the wishy-washy version of a kiss that Liv had gotten from William the day she left. Not even close. This kiss had heart. And soul. It had soft lips and caressing hands and breathless whimpers—mostly from her.

It was the kind of kiss that a girl remembered her entire life, the one she looked back on as her first *real* kiss. And she was kissing him back just as enthusiastically. Her arms went around Aaron's neck, fingers tunneled through his hair. She was practically *attacking* him, but he didn't seem to mind. She felt as though she needed this, needed to feed off his energy, like a plant absorbing the sunlight.

She kept waiting for him to break the kiss, to laugh at her and say, *Just kidding* or *I can't believe you fell for that!* As if it was some sort of joke. What other reason would he have for kissing someone like her? But he didn't pull away. He pulled *her* closer. Her breasts crushed against the solid wall of his chest, tingling almost painfully, and just like that, she was hotter and more turned on than she'd ever been in her life.

But what about William?
William who?

Aaron's hands were caressing her face, tangling through her hair, pulling the band free so it spilled out around her shoulders. He pulled her closer and she nearly gasped when she felt the length of his erection, long and stiff against her belly. Suddenly the reality of what she was doing, where this was leading and the eventual conclusion, penetrated the lusty haze that was clouding her otherwise-rational brain. In the back of her mind a guilty little voice asked, *Is this how you treat the man who asked you to marry him?*

She didn't want to think about that. She wanted to shut him out of her mind, pretend William didn't exist. But he *did* exist, and he was back in the States patiently awaiting an answer from her. Trusting that she was giving his proposal serious thought.

She broke the kiss and burrowed her head against Aaron's shoulder, feeling the deep rise and fall of his chest as he breathed, the rapid beat of his heart. Her own breath was coming in shallow bursts and her heart rate had climbed to what must have been a dangerously high level. Had anyone under the age of seventy ever actually died of heart failure brought on by extreme sexual arousal?

"What's wrong?" he asked, genuine concern in his voice.

She struggled to catch her breath, to slow her pounding heart. "We're moving too fast."

He chuckled. "Um, technically, we haven't actually done anything yet."

"And we shouldn't. We *can't*."

He was quiet for several seconds, then he asked, "Are you saying you don't want to? Because, love, that kiss was hot as hell."

He called her *love*. No one had ever used a term of endearment like that with her. Certainly not her foster parents. Not even William. It made her feel special. Which made what she had to do next that much harder.

"I want to," she said. "A lot."

He rubbed his hands softly up and down her back. "Are you…afraid?"

She shook her head against his shoulder. She was anything but frightened, although maybe she should have been, because nothing about this made any sense. It wasn't logical, and her entire life revolved around logic and science.

Maybe that was what made it so appealing.

"There's something I haven't told you," she said.

"What is it?"

She swallowed the lump in her throat and looked up at him. "I'm kind of…engaged."

Seven

"**Y**ou're *engaged?*" Aaron backed away from Liv, wondering why this was the first time he'd heard this. Especially when he considered all of the blatant flirting that had been going both ways between them the past couple of days. Well, some of it went both ways, but in all fairness he was always the one to initiate it.

"Um…sort of," she said, looking uneasy.

Sort of? "Wait, how can a person be *sort of* engaged? And if you are engaged, why aren't you wearing a ring?"

"We kinda didn't get to that part yet."

He narrowed his eyes at her. "What part did you get to exactly?"

"He asked me, and I told him I would think about it."

There was this feeling, low in his gut. A surge of sensation that he didn't recognize. The he realized he was jealous. He envied a complete stranger. "Who is *he?*"

"His name is William. We work together."

"Another scientist?"

She nodded. "He's my mentor."

"Are you in love with him?" he asked.

She hesitated a moment, then said, "He's a good friend. I have an immense amount of respect for him."

Was that relief he'd just felt? "That isn't what I asked you."

She chewed her lip, as though she was giving it deep consideration, then she said, "Love is highly overrated."

Normally he would have agreed, but this was different. *She* was different. He couldn't imagine Liv being happy with a man she only *respected*. She deserved better. She'd fought all of her life to get exactly what she wanted. Why quit now?

And how did he know *what* she wanted when he barely knew her?

Somehow, he just did. And she was special. He couldn't even vocalize exactly why. It was just something he knew deep down.

"He must be a damned good shag, then," Aaron said, aware of how peevish he sounded.

He expected a snappy response, a firm, *Butt out, buster,* or *Mind your own business.* Instead Liv bit her lip and lowered her eyes. It didn't take him long to figure out what that meant.

He folded his arms across his chest and said, "You haven't slept with him, have you?"

"I didn't say that."

But she didn't deny it, either. "Out of curiosity, how long have you been dating this William fellow?"

Her gaze dropped to her feet again and in went the lip between her teeth. She didn't say a word. But her silence said it all.

"Are you telling me that you two have never even dated? Let me guess, you've never kissed him, either?"

She leveled her eyes on him. "I have so!"

He took a step toward her. "I'll bet he doesn't make you half as hot as I do."

He could tell by her expression, from the sudden rush of color to her cheeks, that he was right.

"I wasn't *that* hot," she said, but he knew it was a lie.

"You won't be happy," he said. "You're too passionate."

She looked at him like he was nuts. "I've been accused of a lot of things, but being passionate is not one of them."

He sighed. "There you go, selling yourself short again."

She shook her head in frustration. "I can't believe we're having this conversation. I hardly even know you."

"I know. And that's the bizarre part, because for some reason I feel as though I've known you forever." He could see by her expression that she didn't know how to respond to that, and she wasn't sure what to make of him. And oddly enough, neither did he. This wasn't at all like him.

She grabbed the knob and opened her door. "I should get to sleep."

He nodded. "Promise me you'll think about what I said."

"Good night, Aaron." She slipped inside her room and closed the door behind her.

He turned and walked in the direction of his own room. What he'd told her wasn't a lie. He'd never met anyone quite like her. She sincerely had no idea how unique, how gifted she was.

At first he'd planned only to seduce Liv and show her a good time while she was here, but something had happened since then. Something he hadn't expected. He really *liked* her. And the idea of her marrying this William person—a man she obviously didn't love— disturbed him far more than it should have.

Liv closed the door and leaned against it, expelling a long, deep breath.

What the heck had just happened out there? What did he want from her? Was he just trying to seduce her? To soften her up with his sweet words? Or did he really mean what he said? Did he really think she was interesting and fun? And *beautiful.* And if she really was, why had no one told her until now?

Just because no man had said the words, it didn't mean it wasn't true. And although she would never admit it to his face, he was right about one thing, no man had ever made her even close to as hot as he just had. With barely more than a kiss. Had it gone any further, she may have become the first scientifically genuine victim of spontaneous human combustion.

And oh how she had wanted it to go further. But to what end? A brief, torrid affair? Yeah, so what if it was? What was so wrong with that? They were consenting adults.

Yeah, but what about William?

So what if William wasn't an above-average kisser, and who cared that he didn't get her all hot and bothered the way Aaron did. William was stable and secure, and he respected her, and she was sure that he thought she was beautiful, too. He just wasn't the type of man to express his feelings. She was sure that once they were married he would open up.

But what if he didn't? Was that enough for her?

She heard a muffled jingle coming from her backpack and realized her phone was ringing. She pulled it out and saw that it was, *speak of the devil,* William. She hadn't spoken to him since she left the States. No doubt he was anxious for an answer.

She let it go to voice mail. She would call him

back tomorrow once she'd had a night to think things through. When she'd had time to forget how Aaron's lips felt against hers, and the taste of his mouth, and what it had been like to have his arms around her, his fingers tangling in her hair.

What if she never forgot? Could she go through life always wondering *what if?* Would it really be so awful, for once in her life, to do something just because she wanted to. Because it felt good. It wasn't as if he would want a relationship, and frankly, neither would she. Just one quick roll in the hay. Or maybe two. Then she could go home to William, who would never be the wiser…and live the rest of her life in guilt for betraying him.

Ugh.

But if they weren't technically engaged yet, could it really be counted as cheating?

As she was changing into her pajamas, her cell phone rang again. It was William. She considered letting it go to voice mail again, then decided she at least owed him a few words.

When she answered, his voice was filled with relief.

"I thought maybe you were avoiding me." He sounded so apprehensive and vulnerable. So unlike the confident, steadfast man she was used to, and the truth was, hearing him that way was just the slightest bit…off-putting. It knocked the pedestal she'd always kept him up on down a notch or two.

"Of course not," she said. "I've just been very busy."

"Is this a bad time? I could call back later."

"No, this is fine. I was just getting ready for bed. How have you been?"

"Swamped." He gave her a rundown on everything that had been going on in the lab since she left.

When he'd finished his dissertation, she asked him again. "How are *you,* William?"

"Me?" He sounded confused, probably because they never really talked about their personal lives.

"Yes, *you.*"

Finally he said, "Good. I'm good."

She waited for him to elaborate, but he didn't. Instead he asked, "How are *you?*"

Exhausted, but excited, and having more fun than I've ever had in my life, not to mention nursing a pretty serious crush, and considering an affair with, of all people, a prince.

But she couldn't tell him that. "I'm…good."

"The reason for my call," he said, getting right to the point—because William *always* had a point. "I was just wondering if you'd given any thought to my proposal."

He said it so drily, as though he were referring to a work proposal and not a lifetime commitment.

"I have," she said. "It's just…well, I've been so busy. I'd like a little more time to think it over. It's a huge decision."

"Of course. I don't mean to rush you. I realize that it probably came as something of a surprise."

"A little, yes. I never realized you had those kinds of feelings for me."

"You know that I deeply respect you. Both personally and professionally. We make a good team."

Yes, but a good professional relationship and a good marriage were two entirely different animals. Again she had to wonder, did she want to marry a man who respected her, or one who loved her? A man whom she worked well with, or one who found her so sexually appealing he couldn't keep his eyes, or hands, off her? One who made her feel all warm and breathless and squishy inside, the way Aaron did.

Don't even go there, she warned herself. Aaron had no place in this particular equation. Besides, for all she knew William would be fantastic in bed. She'd always considered good sex more of a perk than a necessity.

If that was true, why wasn't she jumping at his offer?

"Can I ask you a question, William?"

"Of course."

"Why now? What's changed from, say, two months ago?"

"Well, I've been doing a lot of thinking lately. I've always imagined that one day I would get married and have a family. And as you know, I'm not getting any younger. It seemed like a good time."

It sounded so logical, but that hadn't exactly been what she was hoping for.

"I guess what I want to know is, why me?"

"Why you?" he said, sounding puzzled. "Why not you?"

"What I mean is, was there a particular reason you asked *me?*"

"Who else would I ask?"

She was seriously fishing here, and he just didn't seem to get it. She wasn't desperate enough to beg for a kind word or two. Like, *You're beautiful* or *I love you.* That would come with time.

Then why, deep down, was a little voice telling her that this was all wrong?

"Things are just so crazy right now," she told him. "Can you give me a few weeks to think about it?"

"Of course," he said, his tone so patient and reasonable that it filled her with shame. "Take your time."

They made random and slightly awkward small talk for several minutes, and William seemed almost relieved when she said she had to go.

She hung up wondering what kind of marriage would they have if the only thing they ever talked about was work? And even worse, he didn't seem all that interested in getting to know her on a personal level. Would that just take time? Or should the years she had already known him have been time enough?

She thought of Aaron, who asked her questions and seemed genuinely interested in getting to know her. Why couldn't William be more like that?

Thoughts like that wouldn't get her anywhere.

William would never be like Aaron—a rich, charming prince. Which was a good thing, because as she'd reminded herself so many times now, Aaron, and men like him, were out of her league. Granted, she had never actually had a relationship with a man like Aaron, but she wasn't so naive that she didn't know the way these things worked. Even if Aaron did find her interesting at first, see her as a novelty, it wouldn't take him long to grow bored with her, for him to realize that she wasn't as special as he thought. Then he would be back to pursuing a proper mate. A woman with the right family and the proper breeding.

Yet she couldn't help but think of all the fun they could have in the meantime.

Eight

Liv was on her way to breakfast the following morning when she was greeted—more like accosted—by one of Aaron's sisters at the foot of the stairs on the main floor. Was it Friday already?

She was nowhere near as tall as her brother and had a slim, frail-looking build, and while they didn't exactly look alike, there was a strong family resemblance. She was dressed in a pale pink argyle sweater and cream-colored slacks and wore her hair pulled back in a low bun. In the crook of one arm she cradled a quivering ball of fur with bulging eyes. A dog, Liv realized. Probably a shih tzu.

The first impression that popped into Liv's head

was sweet and demure. Until the princess opened her mouth.

She squealed excitedly when she saw Liv and said, "You must be Olivia! I'm Aaron's sister Louisa."

Liv was so stunned by her enthusiasm—weren't princesses supposed to be poised and reserved?—she nearly neglected protocol and offered a hand to shake.

"It's nice to meet you, Your Highness," she said, dipping into a slightly wobbly curtsy instead. She had barely recovered when Louisa grabbed her hand and pumped it enthusiastically.

"Call me Louisa." She scratched the canine behind its silky ears. "And this is Muffin. Say hello, Muffin."

Muffin just stared, his little pink tongue lolling out of his mouth.

"I can't tell you how excited we are to have you here," she said, smiling brightly. "Aaron has told us *wonderful* things about you."

Liv couldn't help but wonder exactly what he'd told them. She would be mortified if he'd said something about their kiss last night. Having had the entire night to think it over, she decided that it would definitely never happen again. At least, not until she'd decided what to do about William. Although, probably not then, either. What she needed to concentrate on was the job she had come here to do.

"Has my brother been a good host?" Louisa asked.

Good didn't even begin to describe the sort of

host he'd been. "He has," Liv assured her. "He's made me feel very welcome."

"I'm so glad. I can't *wait* for you to meet the rest of the family! Everyone is so excited that you're here."

"I'm anxious to meet them, too."

"Well, then, let's go. Everyone should be having breakfast."

Everyone? As in, the *entire* family? Louisa expected her to meet them all at once?

Her heart slammed the wall of her chest. She never had been much good in groups of people. She preferred one-on-one interaction. She opened her mouth to object, but Louisa had already looped an arm through hers and was all but dragging her in the direction of the dining room. Liv felt like a giant beside her. Too tall, awkward and totally unrefined.

This was a nightmare.

"Look who I found!" Louisa announced as they entered the dining room. She probably didn't mean to, but she gave the impression that Liv had been aimlessly wandering the halls when this was the first morning she *hadn't* gotten lost.

She did a quick survey of the room and realized that other than Geoffrey, who was serving breakfast, there were no familiar faces. Where was Aaron?

Aaron's brother and his wife sat at one side of the table, while his other sister sat across from them.

"Everyone, this is Olivia Montgomery," Louisa

gushed. "The scientist who has come to save our country!"

Wow, no pressure there. She stood frozen beside Louisa, unsure of what to say or do. Then she felt it. The gentle and soothing pressure of a warm hand on her back. Aaron was standing there to rescue her.

She turned to him, never so happy in her life to see a familiar, friendly face. He was dressed to work in the field, in jeans and a soft-looking flannel shirt over a mock turtleneck.

He must have sensed how tense she was because he said under his breath, so even Louisa wouldn't hear, "Relax, they won't bite."

Miraculously, his deep, patient tone did just that. Her tension and fear seemed to melt away. Most of it at least. As long as Aaron was there, she was confident the introductions would go well. He would never feed her to the wolves.

His hand still on her back, he led her to the table where his brother sat.

"Liv," Aaron said, "meet my brother, Prince Christian, and his wife, Princess Melissa."

"Your Highnesses," she said, dipping into a near-perfect curtsy.

Prince Christian rose to his feet and reached out to shake her hand. She shifted her backpack to the opposite shoulder and accepted it.

His grip was firm and confident, his smile genuine. "I know I speak for everyone when I say it's an honor and a relief to have you here with us."

She pasted on her face what she hoped was a confident and capable smile. "I'm honored to be here."

"If there's anything you need, anything at all, you need only ask."

How about a valium, she was tempted to say, but had the feeling he might not appreciate her brand of humor. Instead she said, "I will, thank you."

"My parents send their regards and apologies that they weren't here to welcome you. They'll return in several days."

Liv wasn't sure if she was supposed to know the facts surrounding their father's situation, so she only nodded.

"You've already met Princess Louisa," Aaron said. "And this is my other sister, Princess Anne."

Louisa and Anne may have been twins, but they didn't look a thing alike. Anne was darker. In color, and considering her guarded expression, in personality, as well.

"Your Highness," Liv said, curtsying in her direction. She was getting pretty good at this.

"I understand you think you can find a cure for the diseased crops," Anne said, sounding slightly antagonistic, as though she questioned Liv's credentials. Was Anne trying to intimidate her? Put her in her place?

It was one thing to question Liv personally, but as a scientist, they wouldn't find anyone more capable.

She lifted her chin a notch. "I don't *think* I can, Your Highness. I *will* find a cure. As I told Prince Aaron, it's simply a matter of time."

A vague smile pulled at the corners of Anne's mouth. If it had been some sort of test, it appeared Liv had passed.

"Shall we sit?" Aaron said, gesturing to the table.

She turned to him. "Actually, I was planning to get right to work."

He frowned. "You're not hungry?"

Not anymore. The idea of sitting and eating breakfast surrounded by his entire family was only slightly less intimidating than facing a firing squad. "If I could get a carafe of coffee sent down to the lab that would be great."

"Of course." He addressed the butler. "Geoffrey, would you take care of that, please?"

Geoffrey nodded, and although Liv couldn't say for sure, he might have looked a bit peeved.

"It was nice to meet everyone," Liv said.

"You'll join us for dinner?" Princess Melissa asked, although it came across as more of a statement than a question.

Before she could form a valid excuse to decline, Aaron answered for her, "Of course she will."

She wanted to turn to him and say, *I will?,* but she held her tongue. Besides, much as she'd like to, she couldn't avoid them forever.

She would feel so much more comfortable if they

treated her like the hired help rather than a guest and left her to her own devices.

"I'll walk you down to the lab," Aaron said, and though her first instinct was to refuse his offer, she didn't want everyone to think there was a reason she shouldn't be alone with him. Like the fact that she was scared to death he would kiss her again. And even more terrified that if he did, she wouldn't be able to make herself stop him this time.

He led her from the room, and when they were in the hall and out of earshot he said, "I know they can be intimidating, especially Anne, but you can't avoid them forever. They're curious about you."

"I just want to get an early start," she lied, "before my assistant arrives."

He shot her a we-both-know-that's-bull look.

"You don't have to walk me to the lab."

"I know I don't." His slightly mischievous grin said he was going to regardless, and the warmth of it began melting her from the inside out. When he rested a hand on her back to lead her there, her skin tingled under his touch.

If this was the way things would be from now on, she was in *big* trouble.

"I think we need to talk," Aaron told Liv as they walked through the kitchen to the basement door.

"About what?" she asked and he shot her a what-do-you-think look. She frowned and said, "Oh, *that*."

"In the lab," he said, "where we can have some privacy." She nodded and followed him silently through the kitchen and down the stairs. She wasn't wound nearly so tight as she'd been facing his family. She'd been so tense when he stepped into the dining room that he was hesitant to touch her for fear that she might shatter.

She trailed him down the stairs and waited while he punched in the door code. When they were in the lab with the door closed, she turned to him and said, "I've decided that what happened last night can't ever happen again."

So, she thought she would use the direct approach. That shouldn't have surprised him. And he was sure she had what she considered a very logical reason for her decision.

He folded his arms across his chest. "Is that so?"

"I'm serious, Aaron." She did look serious. "I talked to William last night."

An unexpected slam of disappointment and envy pegged him right in the gut.

"You've made your decision, then?" he asked, knowing that if she'd said yes to the engagement, he would do everything in his power to talk her out of it. Not for himself of course, but for her sake.

All right, maybe a *little* for himself.

"I haven't made a decision yet, but I told William that I'm still considering it. And until I accept or refuse his proposal, I don't feel it's right to…*see* anyone else."

He grinned. "See."

"You know what I mean."

"Why?"

His question seemed to confuse her. "Why?"

"You're not engaged. Admittedly you're not even *dating* him. So, logically, *seeing* me or anyone else wouldn't technically be considered infidelity."

She frowned. "You're splitting hairs."

"Not to mention that, if you really *wanted* to marry him, why would you need time to think about it? Wouldn't you have said *yes* as soon as he asked?"

She looked troubled, as though she realized he was right, but didn't want to admit it. "It's…complicated."

"And you think it will be less complicated after you're married? You think he'll miraculously change?"

"That's not what I meant."

"It doesn't work that way, Liv. Problems don't go away with the vows. The way I hear it, they usually get worse."

She expelled a frustrated breath. "Why do you even care? Or is this just your way of trying to get me in bed?"

He grinned. "Love, if I wanted in your knickers, I'd have been there last night."

Her cheeks blushed bright pink.

He took a few steps toward her. "I'm not going to insult your highly superior intelligence and say I don't want to get you into bed. But more than that, I like you, Liv, and I don't want to see you make a mistake."

"Ugh! Would you please stop saying that I'm making a mistake?"

"Are you afraid you're going to start believing me?"

"You think that my sleeping with you *wouldn't* be a mistake?"

He knew now that she'd at least been thinking about it. Probably as much as he had. "No, I don't. In fact, I think it would be beneficial to us both."

"Well, you're not exactly biased, are you?" She collapsed in her chair and dropped her head in her hands. "I want to do the right thing, and you're confusing me."

"How could anything *I* say confuse you? Either you want to marry him, or you don't."

"I don't know if I want to marry *anyone* right now!" she nearly shouted, looking shocked at her own words.

Then why fret over it? "If you're not ready to get married, tell him no."

She looked hopelessly confused and completely adorable. He could see that she wasn't used to not having all the answers. For some reason it made him like her that much more.

She gazed up at him, eyes clouded by confusion. "What if I don't get another chance?"

"To marry William?"

"To marry *anyone!* I do want to get married someday and have a family."

"What's stopping you?"

"What if no one else ever asks?"

That was the most ridiculous thing he'd ever heard. She was an attractive, desirable woman that any man would be lucky to have. If she spent some time outside of her lab and living her life, she might already know that. Men would probably be fighting each other to win her hand.

He knelt down in front of her chair, resting his hands on her knees. "Liv, trust me, someone will ask. Someone you want to marry. Someone you *love*."

She gazed into his eyes, looking so young and vulnerable and confused. What was it about her that made him want take her in his arms and just hold her? Soothe her fears and assure her that everything would be okay. But even if he'd wanted to, she didn't give him the chance. Instead, she leaned forward, wrapped her arms around his neck and kissed him.

Nine

That guilty little voice inside Liv was shouting, *Don't do it, Liv!* But by then it was already too late. Her arms were around Aaron's neck and her lips were on his. She was kissing him again, and he was kissing her back. The feel of his mouth, the taste of him, was already as familiar as it was exciting and new. Maybe because she'd spent most of the night before reliving the first kiss and fantasizing what it would feel like to do it again. Now she knew. And it was even better than she remembered. Better than she could ever have imagined.

Aaron cupped her face in his hands, stroking her cheeks, her throat, threading his fingers through her hair. She hooked her legs around his back, drawing him closer, clinging to him. She might have been embarrassed by her brazen behavior, but she felt too hot and needy with desire to care. She needed to feel him. She just plain *needed* him. Nothing in her life had ever felt this good, this…right. She hadn't even known it was possible to feel this way. And she wanted more—wanted it all. Even though she wasn't completely sure what *it* was yet. Was this just physical, or was there more to it?

Of course not. What did she think, they were going to have some sort of relationship? She didn't want that any more than he did. Her work was too important to her.

That didn't mean they couldn't have a little fun.

She tugged the tail of his flannel from the waist of his jeans, but he grabbed her hands and broke the kiss, saying in a husky voice, "We can't."

Shame burned her cheeks. Of course they couldn't. Hadn't she just told him that very same thing? What the hell had she been thinking? Why, the instant she was near him, did she seem to lose all concept of right and wrong?

She jerked her hands free and rolled the chair backward, away from him. "You're right. I'm sorry. I don't know what I was thinking. This isn't like me at all."

He looked puzzled for a moment, then he grinned and said, "I don't mean *ever.* I just meant that we can't *here*. Any minute now Geoffrey is going to walk through that door with your coffee, not to mention the lab assistant who's due here this morning."

"Oh, right," she said, feeling, of all things, relieved. When what she should have felt was ashamed of herself, and regretful for once again betraying William. Although, as Aaron had pointed out, she and William weren't technically a couple.

You're rationalizing, Liv. When there was absolutely nothing rational about this scenario. This was not the way the world was supposed to work. Brainy, orphaned scientists did not have flings with rich, handsome princes. No matter what the storybooks said.

Nothing that felt this wonderful could possibly be good for her.

"We can't do this again," she told him. "Ever."

Aaron sighed. "We're back to that again?"

"It's wrong."

Aaron rose from his knees and tucked his shirt back in. "It felt pretty good to me."

"I'm serious, Aaron."

"Oh, I know you are."

So why didn't he look as though he was taking her seriously? Why did she get the feeling he was just humoring her?

"I have to get to work," he said. "I'll see you at dinner?"

Was that a statement or a request? She could say no, but she suspected he wouldn't take no for an answer, and that if she tried to skip it, he would come down to the lab and fetch her. At least with his family around he wouldn't try anything physical with her. At least, she hoped he wouldn't. She seriously doubted his family would approve of Aaron messing around with the hired help. Especially one who ranked so abysmally low in the social ladder.

"Seven sharp," she said.

He leaned over and before she could stop him, he gave her a quick kiss—just a soft brush of his lips against hers, but it left her aching for more—then he walked to the door. As he opened it, he turned back to her and said, "Don't forget about the poker game tonight." Then he left, the door closing with a metallic click behind him.

Ugh. She had forgotten all about that. But she already said she would play, so she doubted he would let her back out now.

As much as she didn't want to spend the evening with his family, she dreaded even more spending it alone with him.

She turned to her desk, reaching for the pen she'd left beside her keyboard, but it wasn't there. She searched all over the desk, under every paper and text. She even checked the floor, in case it had somehow rolled off the desk, but it wasn't there. It was as if it had vanished into thin air.

She got a new one from her backpack, and as she was leaning over she heard a noise behind her, from the vicinity of the door. She thought maybe it was Geoffrey with her coffee, or her lab assistant, but when she turned, there was no one there.

And the damn door was open again.

After breakfast Aaron pulled Chris aside and asked, "So, what did you think of Liv?"

"Liv?"

"Miss Montgomery."

Chris raised one brow. "We're on a first-name basis, are we?"

Aaron scowled a him. "I'm being serious."

Chris chuckled. "I'll admit she's not at all what I expected. She doesn't look like a scientist and she's much younger than I imagined. She does seem quite confident, though, if not a bit...*unusual.*"

"Unusual?"

"Not the typical royal guest."

Despite having thought that very same thing, Aaron felt protective of Liv. "What does that matter, so long as she gets the job done?"

Chris grinned. "No need to get testy. I'm just making an observation."

"An observation of someone you know nothing about." Knowing his siblings had the tendency to be more judgmental, Aaron wouldn't tell them about Liv's past. Not that he believed she had anything to be ashamed of—quite the contrary in fact—but the things she'd told him had been in confidence. If they wanted to know more about her, they would have to ask themselves—which he didn't doubt they would.

"If I didn't know better, I might think you fancy her," Chris said. "But we all know that you prefer your women with IQs in the double digits."

Even though he couldn't exactly deny the accusation, Aaron glared at him. "By the way, I invited her to our poker game tonight."

Chris looked intrigued. "Really? She doesn't strike me as the card-playing type."

Aaron wanted to ask, *What type does she strike you as?,* but he was afraid he might not like the answer he got. "Are you saying you don't want her to play?"

Chris shrugged. "It's fine with me. The more the merrier." He looked at his watch. "Is there anything else? I have a conference call in fifteen minutes."

"No, nothing else."

Chris started to turn away, then stopped and said, "I almost forgot to ask, have there been any new developments since I left?"

Aaron didn't have to ask Chris what he meant. It had been in the back of everyone's minds for months now. The person who referred to himself as the Gingerbread Man. "No e-mails, no security breaches. Nothing. It's as if he disappeared into thin air."

Chris looked relieved. "I hope that means it was a harmless prank, and we've heard the last of him."

"Or it could mean that he's building up to something big."

His relief instantly turned to irritation. "Always the optimist."

Aaron grinned. "I like to think that I'm realistic. Whoever he was, he went through an awful lot of trouble breaching our security systems. All I'm saying is that we should keep on our toes."

"I'll keep security on high alert, but at some point we'll have to assume he's given up."

"Call it a hunch," Aaron said, "but I seriously doubt we've seen or heard the last of him."

In her life Liv had never met such an inquisitive group of people. It must run in the family because during dinner she was overwhelmed by endless questions from every side of the table. And like their brother, they seemed genuinely interested in her answers. They asked about her work and education mostly, and they were nothing if not thorough. By the end of the evening she felt picked over and prodded, much like one of the soil samples she'd studied that afternoon. It could have been worse. They could have completely ignored her and made her feel like an outsider.

"See?" Aaron whispered as they walked to the game room to play cards. "That wasn't so bad."

"Not too bad," she admitted.

As they took seats around the table, Geoffrey took

drink orders while Prince Christian—Chris, as he'd asked her to address him—divvied out the chips.

"We start with one hundred each," Aaron told her. "I can front you the money."

She hadn't realized they would play for real money. In college and grad school the stakes had been nickels and dimes, but one hundred euros wasn't exactly out of her budget range. She'd checked the exchange rate before leaving the U.S. and one hundred euros would be equivalent to roughly one hundred thirty-one dollars, give or take.

"I can cover it," she told him.

He regarded her curiously. "You're sure?"

Did he think she was that destitute? "Of course I'm sure."

He shrugged and said, "Okay."

She was rusty the first few hands, but then it all started to come back to her and she won the next few rounds. A bit unfairly, she would admit, even though it wasn't exactly her fault. Besides, she was actually having fun.

Louisa apparently didn't play cards. She sat at the table with her dog, to her siblings' obvious irritation, chatting.

"Where are you from originally?" she asked Liv. She was definitely the friendlier of the twins. A glass-is-half-full kind of girl. And Liv used the term *girl* because Louisa had so sweet a disposition.

"I'm from New York," Liv told her.

"Your family still lives there?" she asked.

"Five card draw, nothing wild," Chris announced, shooting Louisa a look as he shuffled the cards.

"I don't have family," Liv said.

"Everyone has some family," Melissa said with the subtle twang of a Southern accent. Aaron had mentioned that she was born on Morgan Isle, the sister country of Thomas Isle, but had been raised in the U.S. in Louisiana.

"None that I know of," Liv told her. "I was abandoned as a small child and raised in foster homes."

"Abandoned?" Melissa repeated, her lower lip beginning to quiver and tears pooling in her eyes. "That's *so* sad."

"Easy, emotio-girl," Chris said, rubbing his wife's shoulder. When the tears spilled over onto her cheeks, he put down the cards he'd been dealing, reached into his pants pocket and pulled out a handkerchief. Neither he nor anyone else at the table appeared to find her sudden emotional meltdown unusual.

Melissa sniffed and dabbed at her eyes.

"You all right?" he asked, giving her shoulder a reassuring squeeze.

She gave him a wobbly nod and a halfhearted smile.

"You'll have to excuse my wife," Chris told Liv. "She's a little emotional these days."

"Just a little," Melissa said with a wry smile. "It's these damn fertility drugs. I feel like I'm on an emotional roller coaster."

"They're trying to get pregnant," Aaron told Liv.

"She's a scientist, genius," Anne said. "I'm sure she knows what fertility drugs are for."

Aaron ignored her.

"I don't know much about it myself, although I have a colleague who specializes in fertility on a genetic level," Liv said. "I never realized how common it is for couples to have some fertility issues."

"We're trying in vitro," Melissa said, tucking the handkerchief in her lap while Chris finished dealing. "Our doctor wanted us to wait and try it naturally for six months, but I'm already in my midthirties and we want at least three children, so we opted for the intervention now."

"We do run the risk of multiples," Chris said. "Even more so because obviously twins run in the family. But it's a chance we're willing to take."

It surprised Liv that they spoke so openly to a stranger about their personal medical issues, although she had found that, because she was a scientist, people assumed she possessed medical knowledge, which couldn't be further from the truth. Unless the patient happened to be a plant.

"I'll open for ten," Aaron said, tossing a chip in the pot, and everyone but Anne followed suit.

She threw down her cards and said, "I fold."

"I can hardly wait to have a little niece or nephew to spoil. Or both!" Louisa gushed. "Do you want children, Olivia?"

"Someday," Liv said. After she'd had more time to develop her career, and of course she would prefer to be married first. Would William be that man? Would she settle out of fear that she would never get another chance? Or would she take a chance and maybe meet a man she loved, and who loved her back? One who looked at her with love and affection and pride, the way Chris looked at Melissa. Didn't she deserve that, too?

If she never married and had kids, would it be that big of a tragedy? She always had her work.

"I love kids," Louisa said. "I'd like at least six, maybe eight."

"Which is why when you meet men, they run screaming in the opposite direction," Anne quipped, but her jab didn't seem to bother her sister.

"The right man is out there," Louisa said, with a tranquil smile and a confidence that suggested she had no doubt. She was probably right. What man wouldn't want to marry a sweet, beautiful princess? Even if it meant having an entire brood of children.

"We all know that Aaron doesn't want kids," Anne said, shooting Liv a meaningful look.

Did she suspect that something was going on between Liv and her brother? And if so, did she honestly believe that Liv would consider him as a potential father to her children? Nothing could be further from the truth. If they did have a fling, which was a moot point because she had already decided they wouldn't, she would never expect more than a brief affair.

Unsure of how to react, Liv decided it was best to give her no reaction at all and instead studied her cards.

"I'm just not cut out to be a family man," Aaron said to no one in particular. If he caught the meaning of his sister's statement, he didn't let on. Or maybe he was saying it for Liv's benefit, just in case she was having any delusions of grandeur and thought they had some sort of future together.

"You would have to drop out of the girl-of-the-month club," Anne said with a rueful smile and a subtle glance in Liv's direction.

"And miss out on that fantastic yearly rate they give me?" Aaron said with a grin. "I think not."

"Are we going to talk or play?" Chris complained, which, to Liv's profound relief, abruptly ended the conversation.

Louisa tried occasionally to engage them in conversation, earning a stern look from her oldest brother each time. She finally gave up and said good-night around ten. Half an hour later Melissa followed. At eleven-thirty, when Liv was up by almost two hundred euros, they packed it in for the night.

"Good game," Chris said, shaking her hand, and added with a grin, "I hope you'll give us a chance to win our money back next week."

"Of course," she said, although she would have to throw the game to make it happen.

"I'll walk you to your room," Aaron said, gesturing to the door, and he had a curious, almost sly look on his face. Something was definitely up.

"Why are you looking at me like that?" she asked.

"Because we finally get some time alone."

Ten

The idea of being alone with Aaron again both terrified and thrilled Liv, then he went and added another level of tension by saying, "You do realize that counting cards is considered cheating."

Oh damn.

She really hadn't thought anyone was paying that close attention. They were playing for only a couple hundred euros, so what was the harm?

She plastered on a look of pure innocence that said, *Me? Cheat?* But she could see he wasn't buying it.

She sighed and said, "It's not my fault."

He raised one disbelieving brow at her.

"I don't even do it consciously. The numbers just kind of stick in my head."

"You have a photographic memory?"

She nodded.

"I wondered how you managed to memorize the code for the lab door so quickly. Although for the life of me I don't understand how you kept getting lost in the castle."

"It only works with numbers."

For a second she though he might be angry, but he shot her a wry smile instead. "At least you made a bit of money for your research."

He apparently had no idea of the going rate for genetic research. "A couple hundred euros won't get me very far."

"You mean thousand," he said.

"Excuse me?"

"A couple hundred thousand."

She nearly tripped on her feet and went tumbling down the stairs. "That's not even funny."

He shrugged. "I'm not trying to be funny."

"You're serious?"

"*Totally* serious."

"You said we were starting with one hundred."

"We did. One hundred thousand."

She suddenly felt weak in the knees. All this time she thought she'd been betting a dollar or ten, it had actually been thousands? What if she'd lost? How would she have ever paid her debt?

"I'll give the money back," she said.

"That would look suspicious. Besides," he reminded her, "you already told Chris you would play again next Friday."

Damn it, she had, hadn't she? If the rest of the family figured it out, they might think her some sort of con artist. Next week she would just have to lose on purpose, claim that her first time must have been beginner's luck, then pretend to be discouraged and vow never to play again. Only she and Aaron would know the truth.

When they reached her room she opened the door and stepped inside. A single lamp burned beside the bed and the covers had been turned down. Standing in the doorway, she turned to him and said, "I had fun tonight."

He leaned against the doorjamb, wearing that devilish, adorable grin. "Aren't you going to invite me in?"

"No."

"Why not?"

"I told you earlier, we can't be…intimate." Just saying the word made her cheeks flush.

"You said it, but we both know you didn't mean it." He leaned in closer. "You want me, Liv."

She did. So much that she ached. He smelled so good and looked so damn sexy wearing that wicked, playful smile, and he was emitting enough phero-mones to make any woman bend to his will.

"That doesn't make it right," she told him, but

with a pathetic degree of conviction. She didn't even believe herself.

Which was probably why, instead of saying good-night and closing the door in his face, Liv grabbed the front of his shirt, pulled him into her room and kissed him.

He reacted with a surprised, "Oomf," which she had to admit gave her a decadent feeling of power. But it took him only seconds to recover, then he was kissing her back, pulling her into his arms. He shut the door and walked her backward to the bed, tugging the hem of her shirt free from the waist of her pants. She did the same to him, their arms getting tangled. They broke the kiss so that they could pull the shirts over their heads, and the sight of his bare chest took her breath away. He didn't even seem put off by her very plain and utilitarian cotton bra. His eyes raked over her, heavy with lust, and when his hands settled on her bare skin, she shuddered. He was so beautiful, so perfect, she could hardly believe it was real. That he wanted someone like her.

It's just sex, she reminded herself, although deep down, it felt like more.

He tugged the band from her hair and it spilled down around her bare shoulders.

"You're beautiful," he said, looking as though he sincerely meant it. She wished she could see what he saw, see herself through his eyes for one night.

He lowered his head, brushing his lips against the

crest of one breast, just above the cup of her bra. She shuddered again and curled her fingers through his hair.

"You smell fantastic," he said, then he ran his tongue where his lips had just been, up one side and down the other, and a moan slipped from between her lips. "Taste good, too," he added with a devilish grin.

"What are we doing?" she asked.

He regarded her curiously. "As a scientist, I'd have thought someone would have explained it to you by now."

She couldn't help but smile. "I know *what* we're doing. I just don't understand *why*."

"I don't know what you mean."

"Why me?"

She expected him to tease her, to tell her that she was underestimating herself again; instead his expression was serious.

"Honestly, I'm not sure." He caressed her cheek with the backs of his fingers. "All I know is, I've never wanted a woman the way I want you."

She might have suspected it was a line, but his eyes told her that he was telling the truth. That he was just as stunned and confused by this unlikely connection as she was.

Then he kissed her and started touching her, and she didn't care why they were doing it, her only thought was how wonderful his hands felt on her skin, how warm and delicious his mouth felt as he tasted and nipped her. With a quick flick of his fingers he unhooked her bra, and as he bared her breasts, he didn't seem to notice or care how voluptuous she wasn't, and as he drew one nipple into his mouth, flicking lightly with his tongue, she didn't care, either. He made her feel beautiful and desirable.

There was this burning need inside her like she'd never felt before, a sweet ache between her thighs that made her want to beg him to touch her, but he was still concentrating all of his efforts above her waist—and it was driving her mad.

Thinking it might move things along, she ran her hand down his chest to his slacks, sliding her fingers along his waistline, just below the fabric, then she moved her hand over his zipper, sucking in a surprised breath when she realized how long and thick he felt. She should have expected that he would be perfect everywhere.

She gave his erection a gentle squeeze and he groaned against her cleavage.

He reached behind him and she wasn't sure what he was doing, until he tossed his wallet down on the mattress. Intelligent as she was, it took her several seconds to understand why, and when she did—when she realized that he kept his condoms in there—the reality of what they were doing and exactly where this was leading hit her full force.

The fading flower who in college wouldn't even let a man kiss her until the third date was about to have sex with a man she'd known only four days. A playboy prince who without a doubt was far more experienced than she could ever hope to be.

So why wasn't she afraid, or at least a little wary? Why did it just make her want him that much more?

"Take them off," he told her, his voice husky.

She gazed up at him, confused. Only when she saw the look on his face did she realize how aroused he was, and that she was rhythmically stroking him without even realizing it. Reacting solely on instinct.

"My pants," he said. "Take them off now."

With trembling fingers she fumbled with the clasp, then pulled down the zipper. She tugged the slacks down, leaving his boxers in place.

"All of it," he demanded, so she pulled the boxers down, too. "Now, do that again."

She knew what he wanted. He wanted her to touch him again. She took him in her hand and the skin was so hot, she nearly jerked her arm back. Instead she squeezed.

The point of touching him, or at least, part of the point, had been so that he would touch her, too, but so far he was the one getting all of the action. With that thought came a sudden jab of concern that he was one of *those* men. The kind who took pleasure and gave nothing in return. She'd never been with a man who had taken the time to even try to please her, so what made her think Aaron would be any different?

Before she could even complete the thought, Aaron clasped her wrist to stop her. "That feels too good."

Wasn't that the point?

But she didn't argue because he *finally* reached down to unfasten her chinos—much more deftly than she'd managed with his. He eased her pants and panties down together and she kicked them away.

"Lie down," he said, nodding toward the bed. She did as he asked, trembling with anticipation. But instead of lying down beside her, he knelt between her thighs. If she had been more experienced with men, or more to the point, with men like *him,* she probably would have known what was coming next. Instead it was a total surprise when he eased her thighs open, leaned forward and kissed her there. She was so surprised, she wasn't sure what to do, how to react. Then he pressed her legs even farther apart and flicked her with his tongue. The sensation was so shockingly intimate and intense she cried out and arched off the bed. He teased her with his tongue, licking just hard enough to drive her mad, to make her squirm and moan. When she didn't think she could stand much more he took her into his mouth and every muscle from head to toe locked and shuddered in ecstasy, sending her higher and higher, and when it became too much, too intense, she pushed his head away.

She lay there with her eyes closed, too limp to do more than breathe. She felt the bed shift, and the warmth of Aaron's body beside hers. She pried her eyes open to find him grinning down at her. "Everything all right?"

It took all of her energy to nod. "Oh, yeah."

"Are you always that fast?"

"I have no idea."

"What do you mean."

"No man has actually ever done that."

He frowned. "Which part?"

"Either. Both. The few men I've been with weren't exactly…adventurous. And they were more interested in their own pleasure than mine."

"Are you saying no man has ever given you an orgasm?"

"Nope."

"That's just…*wrong*. There's nothing more satisfying for me than giving a woman pleasure."

"Really?" She didn't think it worked that way. Or maybe he was in a class all by himself.

"And you know the best part?" he said.

"Huh?"

He grinned that wolfish smile. "I get to spend the rest of the night proving it to you."

In his life Aaron had never been with a woman so responsive or easy to satisfy as Liv. She climaxed so quickly, and so often, just using his hands and mouth, that it sort of took the challenge out of it. But the way he looked at it, he was helping her make up for lost time. Those other men she'd been with must have been totally inept, completely self-absorbed or just plain stupid. That gave all men a bad rap. He'd never seen anything as fantastic as Liv shuddering in ecstasy, eyes blind with satisfaction.

"I want you inside me," she finally pleaded, gazing up at him with lust-filled eyes, and he couldn't resist giving her exactly what she wanted. He grabbed a condom and tore the package open with his teeth. He looked down at Liv and realized she was staring at his hard-on with a look on her face that hovered somewhere between curiosity and fascination.

"Can I do it?" she asked, holding out her hand.

He shrugged and gave her the condom. "Knock yourself out."

He expected her to roll it on; instead she leaned forward and took him in her mouth. Deep in her mouth. He groaned and wound his hands through her hair, on the verge of an explosion.

She took him from her mouth, looked up at him and grinned.

"I figured it would go on better this way. Besides, I've always wanted to try that."

She could experiment on him anytime. And he truly hoped she would.

He gritted his teeth as she carefully rolled the condom down the length of him.

"Like that?" she asked.

"Perfect," he said, and before he could make another move she lay back, pulling him down on top of her, between her thighs, arching to accept him.

She was so hot and wet and *tight* that he nearly lost

it on the first thrust. And though he was determined to make it last, she wasn't making it easy. Her hands were all over him, threading through his hair, her nails clawing at his back and shoulders, and she wrapped those gloriously long legs around his waist, whimpering in his ear. Then she tensed and moaned and her body clamped down around him like a fist, and it was all over. They rode it out together, then lay gasping for breath, a tangle of arms and legs.

"I had no idea it could be like this," she said.

Neither did he. "You say that as if we're done."

She rose up on one elbow and looked down at him, her expression serious. "I can't marry William."

"That's what I keep telling you," he said. He just hoped she hadn't decided to set her sights on him instead. They had fantastic sexual chemistry, but that didn't change the fact that he had every intention of remaining a free man. William wasn't the right man for her, but neither was he.

"If I wanted to marry him, I would feel guilty right now, wouldn't I?"

"I would think so."

"I don't. Not at all. In fact I almost feel...*relieved*. Like this huge weight has been lifted from my shoulders."

"That's good, right?"

She nodded. "I'm not ready to get married. And even if I was, I can't marry a man I don't love, that I'm not even sexually attracted to. I want more than that."

"You deserve more."

"I do," she agreed, looking as though, for the first time in her life, she finally believed it. "We have to keep this quiet."

"About William?"

"No. About us. Unless…" She frowned.

"Unless what?"

"Well, maybe we shouldn't do this again."

"Don't you think that's a bit unrealistic? Since you got here we haven't been able to keep our hands off each other."

"Then we'll have to be very discreet. Anne already suspects something."

He shrugged. "So what?"

"I'm going to go out on a limb here and assume that your family wouldn't approve of you slumming it with the hired help."

"You're a *guest*," he reminded her. "Besides, I don't give a damn what my family thinks."

"But I do. I spent most of my life trying not to be one of *those* girls. Having sex for the sake of sex."

"This is different."

"Is it really?"

He wanted to say yes, but they were by definition having an affair. And although he hated to admit it, if he were sleeping with a woman of his own social level, his siblings wouldn't bat an eyelash. Liv's humble beginnings and lack of pedigree put her in an entirely different category.

Even though *he* didn't think of her any differently than a duchess or debutante, she was probably right in believing other people would.

It wasn't fair, but it was just the way the world worked. No point in making this any more complicated than necessary.

"They won't hear a word about it from me," he told her.

"Thank you."

"Now," he said with a grin, "where were we?" He pulled her down for a kiss, but just as their lips met, his cell phone began to ring. "Ignore it."

"What if it's something about your father?"

She was right of course. He mumbled a curse and leaned over the edge of the bed to grab it from the floor. He looked at the display and saw that it was Chris. He answered with an irritated, "What?"

"Sorry to wake you, but we need you in the security office."

He didn't tell him that he hadn't been sleeping. And that he had no intention of sleeping for quite some time. He and Liv weren't even close to being finished. "It can't wait until morning?"

"Unfortunately, no. Besides, you wouldn't want to pass up the opportunity to say I told you so."

Eleven

The Gingerbread Man, as he liked to call himself, was back in business.

Posing as hospital housekeeping staff, he'd made it as far as the royal family's private waiting room. Hours after he was gone, security found the chilling calling card he'd left behind. An envelope full of photographs of Aaron and his siblings that the Gingerbread Man had taken in various places. The girls shopping in Paris, and one of Chris taken through the office window of a building where he'd recently had a meeting with local merchants. Every shot of Aaron showed him with a different woman.

It wasn't a direct threat, but the implication was

clear. He was watching them, and despite all of their security, they were vulnerable. And either he'd gotten bolder or he'd made a critical error, because he'd let himself be caught on the hospital surveillance. Aaron stood in the security office with Chris watching the grainy image from the surveillance tape.

"How in the hell did he get so close to the king?" Aaron asked.

"His ID checked out," Randal Jenkins, their head of security, told him. "He must have either stolen a badge from another employee or fabricated one. He never actually looks up at the camera, so he may be difficult to identify."

"We need to tighten down security at the hospital," Chris told him.

"Already done, sir."

"The king knows?" Aaron asked.

"He and the queen were informed immediately as a precaution," Jenkins said. "The London police are involved, as well. They're talking with the hospital staff to see if anyone remembers him, and they're suggesting we take the news public, run the security tape on television in hope that someone will recognize him."

"What do you think?" Aaron asked his brother. "Personally, I'd like to see this lunatic behind bars, but it's your call."

"Take it to the public," Chris told Jenkins. "And until we catch him, no one will leave the castle without a full security detail, and we'll limit any unnecessary travel or personal appearances."

"That will be difficult with the holidays approaching," Aaron said. "Christmas is barely a month away."

"I'm confident that by then he'll be in custody," Chris said.

Aaron wished he shared that confidence, but he had the feeling that it wouldn't be that easy.

Though Aaron assured her that the king was fine and it was nothing more than a security issue that needed his attention, Liv tossed and turned, sleeping fitfully. She roused at 5:00 a.m. so completely awake that she figured she might as well get to work.

The castle was still dark and quiet, but the kitchen was bustling with activity.

"Getting an early start, miss?" Geoffrey asked, sounding almost…friendly.

"I couldn't sleep," she told him.

"Shall I bring you coffee?"

Was he actually being *nice* to her? "Yes, please. If it's no trouble."

He nodded. "I'll be down shortly."

Liv headed down the stairs, grinning like an idiot. Though it shouldn't have mattered what Geoffrey thought of her, she couldn't help but feel accepted somehow, as if she'd gained access to the secret club.

As she rounded the corner to the lab door, she stopped abruptly and the smile slipped from her face.

She distinctly remembered turning out the lights last night before going up for dinner. Now they were blazing. The assistant, a mousy young girl from the university, didn't have a code for the door. As far as Liv knew, no one but herself, Aaron, Geoffrey and the security office had access, and she couldn't imagine what business they might have down there.

She approached the door cautiously, peering through the window. As far as she could see, there was no one there. So why did she have the eerie sensation she was being watched?

"Problem, miss?"

Liv screeched with surprise and spun around, her backpack flying off her shoulder and landing with a thud on the ground. Geoffrey stood behind her carrying a tray with her coffee.

She slapped a hand over her frantically beating heart. "You scared me half to death!"

"Something wrong with the door?" he inquired, looking mildly amused, the first real emotion she had ever seen him show.

"Do you know if anyone was down here last night?" she asked.

"Not that I'm aware of." He stepped past her and punched in his code. The door clicked open and he stepped inside. Liv grabbed her backpack and cautiously followed him.

"I know I turned out the lights when I left last night, but they were on when I came down."

"Maybe you forgot." He set the coffee down on the table beside her desk.

When she saw the surface of her desk, she gasped.

He turned, regarding her curiously. "Something wrong, miss?"

"My desk," she said. The papers and files that had been strewn everywhere were now all stacked in neat piles. "Someone straightened it."

"They're just trying to get your attention," he said, pouring her a cup of coffee.

"Who?" Had someone been snooping down there?

"The spirits."

Spirits?

She had to resist rolling her eyes. It surprised her that a man as seemingly logical as the butler would buy in to that otherwordly garbage. "I don't believe in ghosts."

"All the more reason for them to ruffle your feathers. But you needn't worry, they're perfectly harmless."

It would explain how the door kept opening on its own, when security claimed the log had shown no record of the keypad being used, and maintenance had found nothing amiss with the controls. Yet she still believed it was far more likely that someone was messing with her head or trying to frighten her. Maybe even Geoffrey?

But why?

"Shall I call you for breakfast?" Geoffrey asked.

"I think I'll skip it," she said.

Geoffrey nodded politely, then let himself out of the lab.

Liv wasn't exactly looking forward to facing Aaron's family again. What if someone else had figured out how she'd done so well at poker? Or even worse, what if they knew Aaron had been in her room last night?

If it were possible, she would stay holed up in her lab until the day she was able to go home to the States.

She took her computer out of her backpack and booted it up. As she did every morning, she checked her e-mail first and among the usual spam the filter always missed, she was surprised to find a message from William. There was no subject, and the body of the e-mail said simply, *Just checking your progress.* That was it. Nothing personal like, *How are you?* Or, *Have you made a decision yet?*

She was going to have to tell him that she couldn't marry him. Let him down easy. She would be honest and explain that she just wasn't ready to marry anyone yet, and hope that it wouldn't affect their friendship or their working relationship.

But she couldn't do it through e-mail; that would be far too impersonal, and she hadn't yet worked up the nerve to call him. Maybe it would be better if she waited until she flew home and did it face-to-face.

But was it really fair to string him along? If he knew what she'd been up to last night…

A pleasant little shiver tingled through her body

when she recalled the way Aaron had touched her last night. The way he'd driven her mad with his hands and his mouth. Just thinking about it made her feel warm all over. Even though deep down something was telling her that she would end up regretting it, that she was way out of her league and headed for imminent disaster, she could hardly wait to be alone with him again.

Maybe last night was a total fluke and the next time they had sex it would only be so-so, even though she doubted it. If she kept thinking about it, about *him,* she wouldn't get a thing done today.

She answered William's mail with an equally impersonal rundown of her progress so far, and asked him to please go over the data she planned to send him later that afternoon—a fresh eye never hurt— then she got back to work analyzing the samples her assistant had taken yesterday.

Although she usually became engrossed in her work, she couldn't shake the feeling that she was being watched, and kept looking over to the door. The window wasn't more than ten-by-ten inches square, but a few times she could swear she saw the shadow of a figure just outside. Was it possible that Aaron or one of his siblings had someone keeping an eye on her? What did they think she might be doing down there, other than saving their country from agricultural devastation?

Or maybe it was just her mind playing tricks.

Some time later she heard the sound of the door clicking open, and thought, Here we go again. She was relieved when she heard footsteps moving in her direction. Assuming it was probably Geoffrey fetching the empty coffee carafe, she paid no attention, until she felt a rush of cool air brush past her and the unmistakable weight of a hand on her shoulder. She realized it had to be Aaron, there to say good morning. She pried herself away from her computer and spun in her chair to smile up at him, but there was no one there. She looked over at the door and saw that it was still firmly closed.

She shot to her feet and an eerie shiver coursed through her. It had to be her imagination. Could she have dozed off for a second? Maybe dreamed it?

If she had been sleeping, she wouldn't feel completely awake and alert. She glanced back up at the door and saw distinct movement outside the window, then it clicked and swung open. She sat there frozen, expecting some ghoulish apparition to float through, relieved when it was Aaron who stepped into the lab.

Her apprehension must have shown because when he saw her standing there, he stopped in his tracks and frowned. "You look as though you've just seen a ghost."

"Do you have someone spying on me?"

Taken aback by Liv's question, Aaron said, "Good morning to you, too."

"I'm serious, Aaron. Please tell me the truth."

Not only did she look serious, but deeply disturbed by the possibility. How could she even ask him that? "Of course not."

"You mean it?"

"Liv, if I felt you needed constant supervision, I never would have invited you here."

"Could your brother or one of your sisters have someone watching me?"

"I can't imagine why they would."

She shuddered and hugged herself. "This is too weird."

He walked over to her desk. "What's wrong?"

"I keep getting this feeling like someone is watching me, and when I look up at the window in the door, I see a shadow, like someone is standing just outside."

"Maybe someone on the laundry staff has a crush on you," he joked, but she didn't look amused. "I don't know who it could be."

"You know that the door kept popping open yesterday, and the technician said there wasn't anything wrong with it. Then this morning when I came down here, the lights were on and I know I turned them off last night."

He shrugged. "Maybe you thought you did, but didn't hit the switch all the way or something."

"Then explain how the papers that were strewn all over my desk were stacked neatly this morning."

He frowned. "Okay, that is kind of weird."

"There's something else."

"What?"

She looked hesitant to tell him, but finally said, "This is going to sound completely crazy, but a few minutes before you came in I heard the door open and footsteps in the room, then someone touched my shoulder, but when I turned around no one was there and the door was closed."

He might have thought it was crazy, but he'd heard similar stories from the staff. "Lots of people have reported having strange experiences down here."

"I don't believe in ghosts," she said, but without a whole lot of conviction. "Scientific labs aren't typically hot spots for paranormal activity."

"But how many labs have you been in that used to be dungeons?"

"None," she admitted.

"If it eases your mind, no one has ever been physically harmed down here. Just frightened."

"I don't feel as though I'm in physical danger. It's just creepy to think that someone is watching me. And—" she shuddered again "—*touching* me."

"Do you want to leave?"

"You mean, permanently?"

He nodded. God knows he didn't want her to; they needed her expertise and would be hard-pressed to find someone equally qualified, but he would understand if she had to.

"Of course not," she said, and he felt a little too relieved for comfort.

He tried to tell himself that he was only concerned

for his country's welfare, but he knew that was nonsense. He wanted more time with Liv. At least a few weeks to get her out of his system.

He grinned and told her, "I guess that means I'll just have to protect you."

He wrapped a hand around her hip and tugged her to him. She resisted for about half a second, then gave in and melted into his arms, resting her head on his shoulder. She felt so warm and soft and she smelled delicious. If they weren't in the lab, he would already be divesting her of her clothing.

"I had fun last night," he said and he could swear he felt her blush.

She wrapped her arms around him and hugged herself to his chest. "Me, too. Did you resolve your security problem?"

"In a manner of speaking." Because it wasn't a secret, and she would eventually be informed of the security lockdown, he figured he might as well tell her about the Gingerbread Man.

"That's really creepy," she said, gazing up at him. "Why would someone want to hurt your family?"

Aaron shrugged. "There are a lot of crazy people out there."

"I guess."

He kissed the tip of her nose. "I didn't think I'd find you in the lab. I figured, because it's the weekend, you might not be working today. I thought you might be up to a game of billiards."

"I work every day."

"Even Sunday?"

She gazed up at him and nodded. "Even Sunday."

"That reminds me. Chris wanted to know how long you'll need for the holidays."

She looked confused. "Need for what?"

"To go home."

"Oh, I won't be going home. I don't celebrate Christmas."

"Why not?" he asked, thinking that maybe it was some sort of religious issue.

She shrugged. "No one to celebrate with, I guess."

He frowned. "You must have friends."

"Yes, but they all have families and I would feel out of place. It really is not a big deal."

But it was. It was a very big deal. The thought of her spending the holidays alone disturbed him in a way he hadn't expected. It made him...*angry.* If her so-called friends really cared about her, they would insist she spend the holidays with them.

"If you're worried about me getting in the way, I'll keep to myself," she assured him. "You won't even know I'm here."

What kind of person did she think him to be? "That is the most ridiculous thing I've ever heard," he said, and she looked startled by his sharp tone. "I won't let you spend Christmas alone. You'll celebrate with us."

"Aaron, I don't think—"

"This is *not* negotiable. I'm *telling* you. You're spending the holidays with my family."

She opened her mouth to argue, so he did the only thing he could to shut her up. He leaned forward, covered her lips with his and kissed her.

Twelve

Aaron was making it really difficult for her to tell him no. Literally. Every time they came up for air, and she would open her mouth to speak, he would just start kissing her again. She was beginning to feel all soft and mushy-brained and turned on. Yet she couldn't shake the feeling they were being watched.

She opened one eye and peered at the door, nearly swallowing her own tongue when she saw a face staring back at her through the window. A woman she didn't recognize, with long, curly blond hair wearing some sort of lacy bonnet. Liv's first thought was that someone had discovered their secret, and they were both in big trouble. Then before her eyes the face went misty and translucent and seemed to dissipate and disappear into thin air.

She let out a muffled shriek against Aaron's lip, then ripped herself free so fast that she stumbled backward, tripped over her chair and landed on her rear end on the hard linoleum floor.

"Bloody hell, what's wrong?" Aaron asked, stunned by her sudden outburst.

She pointed to the door, even though whoever, or *whatever,* she'd seen in the window was no longer there. "A f-face."

He spun around to look. "There's no one there."

"It disappeared."

"Whoever it was probably saw you looking and ran off."

"No. I mean, it actually disappeared. One minute it was there, and the next minute it vanished. I don't even know how to explain it. It was as if it…dissolved."

"Dissolved?"

"Like mist." It was scary as hell, but the scientist in her couldn't help feeling intrigued. She had always clung to the belief that there was no such thing as heaven or an afterlife. When you were dead, you were dead. Could this mean there was some sort of life after death?

He looked at the window again, then back to her, still sprawled on the floor. "Are you saying that you saw a ghost?"

"A few days ago I never would have believed it,

but I can't think of any other logical explanation." And for some reason, seeing it with her own eyes, knowing it was real, made her more curious than frightened. She wanted to see it again.

He held out a hand to help her up, and when she was on her feet he tugged her back into his arms. "If someone was watching us, alive or otherwise, they nearly got one hell of a view, because I was about two seconds from ravishing you."

So much for being discreet. "Suppose someone on this plane of existence did happen to come down and look in the window?"

"So we'll cover it," he said, nibbling on her neck. "A sheet of paper and some tape should do the trick."

What he was doing felt deliciously wonderful, but now wasn't the time for fooling around. Although she had the feeling that when it came to women, he was used to getting his way. If he was going to be with her, he was going to have to learn to compromise.

"Aaron, I have to work," she said firmly, planting her hands on his chest.

"No, you don't," he mumbled against her skin.

She gave a gentle but firm shove. "Yes. *I do.*"

He hesitated a moment, then grudgingly let her go. "Do I get to see you at all today?"

Though she could easily work late into the evening, if he had to compromise, then so should she. "How about a game of billiards tonight after dinner?"

He grinned. "And after billiards?"

She just smiled.

"I'm holding you to it," he said, backing toward the door.

"Oh, and about Christmas," she said.

"It's not up for discussion."

"But your family—"

"Won't mind at all. Besides, if Melissa were to get wind of you spending the holidays alone, she would probably have an emotional meltdown."

He was probably right. If Aaron didn't insist she join them, Melissa probably would. Or maybe she was rationalizing.

Compromise, Liv. Compromise.

"Okay," she said, and that seemed to make him very happy.

"See you at dinner," he said as he walked out.

She'd never had what anyone would consider a conventional Christmas holiday. Her foster families never had money for gifts and extravagant meals. If she got candy in her stocking—hell, if she even *had* a stocking—it was a pretty good year. It used to make her sad when the kids at school returned after the holiday break sporting new clothes and handheld video games and portable CD players, but she'd learned to harden her heart.

Even now Christmas was just another day to her. But she would be lying if she said it didn't get a *little* lonely, knowing everyone else was with their families.

But there were definite benefits, too. She didn't

have to fight the holiday crowds shopping for gifts, or have outrageous credit card bills come January. The simpler she kept her life, the better. Although it might be a nice change to spend Christmas somewhere other than alone in the lab. With a real family.

Or maybe, she thought as she sat down in front of her computer, it would make her realize all that she'd been missing.

Liv fidgeted beside Aaron as they neared the king's suite. His parents had returned from England yesterday, several days later than expected due to mild complications caused by the reinsertion of the pump. But he was feeling well, in good spirits and happy to be home with his family.

"Maybe we shouldn't bother them," Liv said, her brow furrowed. "I'm sure the king needs rest."

"He *wants* to meet you," he assured her. She'd grown much more comfortable in the castle this past week. She seemed to enjoy spending time with his siblings, and the feeling was remarkably mutual. Even Anne had lowered her defenses within the past few days and seemed to be making a genuine effort to get to know Liv, and of course Louisa loved everyone.

He took Liv's hand and gave it a reassuring squeeze, and even though no one was around, she pulled from his grasp. He was breaking her rule of no public displays of affection. Although he was quite sure that if his siblings hadn't already begun to suspect their affair, it was only a matter of time. Nearly every moment Liv wasn't in the lab, Aaron was with her and he'd spent every night for the past seven days in her room.

If they did suspect, no one had said a word to him.

"I'm so nervous. I'm afraid that when I curtsy I'm going to fall on my face."

"If you fall, I'll catch you," he assured her. He knocked on the suite door then pushed it open, feeling Liv go tense beside him.

His father had dressed for the occasion, though he was reclined on the sofa. His mother rose to greet them as they entered the room.

"Liv, meet my parents, the King and Queen of Thomas Isle. Mother, Father, this is Olivia Montgomery."

Liv curtsied, and even though it wasn't the smoothest he'd ever seen, she was nowhere close to falling over.

"It's an honor to meet you both," she said, a slight quiver in her voice.

"The honor is all ours, Miss Montgomery," his father said, shaking her hand, which she did gingerly, Aaron noticed, as though she worried she might break him. "Words cannot express how deeply we appreciate your visit."

His mother didn't even offer to shake Liv's hand. Maybe the king's health and all that time in the hospital was taking its toll on her. Although she'd seemed fine yesterday. Just a bit tired.

"My children speak quite highly of you," the king said, and added with a grin, "in fact, I hear you're something of a card shark."

Liv smiled nervously. "I'm sure it was beginner's luck, Your Highness."

"I'm assuming you've had time to work since you arrived," his mother said and her curt tone took him aback.

Liv looked a little stunned as well, so Aaron answered, "Of course she has. I practically have to drag her out of the lab just to eat dinner. She would work around the clock if I didn't insist she take a break every now and then."

She ignored him and asked Liv in an almost-demanding tone, "Have you made any progress?"

As was the case when she talked about her work or someone questioned her professionally, she suddenly became the confident and assertive scientist. The transformation never ceased to amaze him.

"I'm very close to discovering the strain of disease affecting the crops," she told his mother. Usually she explained things to him in layman's terms, so he had at least a little hope of understanding what she was talking about. She must have been trying to make a point because when she explained her latest developments to his mother, she used all scientific terms and jargon. Though the queen had spent the better part of her life farming, botanical genetics was *way* out of her league.

By the time Liv finished with her explanation, his mother looked at least a little humbled.

"Would you mind excusing us, Miss Montgomery," the queen said. "I need to have a word with my son."

"Of course," Liv said. "I need to get back down to the lab anyway. It was a pleasure to meet you both."

"I'll walk you out," Aaron said, leading her from the room.

When they were in the hallway with the door closed, Liv turned to him and said, "I'm so sorry."

Her apology confused him. He should be the one apologizing for his mother's behavior. "For what? I thought you were fantastic."

She frowned, looking troubled. "I was showing off. It was rude of me."

"Love, you've earned the right to show off every now and then."

"Your mother hates me."

"Why would she hate you?"

"Because she knows."

He frowned. "Knows what?"

She lowered her voice, even though they were alone. "That something is going on between us."

"How could she?"

"I don't know, but that was a mother lion protecting her cub. Her message clearly said back off."

"You're being paranoid. I think between my

father's health, the security breach at the hospital and the diseased crops, she's just stressed out."

Liv didn't look as though she believed him, but she didn't push the issue.

"I'll come see you in the lab later." He brushed a quick kiss across her lips, ignoring her look of protest, then let himself back into his parents' suite. He crossed the room to where they still sat, determined to get to the bottom of this.

"What the bloody hell was that about?" he asked his mother.

"Watch your tone," his father warned.

"*My* tone? Could she have been any more rude to Liv?"

"Don't think I don't know what's going on between you two," his mother said.

So Liv had been right. She did suspect something. He folded his arms over his chest. "And what *is* going on, Mother?"

"Nothing that your father and I approve of."

"You haven't even been here, so how could you possibly know what's been going on? Do you have the staff watching me?"

"There's someone I want you to meet," she said. "She's a duchess from a *good* family."

Unlike Liv who had *no* family, was that what she meant? That was hardly Liv's fault. "If you're concerned that I'm going to run off and marry Liv, you can stop worrying."

"It isn't proper. She's not of noble blood."

If his mother had the slightest clue about the behavior of those so-called *proper* women she set him up with, she would have kittens. The spoiled brats whose daddies gave them everything their hearts desired, while they dabbled in drugs and alcohol, and were more often than not sexually promiscuous. Liv was a saint in comparison.

"Maybe you should take the time to know her before you pass judgment."

"I know all I need to. She's not good enough for you," his mother said.

"Not *good* enough? I can safely say she's more intelligent than all three of us combined. She's sweet, and kind, and down-to-earth. And she could very well be saving our *asses* from total financial devastation," he said, earning a stern look from his father. "Can you say that of your princesses or duchesses?"

"The decision has already been made," his mother said. "You'll meet the duchess next Friday."

Since Chris married Melissa, their mother had been determined to find Aaron a wife, and even though he'd told her a million times he didn't want to settle down, the message seemed to go in one ear and out the other. But he'd gone along with the blind dates and the setups because it was always easier than arguing. Easier than standing up for himself.

He thought of Liv, who had fought like hell for everything she'd ever gotten, how strong she was, and wondered what had he ever done but settle? From the day he was born his family told him who he was supposed to be. Well, he was tired of compromising himself, tired of playing by their rules. It ended today.

"No," he said.

She frowned. "No, what?"

"I won't meet her."

"Of course you will."

"No, I won't. No more blind dates, no more setups. I'm finished."

She huffed out a frustrated breath. "How will you ever find a wife if you don't—"

"I don't *want* a wife. I don't want to settle down."

She rolled her eyes. "Every man says that. But when the right one comes along you'll change your mind."

"If that's true, I'll find her without your help."

She gave him her token you-would-be-lost-without-me-to-run-your-life look. "Aaron, sweetheart—"

"I mean it, Mother. I don't want to hear another word about it."

She looked stunned by his demand; his father, on the other hand, looked amused. "He's made his decision, dear," he said. And before she could argue, he sighed and said, "This conversation has worn me out."

"Why didn't you say something?" She patted his shoulder protectively and summoned the nurse, shooting Aaron a look that suggested his father's sudden fatigue was his fault. "Let's get you to bed. We'll talk about this later."

No, they wouldn't, he wanted to say, but for his father's sake he let it drop. She would come to realize that he wasn't playing by her rules any longer.

While the nurse helped his father into bed, his mother turned to him and said, "Please let Geoffrey know that your father and I will be taking dinner in our suite tonight."

"Of course."

She smiled and patted his cheek fondly. "That's a good boy."

A good boy? Ugh. What was he, twelve? He turned and left before he said something he regretted. She seemed to believe she'd won, but nothing could be further from the truth. Knowing Liv had made him take a good hard look at his own life and he didn't like what he was seeing. It was time he made a few changes.

Thirteen

The following Monday was December first and overnight the castle was transformed to a holiday wonderland. Fresh evergreen swags dotted with red berries and accented with big red bows hung from the stair railings, making everything smell piney and festive, and mistletoe hung in every door and archway. Life-size nutcrackers stood guard in the halls and every room on the main floor had a Christmas tree decorated in a different color and theme. From one hung various styles and flavors of candy canes and other sugar confections, while another was festooned with antique miniature toy ornaments. Some were draped in all shades of purple, and others in creamy whites. But the most amazing tree was in the ballroom. It stood at least twenty feet high, decorated in shimmering silver and gold balls.

The outside of the castle was the most incredible of all. What looked to be about a million tiny multicolored lights edged the windows and turrets and lit the shrubs.

Liv had never seen anything like it, and she couldn't help but get drawn into the holiday spirit. For the first time in her life Christmas wasn't something she dreaded or ignored. This time she let herself feel it, get caught up in the atmosphere. And she almost felt as if she had a family. Aaron's siblings made her feel so welcome, and Liv was particularly fond of the king. He was warm and friendly and had a surprisingly thorough understanding of genetic science and an insatiable curiosity. They had many evening conversations about her research, sitting by the fire in the study sipping hot cider.

"Science is a hobby of mine," he once told her. "As a child I used to dream of being a scientist. I even planned to go to university and study it. That was before I was crown prince."

Much the way Aaron had dreamed of being a doctor, she thought. "You weren't always crown prince?"

"I had an older brother, Edward. He would have been king, but he contracted meningitis when he was fifteen. It left him blind and physically impaired, so the crown was passed on to me. It's a bit ironic, really. We would spend hours in this very room, sitting by the fire. I would read to him, or play his favorite music. And now here I am, the incapacitated one."

"But only temporarily," she reminded him.

He just smiled and said, "Let's hope so."

The queen didn't share her husband's affection for Liv. She wasn't cruel or even rude. She was just...indifferent. Liv had overcome enough adversity in her life to understand that she couldn't let herself be bothered by the opinions of one person, but she would be lying if she said it didn't hurt her feelings just a little. Particularly because she was being judged not on the merits of her accomplishments, or even her morals, but on her lack of pedigree.

The Sunday before Christmas a blizzard dropped nearly a foot of snow and Liv let Aaron talk her into trying cross-country skiing. He wanted to take her to their ski lodge on the other side of the island, but with the Gingerbread Man still on the loose, the king insisted they stay on the castle property.

As Liv anticipated, she spent the better part of the first hour sitting in the snow.

"It just takes practice," Aaron told her as he hauled her back up on her feet again, and she actually managed to make it two or three yards before she fell on her face. But he assured her, "You're doing great!"

As inept as she felt, and embarrassed by her lack of coordination, Aaron's enthusiasm was contagious and she found that she was having fun. Since she arrived on Thomas Isle, he had introduced her to so many things that she otherwise would have never tried. If not for him, she would still be in her lab 24/7, working her life away instead of living it.

As much fun as they had been having, Liv knew it wouldn't last. She was in the process of testing compounds in hope of finding one that would kill the disease, and when she found the right combination, there would be no reason for her to stay. Leaving would be hard because she'd grown attached to Aaron. In fact, she felt she may even be in love with him, but that didn't change who they were. Besides, he had made it quite clear that he didn't want to be tied down. It was destined to end, and all she could do was enjoy the time they had left together.

An hour before sundown, exhausted to the center of her bones and aching in places she didn't even know she could ache, Liv tossed down her poles and said enough.

"You have to admit that was fun," he said as they stripped out of their gear.

"Oh, yeah," she said, hissing in pain as she bent over to unclip the ski boots. "Spending an entire day sitting in the snow has always been my idea of fun."

He shot her a skeptical look.

"Okay," she admitted with a shrug that sent spirals of pain down her back. "Maybe it was a *little* fun."

"You were getting pretty good near the end there."

It was her turn to look skeptical.

"I'm serious," he said. "By the end of winter I'll have you skiing like a pro."

The *end* of winter? How long did he expect her to stay? Did he *want* her to stay? And even more important, did *she* want to?

Of course he didn't. It was just an off-the-cuff remark that he probably hadn't thought through.

They walked up the stairs—well, he walked and she limped—to her room.

"I'm going to dress for dinner," he said. "Shall I pick you up on my way back down?"

"I don't think so."

"Are you sure?"

"Not only am I not hungry, but I'm exhausted and everything hurts. I'd like to lie down for a while."

"I'll come by and check on you later." He brushed a quick kiss across her lips, then headed to his room. She still wasn't comfortable with him showing her physical affection where someone might see. Although she didn't doubt that his family knew what was going on. They had just been kind enough not to say anything. She was sure they saw it for what it was. A fling. But she still didn't feel comfortable advertising it.

She went into her room and limped to the bathroom, downing three ibuprofen tablets before she stepped into the shower. She blasted the water as hot as she could stand, then she toweled off and crawled into bed naked. She must have fallen asleep the instant her head hit the pillow because the next thing she remembered was Aaron sitting on the edge of the mattress.

"What time is it?" she asked, her voice gravelly with sleep.

"Nine." He switched on the lamp beside the bed and she squinted against the sudden flood of light. "How do you feel?"

She tried to move and her muscles screamed in protest. "Awful," she groaned. "Even my eyelids hurt."

"Then you're going to like what I found," he said, holding up a small bottle.

"What is it?"

He flashed her one of his sexy, sizzling smiles. "Massage oil."

He eased back the covers, and when he saw that she was naked, he growled deep in his throat. "I swear, you get more beautiful every day."

He'd told her that so many times, so often that she was beginning to believe him, to see herself through his eyes. And in that instant in time everything was perfect.

He caressed her cheek with the backs of his fingers. "I love…"

Her heart jolted in her chest and she thought for sure that he was going to say he loved her. In that millisecond, she knew without a doubt that her honest reply would be, *I love you, too.*

"…just looking at you," he said instead.

The disappointment she felt was like a crushing weight on her chest, making it difficult to breathe. Tell him you love him, you idiot! But she couldn't do that. Love wasn't part of this arrangement. Instead she didn't say a word, she just wrapped her arms around him and pulled him down for a kiss. And when he made love to her, he was so sweet and gentle that it nearly brought her to tears.

She loved him so fiercely it made her chest ache, and she desperately wanted him to love her, too.

She wasn't sure how much longer she could take this.

It took some convincing on his part, but Aaron talked Liv into another afternoon of skiing on Christmas Eve. And despite her reservations she did exceptionally well. So well that he looked forward to introducing her to other recreational activities, like biking and kayaking and even low-level rock climbing. The problem was, she probably wouldn't be around long enough. He was sorry for that, but in a way relieved. He'd grown closer and more attached to Liv than he had any other woman in his life. Dangerously close. And even though he knew he was walking a very fine and precarious line, he wasn't ready to let go yet.

Christmas morning he woke Liv at 5:45 a.m., despite the fact that they had been up half the night making love.

"It's too early," she groaned, shoving a pillow over her head.

He pulled it back off. "Come on, wake up. We're gathering with everyone in the study at six."

She squinted up at him. "*Six?* What for?"

"To open presents. Then afterward we have a huge breakfast. It's been a tradition as long as I can remember."

She groaned again and closed her eyes. "I'd rather sleep."

"It's *Christmas*. And you promised you would spend it with me and my family, remember?"

"I was thinking that you meant Christmas dinner."

"I meant the entire day." He tugged on her arm. "Now come on, get up."

She grumbled about it, but let him pull her to an upright position. She yawned and rubbed her eyes and asked, "What should I wear?"

"Pajamas." At her questioning look, he added, "It's what everyone else will be wearing."

She made him wait while she brushed her hair and teeth, and when they got to the study his siblings and sister-in-law were already gathered around the tree, waiting to open the piles of gifts stacked there. Their father sat in his favorite armchair and their mother beside him at the hearth. Geoffrey stood at the bar pouring hot cider. Christmas music played softly and a fire blazed in the fireplace.

"Hurry up, you two!" Louisa said excitedly.

"I shouldn't be here," Liv mumbled under her breath, standing stiffly beside him, looking as though she were about to go to the guillotine.

"Of course you should." When she refused to move, he took her hand and pulled her over to the tree and sat her by Louisa. The second she was off her feet she pulled her hand from his.

"Merry Christmas!" Louisa gushed, giving Liv a warm hug, and after a slight hesitation, Liv hugged her back. If anyone could make Liv feel like part of the family, it was Louisa. Although right now she just looked overwhelmed. She looked downright stunned when Anne, who wore the santa hat and passed out the gifts, announced, "And here's one for Olivia from the king and queen."

Liv's jaw actually dropped. "F-for me?"

Anne handed it to her. "That's what the tag says."

She took it and just held it, as if she wasn't sure what to do.

"Aren't you going to open it?" Aaron asked.

"But I didn't get anything for anyone."

His mother surprised him by saying, "Your being here is the only gift we need."

Liv bit her lip, picking gingerly at the taped edge of the paper, while everyone else tore into theirs enthusiastically. It was almost as though she had never opened a gift before or had forgotten how. What disturbed him most was that it might be true. When was the last time anyone had given her anything?

She finally got it open and pulled from the layers of gold tissue paper a deep blue cashmere cardigan.

"Oh," she breathed. "It's beautiful."

"You keep the lab so dreadfully cold," his mother said. "I thought it might come in handy."

"Thank you so much."

Anne passed out another round of gifts and this time there was one for Liv from Chris and Melissa, a pair of thick wool socks.

"For skiing," Melissa told her.

Louisa got Liv a silver bracelet decorated with science-themed charms, and Anne gave her a matching cashmere mitten, scarf and hat set. Aaron had gotten her something, too, but she would have to wait until later to get it.

The last present under the tree was for the king and queen from Chris and Melissa. Their mother opened it and inside was what looked like an ultrasound photo. Did that mean…?

"What is this?" their mother asked, looking confused.

"Those are your grandchildren," Chris said with a grin. "All three of them."

"Three grandchildren!" his mother shrieked, while his father beamed proudly and said, "Congratulations!"

"They implanted five embryos," Melissa said. "Three took. It's still very early, but we couldn't wait to tell you. My doctor said everything looks great."

Aaron had never seen his mother look so proud or

excited. She knelt down to hug them both, then *everyone* was hugging Chris and Melissa and congratulating them.

"Isn't it great? I'm going to be an uncle," Aaron said, turning to Liv, but she wasn't smiling or laughing like the rest of them. In fact, she looked as though she might be sick. "Hey, are you okay?"

She shook her head and said, "Excuse me," then she bolted from the room, seven startled pairs of eyes following her.

"What happened?" his mother asked, and Louisa said, "Did we do something wrong?"

"I don't know," Aaron said, but he was going to find out.

Fourteen

Liv reached her room, heart beating frantically and hands shaking, and went straight to the closet for her suitcase. She dropped it on the bed and opened it just as Aaron appeared in the doorway.

"What happened down there?" he asked, looking concerned. "Are you okay?"

"I'm sorry. Please tell everyone that I'm *so* sorry. I just couldn't take it another minute."

He saw her suitcase and asked, "What are you doing?"

"Packing. I have to leave."

He looked stunned. "Was being with my family really that awful?"

"No, it was absolutely wonderful. I had no idea it could be like that. I just… I can't do this anymore."

"What do you mean? I thought we were having fun."

"I was. I *am*. The time we've spent together has been the best in my life."

She started toward the closet to get her clothes, but he stepped in her way, looking so hopelessly confused she wanted to hug him. "So what's the problem?"

Did he honestly have no idea what was going on? "I know it's illogical and totally irrational, but I've fallen in love with you, Aaron."

She gave him a few seconds to return the sentiment, but he only frowned, looking troubled, and it made her inexplicably sad. She hadn't really believed he would share her feelings, but she had hoped. But as she had reminded herself over and over, the world just didn't work that way. Not the world she lived in.

"We don't have any further to go with this," she said. "And I'm just not the kind of person who can tread water. I think it would be better for us both if I leave now. The work I have left to do, I can finish in my lab in the States."

"You can't leave," he said, looking genuinely upset.

"I have to."

"I *do* care about you."

"I know you do." Just not enough. Not enough for her, anyway. She wanted more. She wanted to be part of a family, to feel as if she belonged somewhere. And not just temporarily. She wanted forever.

She wanted it so badly that she ached, but she would never have that with him.

His brow furrowed. "I just… I can't…"

"I know," she assured him. "This is not your fault. This is *all* me. I never meant to fall in love with you."

"I…I don't know what to say."

Just tell me you love me, she wanted to tell him, but Aaron didn't do love. He didn't get serious and settle down. And even if he did, it wouldn't be with someone like her. She didn't fit in. She wasn't good enough for someone like him.

"I'll pack up the lab today," she told him. "Can you arrange for a flight off the island tomorrow?"

"Won't you at least have dinner with us? It's Christmas."

She shrugged. "It's just another day for me."

That was a lie. It used to be, but after this morning it would forever be a reminder of how wonderful it could be and everything she'd been missing out on, and so *desperately* wanted. In a way she wished she'd never met Aaron, that he'd never called for her help. She would still be living in blissful ignorance.

"You should get back to your family," she told him.

"You're sure I can't convince you to spend the day with us?"

"I'm sure."

He looked disappointed, but he didn't push the issue, and she was relieved because she was this close to caving, to throwing herself into his arms and saying she would stay as long as he wanted. Even if he couldn't love her.

"I'll have Geoffrey bring your gifts up and inform you of your travel arrangements," he said.

"Thank you."

"You're *sure* I can't change your mind?"

There was an almost pleading look in his eyes, and she wanted so badly to give in, but her heart just couldn't take it. "I can't."

"I'll leave you alone to pack."

He stepped out of the room, closing the door behind him, and though it felt so final, she knew she was doing the right thing.

She packed all of her clothes, leaving out one clean outfit for the following day, then she went down to the lab to start packing there, feeling utterly empty inside.

She never had seen the ghost again, but she'd made her presence known by occasionally stacking Liv's papers, hiding her pen or opening the lab door. Maybe she should have felt uncomfortable knowing she wasn't alone, but instead the presence was a comfort. She'd even caught herself talking to her, even though the conversation was always one-sided. She realized now that when she was gone she might even miss her elusive and unconventional companion.

She was going to miss everything about Thomas Isle.

Geoffrey came down around dinnertime with a

plate of food. She wasn't hungry, but she thanked him anyway. "I bet you're happy not to have to deal with me anymore," she joked, expecting him to emphatically agree.

Instead his expression was serious when he said, "Quite the contrary, miss."

She was too stunned to say a word as he turned and left. And here she thought he viewed her as a nuisance. The fact that he hadn't only made her feel worse.

She packed the last of her equipment by midnight, and when she went up to her room, waiting for her as promised were the gifts the family had given her and the itinerary for her trip. She sat down at the desk by the window writing them each a note of thanks, not only for the presents, but for accepting her into their home and treating her like family. She left them on the desk where Elise would find them when she cleaned the room.

She climbed under the covers around one-thirty, but tossed and turned and slept only an hour or two before her alarm buzzed at seven. She got out of bed feeling a grogginess that even a shower couldn't wash away. At seven-forty-five someone came to fetch her luggage, then a few minutes later Flynn from security came to fetch her.

"It's time to go to the airstrip, miss," he said.

"Let's do it," she said, feeling both relieved and heartsick. She wanted so badly to change her mind, to stay just a little bit longer and hope that he would see he loved her. But it was too late to turn back now. Even if it wasn't, she knew in her heart that it would be a bad idea.

She followed Flynn down the stairs to the foyer, and when she saw that the entire family lined up to say goodbye, the muscles in her throat contracted so tight that she could barely breathe. This was the last thing she'd expected. She had assumed her departure would be as uneventful as her arrival.

The king was first in line. If she had expected some cold and formal goodbye, a handshake and a "have a nice life," she couldn't have been more wrong. He hugged her warmly and said, "I've enjoyed our talks."

"Me, too," she said, realizing he was the closest thing she had ever had to a father figure. She hoped with all her being that the heart pump was successful and he lived a long, productive life. Long enough to see his daughters marry and his grandchildren grow. She wasn't a crier, but she could feel the burn of tears in her throat and behind her eyes. All she could manage to squeak out was, "Thanks for everything."

The queen was next. She took Liv's hands and air kissed her cheek. "It's been a pleasure having you with us," she said, and actually looked as though she meant it.

"Thank you for having me in your home," Liv said.

Chris and Melissa stood beside the queen. Chris kissed Liv's cheek and Melissa, with tears running in a steady river down her face—no doubt pregnancy hormones at work—hugged her hard. "Watch the mail for a baby shower invitation. I want you there."

If only. It was a lovely thought, yet totally unrealistic. She was sure by then they would have forgotten all about her.

Louisa scooped her up into a bone-crushing embrace. "We'll miss you," she said. "Keep in touch."

Anne hugged her, too, though not as enthusiastically. But she leaned close and Liv thought she was going to kiss her cheek, but instead she whispered, "My brother is a dolt."

Of all the things anyone could have said to her, that was probably the sweetest, and the tears were hovering so close to the surface now that she couldn't even reply.

Aaron was last, and the one she was least looking forward to saying goodbye to. He stood aside from his family by the door, hands in his pants pockets, eyes to the floor. As she approached he looked up at her.

The tears welled closer to the surface and she swallowed them back down. Please let this be quick and painless.

"You'll contact me when you have results," he said, all business.

She nodded. "Of course. And I'll send you updates on my progress. At the rate it's going, you should have it in plenty of time for the next growing season."

"Excellent." He was quiet for a second, then he said in a low voice, "I'm sorry. I just can't—"

"It's okay," she said, even though it wasn't. Even though it felt as though he was ripping her heart from her chest.

He nodded, looking remorseful. She had started to turn toward the door when he cursed under his breath, hooked a hand behind her neck, pulled her to him and kissed her—*really* kissed her—in front of his entire family. He finally pulled away, leaving her feeling breathless and dizzy, said, "Goodbye Liv," then turned and walked away, taking her heart with him.

The flights to the U.S. couldn't have been smoother or more uneventful, but when Liv got back to her apartment and let herself inside it almost didn't feel like home. She'd barely been gone a month, but it felt as if everything had changed, and there was this nagging ache in the center of her chest that refused to go away.

"You just need sleep," she rationalized.

She climbed into bed and, other than a few trips to the bathroom, didn't get back out for three days. That was when she reminded herself that she'd never been one to wallow in self-pity. She was stronger than that. Besides, she needed to see William. She hadn't spoken to or even e-mailed him in weeks. Maybe they could have a late lunch and talk about his proposal and she could let him down easy.

She tried calling him at the lab, but he wasn't there and he wasn't answering his house or cell phone. Concerned that something might be wrong, she drove to his house instead.

She knocked, then a minute later knocked harder. She was about to give up and leave when the door finally opened.

Being that it was the middle of the afternoon, she was surprised to find him in a T-shirt and pajama bottoms, looking as though he'd just rolled out of bed.

"Oh, you're back," he said, and maybe it was her imagination, but he didn't seem happy to see her. Maybe he was hurt that she hadn't readily accepted his proposal. Maybe he was angry that she'd taken so long and hadn't been in contact.

"I'm back," she said with a smile that she hoped didn't look as forced as it felt. She thought that maybe seeing him again after such a long time apart would stir up feelings that had been buried or repressed, but she didn't feel a thing. "I thought we could talk."

"Um, well…" He glanced back over his shoulder, into the front room. "Now's not the best time."

She frowned. "Are you sick?"

"No, no, nothing like that."

Liv heard a voice behind him say, "Billy, who is it?"

A *female* voice. Then the door opened wider and a young girl whom Liv didn't recognize stood there dressed in, of all things, one of William's T-shirts.

"Hi!" she said brightly. "Are you a friend of Billy's?" *Billy?*

"We work in the lab together," William said, shooting Liv a look that said, *Go along with it*. He obviously didn't want this girl to know that she and William had had anything but a professional relationship. Which, if you wanted to get technical, they never really had.

"I'm Liv," Liv said, because William didn't introduce them. She had the feeling he wished she would just disappear. "And you are?"

The girl smiled brightly. "I'm Angela, Billy's fiancée."

Fiancée? William was *engaged*?

She waved in front of Liv's face a hand sporting an enormous diamond ring. "We're getting married in two weeks," she squealed.

"Congratulations," Liv said, waiting to feel the tiniest bit of remorse, but what she felt instead was relief. She was off the hook. She didn't have to feel bad for turning him down.

"Could you give us a second, Angie?" he said. "It's work."

"Sure," she said, smiling brightly. "Nice to meet you, Liv."

William stepped out onto the porch, closing the door behind him. "I'm so sorry. I wasn't expecting you."

If he'd answered his phone, he would have been, but she was pretty sure they had been otherwise occupied. "It's okay," she said. "I only came here to tell you that I can't marry you."

"Yes, well, when you stopped calling, I just assumed…"

"It just wasn't something I wanted to do over the phone. I guess it doesn't matter now."

"I'm sorry I didn't have a chance to prepare you. I mean, it was very sudden. Obviously."

"I'm very happy for you." And jealous as hell that even he had found someone. Not that he didn't deserve to be happy. It just didn't seem fair that it was so easy for some people. Of course, falling in love with Aaron had been incredibly easy. The hard part was getting him to love her back.

He smiled shyly, something she had never seen him do before, and said, "It was love at first sight."

She left William's house feeling more alone than she had in her entire life. She'd gone from having seven people who accepted her as part of the family—even if the queen had done it grudgingly—to having no one.

Fifteen

Aaron sat in his office, staring out the window at the grey sky through a flurry of snow, unable to concentrate on a single damn thing. He should be down in the greenhouse, meeting with the foreman about the spring crops, but he just couldn't work up the enthusiasm to get his butt out of the chair. The idea of another long season of constantly worrying about growth rates and rainfall and late frosts, not to mention pests and disease, gave him a headache. He was tired of being forced into doing something that deep down he really didn't want to do. He was tired of duty and compromise and putting everyone else's wishes ahead of his own. And even though it had taken a few days for him to admit it to himself, he was tired of shallow, meaningless relationships. He was sick of being alone.

He missed Liv.

Unfortunately she didn't seem to share the sentiment. It had been two weeks since she left and he hadn't heard a word from her. Not even an update on her progress. Yet he couldn't bring himself to pick up the phone and call her. Maybe she'd run back to William.

"Are you going to mope in here all day?"

Aaron looked up to see Anne standing in his office doorway. "I'm working," he lied.

"Of course you are."

He scowled. "Do you need something?"

"I just came by to let you know that I talked to Liv."

He bolted upright in his chair. "What? When?"

"About five minutes ago. She wanted to update us on her progress. And inquire about father's health."

"Why did she call you?"

Anne folded her arms across her chest. "Gosh, I don't know. Maybe because you *broke her heart.*"

"Did she say that?"

"Of course not."

"Well," he said, turning toward the window, "she always has William to console her."

"William?"

"He's another scientist. He asked her to marry him before she came here." Not that Aaron believed for a minute she would actually marry William. Not when she admitted she loved Aaron.

"Oh, so *that* was what she meant."

He swiveled back to her. "What?"

"She mentioned that, with the wedding coming up, it might be several weeks before we get another update. I just didn't realize it was *her* wedding."

She was actually going to do it? She was going to compromise and marry a man she didn't love? How could she marry William when she was in love with Aaron?

The thought of her marrying William, or anyone else for that matter, made him feel like punching a hole in the wall. And why? Because he was jealous? Because he didn't like to lose?

The truth hit him with a clarity that was almost painful in its intensity. He loved her. She couldn't marry William because the only man she should be marrying was him.

He rose from his chair and told Anne, "If you'll excuse me, I need to have a word with Mother and Father."

"Something wrong?" Anne said with a grin.

"Quite the opposite." After weeks, maybe even *years* of uncertainty, he finally knew what he had to do.

Aaron found his parents in their suite watching the midday news. "I need to have a word with you."

"Of course," his father said, gesturing him inside.

He picked up the remote and muted the television. "Is there a problem?"

"No. No problem."

"What is it?" his mother asked.

"I just wanted to let you both know that I'm flying to the States today."

"With the Gingerbread Man still on the loose, do you think that's wise?" his father asked.

"I have to see Liv."

"Why?" his mother demanded.

"So I can ask her to marry me."

Her face transformed into an amusing combination of shock and horror. "*Marry* you?"

"That's what I said."

"*Absolutely not.* I won't have it, Aaron."

"It's not up to you, Mother. This is my decision."

"Your father and I know what's best for this family. That girl is—"

"Enough!" his father thundered, causing both Aaron and his mother to jolt with surprise. It had been a long time since he'd been well enough to raise his voice to such a threatening level. "Choose your words carefully, my dear, lest you say something you'll later regret."

She turned to him, eyes wide with surprise. "You're all right with this?"

"Is there a reason I shouldn't be?"

"I know you're fond of her, but a *marriage?* She isn't of noble blood."

"Do you love her, Aaron?" his father asked.

"I do," he said, never feeling so certain of anything in his life.

He turned and asked Aaron's mother, "Do you love our son?"

"What kind of question is that? Of course I do."

"Do you want him to be happy?"

"You know I do. I just—"

"Since Liv has come into his life, have you ever seen him so happy?"

She frowned, as though she didn't like the answer she had to give. "No…but…"

He took her hand. "She's not of noble blood. Who cares? She's a good person. Thoughtful and sweet and kind. If you'd taken any time to get to know her, you would realize that. Royal or not, our son loves her, so she deserves our respect. And our *acceptance*. Life is too short. Shouldn't he spend it with someone who makes him happy? Someone he loves?"

She was silent for a moment as she considered his words, and finally she said, "I want to state for the record that I'm not happy about this."

Aaron nodded. "So noted."

"However, if you love her and she loves you, I suppose I'll just have to learn to accept it."

"You have our blessing," his father told him.

"There's one more thing. I'm going back to school."

His mother frowned. "What for?"

"Because I still need a few science credits before I can apply to med school."

"*Med* school? At your age? What in heaven's name for?"

"Because I've always wanted to."

His father mirrored her look of concern. "But who will oversee the fields?"

"I'm sure we can find someone capable to fill my position. You'll manage just fine without me."

The king didn't look convinced. "Why don't we discuss this when you get back? Maybe we can reach some sort of compromise."

He wanted to tell his father that he was through compromising, but this was a lot to spring on them in one day. It would be best if he gave it some time to sink in.

"All right," he agreed. "We'll talk about it when I get home."

"I want you to take a full security detail with you," his father said. "I know we haven't had any more threats, but I don't want to take any chances."

"Of course," he agreed, and as he left his parents' suite to make the arrangements, he felt an enormous weight had been lifted from his shoulders. That for the first time instead of just watching his life pass by before him, he was finally an active participant. And he knew with a certainty he felt deep in his bones that until he had Liv by his side, life would never be complete.

And he would do anything to get her back.

* * *

It was late in the evening when his limo pulled up in front of Liv's apartment. The building was very plain and unassuming, which didn't surprise him in the least. Hadn't she claimed to spend most of her time in the lab? He hoped she wasn't there now, or, God forbid, at William's place. Not that he wouldn't hunt her down and find her wherever she happened to be. And if William tried to interfere, Aaron might have to hurt him.

Flynn opened the door for him.

"I'm going in alone," Aaron told him.

"Sir—"

"I don't imagine there's an assassin staked out on the off chance that I drop by. You can wait outside."

He nodded grudgingly. "Yes, sir."

Aaron went inside and took the stairs up to the third floor. Her apartment was the first on the right. There was no bell, so he rapped on the door. Only a few seconds passed before it opened, and there stood Liv wearing flannel pajama bottoms and a faded sweatshirt, looking as sweet and sexy and as irresistible as the first time he'd met her.

She blinked several times, as if she thought she might be imagining him there. "Aaron?"

He grinned. "The one and only."

She didn't return his smile. She just looked…confused. In every scenario he had imagined, she had immediately thrown herself into his arms and thanked him for saving her from a life of marital disaster. Maybe this wouldn't be quite as easy as he'd anticipated.

"What are you doing here?" she asked.

"Can I come in?"

She glanced back inside the apartment, then to him, looking uneasy. Had it not occurred to him that William could be there, in her apartment?

"Is someone...*with* you?" he asked.

She shook her head. "No, it's just that my apartment is kind of a mess. I'm getting ready to do some redecorating."

"I won't hold it against you," he said.

She stepped back and gestured him inside. Her apartment was small and sparsely furnished. And what furniture she did have was covered in plastic drop cloths.

"I was getting ready to paint," she explained. She didn't offer to take his coat, or clear a seat for him. "What do you want?"

"I'm here to prevent you from making the worst mistake of your life."

She frowned and looked around the room. "Painting my apartment?"

She looked so hopelessly confused that he had to smile. "No. I'm here to stop you from marrying a man you don't love."

"Why would you think I'm getting married?"

It was his turn to look confused. "Anne said..."

Before he could finish the sentence, reality slapped him in the face. Hard. He'd been set up. Anne was trying to get him off his behind, so he would go after Liv. And he'd given her just the ammunition she needed when he told her about William.

The next time he saw his sister, he was going to give her a big hug.

"I take it you never said anything to my sister about a wedding?"

She shook her head.

"So, you're definitely not marrying William," he confirmed, just to be sure.

"I should hope not, considering he's engaged to someone else."

That was by far the best news Aaron had had all day.

"What difference does it make?" she asked. "Why do you care who I marry?"

"I care," he said, taking a step toward her, "because the only man you should be marrying is me."

Her eyes went wide with disbelief. "I beg your pardon?"

"You heard me." He got down on one knee and pulled the ring box from his coat pocket. He opened it, offering her the five-carat-diamond family ring that sat nestled in a bed of royal-blue velvet. "Will you, Liv?"

For several excruciating seconds that felt like hours, she just stared at him openmouthed, and he began to wonder if she'd changed her mind about him, if, now that they'd been apart for a while, her affection for him had faded. For an instant he genuinely worried that she would actually tell him no.

But when she finally spoke, she said, "You don't want to get married. You're not cut out to be a family man. Remember?"

"Liv, you told me that you love me. Is that still true?"

She bit her lip and nodded.

"And I love you. It took me a while to admit it to myself, but I do. And I couldn't imagine spending the rest of my life with anyone else."

A smile twitched at the corner of her mouth. "What about that excellent rate you get from the girl-of-the-month club?"

He grinned. "I already cancelled my subscription. The only girl I want in my life is you. Now, are you going to make me kneel here all night?"

"But what about your parents? They'll never let you marry a nonroyal."

"They've already given their blessing."

Her eyes went wide. "Your *mother* gave her blessing? Did you have to hold a gun to her head?"

"I'll admit she did it grudgingly, but don't worry, she'll come around. If we give her a grandchild or two, she'll be ecstatic."

"You want that?" she asked. "You really want children?"

"Only if I can have them with you, Liv."

That hint of a smile grew to encompass her entire face. "Ask me again."

He grinned. "Olivia, will you marry me?"

"Yes." She laughed as he slid the ring on her finger, then he pulled her into his arms. "Yes, Your Highness, I definitely will!"

* * * * *

"You know, Vanessa," Brock said, "I was in a devil of a mood when I got here..."

"Ready to take my head off?" she asked nervously.

"Well, I'm definitely ready to take *something* off," he said quietly.

She remained silent. Even as he set his glass down on the counter. Even as he walked toward her. Even as he stood toe to toe with her, backing her against the granite countertop.

"My mood *is* improving," he said, touching a strand of her hair and looking down at her mouth.

Her heart raced. She didn't know what to do. She'd spent the day sabotaging his business, but now, as he bent his head, she wanted to feel his lips claim hers again. A thrilling sensation swept through her.

"This is crazy..." she whispered.

"Why?" he asked, his sexy sandalwood scent surrounding her senses.

Because I'm doing my best to ruin you...

RESERVED FOR
THE TYCOON

BY
CHARLENE SANDS

Published in Great Britain 2010
Harlequin Mills & Boon Limited,
Eton House, 18-24 Paradise Road, Richmond, Surrey TW9 1SR

© Charlene Swink 2009

ISBN: 978 0 263 88189 9

51-1210

Harlequin Mills & Boon policy is to use papers that are natural, renewable
and recyclable products and made from wood grown in sustainable forests.
The logging and manufacturing processes conform to the legal environmental
regulations of the country of origin.

Printed and bound in Spain
by Litografia Rosés S.A., Barcelona

Charlene Sands resides in Southern California with her husband, school sweetheart and best friend, Don. Proudly, they boast that their children, Jason and Nikki, have earned their college degrees. The "empty nesters" now have two cats that have taken over the house.

Charlene has written twenty-five romances and is the recipient of the 2008 Booksellers' Best Award, the 2007 Cataromance Reviewer's Choice Award and the 2006 National Readers' Choice Award. When not writing, she enjoys sunny California days, Pacific beaches and sitting down with a good book.

She blogs regularly on the all-western site www.petticoatsandpistols.com, and you can also find her at www.myspace.com/charlenesands.

Charlene invites you to visit her website at www.charlenesands.com to enter her contests and see what's new.

To my dear mother-in-law, Nancy,
Whose support and love mean a great deal to me.
You are very close to my heart.

Dear Reader,

I've never met a tropical island I didn't like! Maui is one of my favorites, with its stunning golden sunsets and deep aqua blue waters.

I've always wanted to write a story filled with deception in its simplest form. With Brock Tyler and Vanessa Dupree you'll meet two people who are as cunning as they are appealing. I enjoyed plotting their escapades, where nothing is as it seems and their cagey games of cat and mouse end only when they enter the bedroom. There, the sizzling heat of the tropics is turned up and emotions run very high.

Make your reservation to be swept away with surprising twists and turns and, of course, romance.

"Suite" reading!

Charlene

One

Getting the job at Tempest Maui Hotel as event planner had been a breeze. With her impressive résumé in hand, Vanessa Dupree walked right into today's interview with confidence and answered the hotel tycoon's questions with all of the intelligence and charm she possessed. Then she smiled winningly with promise in her eyes. Promises that arched Brock Tyler's dark eyebrows a bit and had his gaze wandering to her "other" assets.

Vanessa silently fumed. Brock was a charmer, all right. Black hair, perfectly groomed, dark eyes that could mesmerize and classy clothes covering a fit body; it was a small wonder her younger sister fell for him back in New Orleans.

He didn't know that Melody Applegate and Vanessa Dupree were related and that's exactly how she intended on keeping it. Vanessa shoved the image of her heartbroken sister, teary-eyed and devastated, out of her mind, for now.

She rose from her seat. "Thank you for the opportunity, Mr. Tyler. You won't be sorry you hired me."

The lie flowed easily from her lips.

He stood up and instead of reaching across his desk for a handshake, walked around to grasp her hand and give a gentle but firm tug. "The success of this hotel is very important to me. I handpick all my employees. Welcome to the team, Miss Dupree."

Vanessa squirmed a little under his steady gaze. He stood a head taller than her and she felt his dominating presence far more than when a bamboo-accented desk separated them. The man oozed sexual prowess with every movement he made and his hand touching hers brought queasy jitters to her stomach. "Thank you."

"I'll see you tonight for dinner."

"Dinner?" Vanessa's voice squeaked. The man worked fast.

"There's an employee dinner meeting every Wednesday night. Seven o'clock in the Aloha conference room."

"Right," she said, steadying her nerves. "I'll be there."

Brock nodded and walked her to the door, his eyes

flickering from her tightly pulled back platinum hair, down the bodice of her navy-blue business suit, lingering a second on her breasts, then to the hem of her dress. "We dress more casual here. We want the guests to feel relaxed. No more business suits and…let your hair down."

Sizzling heat rivaling the Hawaiian sun raced through her system when his gaze returned to her hair. She touched a strand absently. "It's natural. The color, I mean."

Good heavens, Vanessa. Get a grip.

Those dark brows rose again, but he didn't voice his doubt.

"My mother always said it was a freak of nature. No one in the family has this color hair."

He looked at her hair again and nodded. "Pretty."

"Oh, I wasn't fishing for a compliment, Mr. Tyler."

Though that's exactly how she'd sounded.

"No, I doubt you'd have to hunt down compliments, *Vanessa.*"

The soft tone of his voice when he spoke her name brought another round of jitters to her stomach.

He was good, she surmised.

Sexy. Rich. Powerful.

But Vanessa wouldn't let that discourage her from her mission. She thought of the pain he'd caused Melody last month. Her sister had been beside herself with grief. She'd fallen hard and fast for her tycoon employer in New Orleans and Brock had discarded her like yesterday's newspaper. To him, she was old news. Vanessa had never seen her sister cry so much or so hard. She'd been destroyed by his abrupt dismissal and rejection. He hadn't cared that he'd broken her young naive heart after dating her for weeks and leading her on.

Vanessa had firsthand experience with this kind of man. She'd been dumped a few times and she remembered how much that had hurt. She learned how to weed out the insincere men and steer clear. Melody, on the other hand, being six years her junior, hadn't the experience to handle a man like Brock Tyler.

Vanessa had always championed her younger half sister's cause. She'd watched out for her. She'd protected her all of her life. In most respects, she'd mothered Melody when their own mother had become too ill to do it. Vanessa had taken over the role then and those tendencies were hard to change.

Compelled by anger and a sense of justice, Vanessa couldn't pass up this chance to finally give Brock Tyler a taste of his own medicine. The event planner position had fallen into her lap. She'd always wanted to see Hawaii, and now she'd be here for a time, subletting a little condo on the island. All things had fallen into place.

Yet, after meeting Brock Tyler, Vanessa understood the challenge. It wouldn't be easy. He'd be a worthy adversary but that wouldn't deter her. She'd come to the island for one reason and one reason only.

To ruin Brock Tyler.

* * *

"Vanessa Dupree is teaching the class?" Brock Tyler watched his new event planner on an exercise mat lift one firm, gorgeous leg over her head on Tempest Maui's sandy beachfront.

"Yes, sir." Akamu Ho, his hotel manager, nodded. "Pilates. She didn't want our guests to miss out when Lucy called in sick this morning."

"Enterprising woman." His newest employee had spunk and a great résumé. From the moment they'd met in the interview, Brock had been intrigued. He'd debated about hiring her. His instant attraction to her had knocked his well-honed senses off the charts. Not that Brock had trouble mixing business with pleasure normally, but he couldn't jeopardize the success of Tempest Maui. His focus and all of his attention had to be directed to the newly renovated hotel.

Brock walked from the plush Garden Pavilion onto the sands of Tranquility Bay toward the dozen guests working out on the beach. When Vanessa spotted him, she wiggled three fingers in a wave.

Her natural smile and that Marilyn Monroe hair were eye-stopping enough, but add the skimpy black spandex shorts with her tanned midriff exposed and Brock had a helluva time containing his lust.

He leaned against a tall palm tree and waited for her to finish. After leading the class in a cooldown exercise that had his blood heating up, she dismissed the class. He walked over to her, helping her pick up the mats and stack them in one pile on the sand. "So you're a Pilates expert, too? I didn't see that in your résumé."

Her low rumble of throaty laughter brought images of hot sex on the sand. "I'm not an expert. I just enjoy exercise. I've always been flexible."

Brock cleared his throat, but that image of sex with her on the sand went from hazy to vivid in two seconds flat.

"When Lucy called in sick with a high fever, I didn't want to disappoint the guests. I let them know I wasn't an expert or anything, but I could lead them in a class."

She picked up a towel and wiped sweat from her forehead. Beads of perspiration coated her body and brought a shimmering sheen to her tanned skin.

"They all thanked me," she said with a slight shrug. "I think they enjoyed it."

"I'm sure they did," Brock said, trying to keep his mind on the reason he'd come out here. "In just the week you've worked here, you've made an impression. Stepping in today for Lucy shows you've got team spirit and the hotel's interests in mind."

With the towel placed around her neck, she gazed into his eyes, squinting a bit in the sunlight. "Are you saying you're glad you hired me?"

She surprised him with her blunt assessment. "I'm a good judge of character."

Then he focused on the reason for approaching her in the first place, setting aside the fact that he'd have watched her do her *flexible* exercises for no other reason than pure fascination. "Actually, I need to speak with you about some upcoming events that are important to the hotel."

"Okay. Should I shower and change and meet you in your office?"

That had been his plan initially, but now it seemed sacrilegious to ask a gorgeous woman to change out of revealing spandex. "No, let's walk the beach. I've got a full schedule today and doubt I'll get outside again before the sun sets."

That much was true. Brock didn't spend enough time outside on these gorgeous Hawaiian days. Whenever he could, he'd go out on his yacht, harbored in Tranquility Bay to get away from the mounds of paperwork he'd encountered since the renovation project began months ago. Now he had a wager with his brother Trent, for ego's sake more than anything else, to make a bigger success of his hotel than Trent had with Tempest West in Arizona. The two had always been competitive and with the added bonus of his late father's beloved classic Thunderbird as the prize, Brock had everything to gain by seeing that his hotel prospered.

They walked in morning sunshine along the warm sand, the ocean humming more like a small kitten than a lion's roar.

Brock got right to the point. "These first few events will make or break our hotel's reputation. As you know, this hotel had been closed down for more than a year due to poor management. Certainly not because of location. My brothers and I saw the hotel's great potential as a destination spot for weddings, conventions, fashions shows and major parties. The renovations are complete and now it's up to all of us, including you, to see that we succeed, Vanessa."

Vanessa nodded, her head down. "I understand that, sir."

He winced at her serious tone. He was used to commanding respect from his employees, but somehow, the "sir" coming from Vanessa's sensual lips didn't sound quite right. "Call me Brock."

When she glanced up, he smiled. "We'll be working closely from now on. You and I might as well drop the formalities."

"Okay...Brock." She cast him a quick coy smile.

Brock couldn't quite figure her out. Several times this week he'd caught her watching him, but the minute their eyes met she'd looked away abruptly. What had he witnessed in those pretty blue eyes?

"We have a wedding next week. It's a big expensive affair and the hotel has booked over three hundred guests. You've been working with the wedding coordinator, I suspect?"

"Yes, since the moment I hired on. I have the details covered, Mr....uh, Brock."

"Good."

"I've done wedding coordinating before. I've got it under control."

Her qualifications were impeccable. She'd had experience in event planning for a large corporation as well as a major hotel chain, working at one time for a competitor, actually. Brock had been fortunate she'd come along when she had.

"I'm counting on your expertise to make this happen."

"I'm good at making things…*happen*." She spoke that last word softly, the woman oozing sensuality.

Brock stopped to gaze into her eyes. A little, throaty laugh escaped and he didn't mistake the demure look she cast him. "How good?" he asked, all thought of business now out of his mind.

"Oh, very good," she whispered, her gaze dropping to his mouth.

Brock was ready to pull her into his arms and crush his lips to hers, until she took a step back. "About the other events?"

"We'll talk about those later," he said, keeping his frustration at bay. He'd almost kissed her. Hell, he wanted to, but she'd backed off.

"Is there anything else you'd like to discuss with me?"

He shook his head. "No. Just concentrate on the wedding."

"Okay. Well, I'd better get to that shower now. I have work to do." She turned and jogged away, leaving him a stunning view of her backside and wondering what she'd do if he'd joined her in the shower.

* * *

Vanessa drove her MINI Cooper to Lucy's small home in a residential part of the island. She parked her car and carefully juggled a pot of homemade chicken soup and a bag of navel oranges. Knocking had been tricky, but she managed and waited for Lucy to open the door.

"Hi. Did I catch you napping?"

Lucy looked miserable. Her long raven hair was disheveled and her eyes were watery. "No, I'm up. Are you sure you want to come in? I don't know what I have, but it's nasty."

"I'm sure. Don't worry, I never get sick. I brought you the cure. Hot chicken soup and fresh-squeezed orange juice. I'm the squeezer," she added, chuckling.

Lucy opened the door wider and Vanessa entered. "You're so sweet to do this, but remember I warned you."

"I'll take my chances."

Lucy shook her head and sighed. "You fill in for me today with my class and now you bring me nourishment. How can I ever thank you?"

"You can tell me where can I put these things."

"Oh, follow me."

They walked into a big kitchen area, which seemed to also serve as her main living space, an oblong bay window caught a view of the Pacific Ocean between rooftops. Vanessa set the bag of oranges on the bright-white-tiled countertop and handed Lucy the soup container. "This place is great."

"Thanks," she said, her eyes sparking with pride as she set the soup pot onto a four-burner range. "It's small and affordable and I couldn't resist the view. Any place here with a view goes for a bundle, so I consider myself lucky."

"How are you feeling?"

"My fever's gone. Now I'm just exhausted." Lucy plopped into a dark cane chair and gestured for Vanessa to also sit at the kitchen table.

Vanessa shook her head. "No, let me heat up the soup and squeeze you some juice. I'll have it all ready in no time."

"This is very nice of you," Lucy said.

"You were friendly to me all week at the hotel and I…well, I don't have any friends on the island yet. Besides, I'm kind of a nurturer. My younger sister would say too much so. Just kick me out when you want to rest."

"Fair deal."

Vanessa turned the knob on the gas range to simmer then found a knife from a block on the counter. "Do you have a juicer?"

"Just a manual one in that drawer behind you."

Vanessa found the juicer and began twisting cut oranges onto the cone-shaped device.

"So how did the class go?"

"You mean after I told the disappointed guests that you were out sick? I guess it went okay. Not too many grumbles," Vanessa said, smiling while pressing half an orange down, squeezing out every last ounce of juice. "I didn't expect the big boss to show up."

"Mr. Tyler was there?" Lucy's expression brightened.

"Yep. He watched me through the class, probably making sure I didn't scare any guests away."

"He's dedicated to the hotel," Lucy said, dreamy-eyed. "He's got some sort of competition going with his brother. He told the staff about it when we all hired on. Big bonuses for all of us if the hotel does well."

Vanessa couldn't conceal a frown. "Is that so?"

He'd brought devastation to Melody without blinking an eye, walking out on her when she'd needed him the most. He'd abandoned her for another woman and now Vanessa couldn't wait to work on her plan to screw up the beloved Tempest Maui.

To think he'd almost kissed her today. And she'd almost allowed it to happen. She'd been drawn to those dark, promising eyes, and that killer smile could do a weaker woman in. He was attracted to her and she decided that it could only work to her advantage.

Maybe next time, she would allow him to kiss her.

"Yeah, he's been a good boss so far. He's given me free rein to run the gym the way I see fit and I appreciate his confidence in me. I think every female employee from sixteen to sixty has a major crush on him."

Vanessa's jaw dropped. "Really?"

Lucy bit her lip guiltily and nodded. So Lucy could be included in with the smitten females.

"Really," she confessed. "Aren't you slightly attracted to him?"

"Me?" Vanessa's voice elevated so much, she coughed to hide her scorn. "I hardly know him."

"You've just been here a short while. Give it time. You'll see."

"I hope not," she whispered softly.

"What?"

"Nothing. Your juice is ready," she said, pouring her a nice tall glass. "Drink up." She handed Lucy the glass and then turned to the range and stirred the soup. "I'll have you feeling better in no time."

Two

Two days later, Vanessa tied the laces on her running shoes, did a few warm-up stretches on the sand and began jogging along the coast of Tranquility Bay. Early breezes cooled the air considerably and made her morning jog all the more pleasurable. She waved at guests she recognized on the beach, early birds like herself, who enjoyed the sunrise and came out for a walk or to sit quietly on the beach before the day erupted. She recognized a few she knew were here for the wedding taking place on Saturday afternoon and fought the guilt she felt over causing them any discomfort. This was the bride's third marriage and the groom's fourth, millionaires who had nothing better to spend their money on than an elaborate party for themselves, she rationalized.

Vanessa jogged to the south tip of the bay where a parking lot of boats were moored in the marina and seagulls squawked out of unison while perched atop buoys. Stunning blue-green waters shimmered, in great contrast with her hometown's mighty muddy waterway, the Mississippi River.

"Vanessa?" Brock's voice broke through her thoughts and she nearly stumbled when she caught sight of him in blue jeans and a white T-shirt, walking down the long wood dock, heading straight for her.

She halted, but jogged in place, waiting for him to come down the steps to join her on the path. She wished he didn't look so darn appealing—tanned and healthy, even without his millionaire attire on. "Hello." She stopped, trying not to ogle his perfect biceps.

"Good morning. Enjoying your jog?"

She was, up until a minute ago. "Yes, it's a habit of mine."

"Running?"

"It clears my head. Gets me ready for work." She'd run in half marathons for most of her adult life, she didn't add. "What brings you here?" she asked, being polite since conversation seemed to be on his mind this morning.

"I'm checking out Rebecca."

Rebecca? Of course, another woman. He probably

had one in every port. What could she say to that? "Well, I'd better be on my way."

"Rebecca's my boat," he said with a sly grin. "I named her after my mother." He pointed to the impressive yacht in the farthest slip in the marina. "She's been under repair."

Her heart melted into a puddle of warmth. His uncharacteristic gesture touched her in an elemental way. "I'm sorry to hear you lost your mother."

Brock tossed his head back and chuckled. "My mother's very much alive. Probably going to get married again soon. But I appreciate your kindness."

Vanessa blinked away her puzzlement, then felt foolish for her assumption. The man twisted her into knots. She needed an easy escape. "I've got a lot of details to go over for the Everett wedding, I'd better head back now."

"Just a sec," he said, taking her wrist gently. "Come see the boat," he said. "I could use your opinion about something."

"My opinion?" Vanessa nearly gasped. "I don't know a thing about boats."

"You're a woman. You'll have an opinion, believe me."

What choice did she have? "Okay." And just like that, Brock slipped his fingers from her wrist to her palm and guided her up the dock that way, holding her hand.

Tingles mingled with wariness, putting Vanessa on

guard. He had a firm grip, one that made a girl feel protected and safe. "Hah," she mumbled aloud.

"What?"

"Oh, it's lovely here," she said, covering her verbal blunder.

Thankfully, he didn't comment. And once they reached the end of the dock, he climbed onto the boat and turned to help her aboard. His touch brought unwelcome trembles and that knot inside twisted tighter. He released her immediately and smiled. "This is it. The *Rebecca.*"

A question entered her mind and Vanessa had to ask, "Why'd you name the boat after your mother?"

He scratched the back of his head, drew his brows together and replied almost reluctantly, "I lost a bet with my brother."

"You…" And then it hit her. Those warm feelings she'd held for him minutes ago vanished and the relief she felt brought a smile to her lips. "You lost a *bet?*"

"I know," he said, smiling, too. "Terrible, isn't it? Trent and I have ongoing bets and it usually takes my older brother Evan to referee. My mother doesn't know that, though, and it made her happy when I told her. So all was not lost. I'm used to the name, but the one I picked fit me better."

Brock's honesty seemed genuine…and human. She couldn't get caught up in that moment of sincerity, she reminded herself. "Which was?"

"Winning B.E.T."

"Catchy," she said. "Stands for Brock Elliot Tyler, right?"

"You've done your homework. I like that," he said, his dark eyes gleaming in a way that made her heart pound against her chest.

She shrugged. "It's not rocket science to know your employer's full name."

Brock frowned and cast her a piercing look. "Can we pretend I'm not your employer right now?"

But you are, she wanted to scream. "Um, sure."

He took her hand again and she followed him to the opposite end of the boat where a lavish table was set for two. "This is where I need your opinion. Can't decide on whether to have eggs Benedict or a veggie omelet for breakfast. Which do you prefer?"

She stared at him in disbelief. "Are you inviting me for breakfast?"

His eyes flickered to the table, then back to her and then the thought struck. "You knew I'd be running this way this morning?" She pointed toward the place where they'd first met. "And you planned this?"

He shrugged. "I've seen you run every day this week. Today I thought I'd ask you to join me for breakfast."

Vanessa was flattered and confused. "You could have called me up and asked me."

"Would you have said yes?"

She opened her mouth to respond, then clamped it shut. Self-conscious, she touched her hair and shoved the tresses that had come loose back into her ponytail. "I'm hardly dressed for—"

His gaze roamed over her gray sweatpants and tank top, appreciation evident in his eyes. "You look... *good,* Vanessa. There's no formality here, I'm in jeans."

She'd noticed. They fit him so well, hugging his waist and outlining his perfect butt. "Why?"

He scrubbed his face, running a hand down his jawline. "It's just breakfast on my boat. Are you hungry?"

"I could eat," she said, smiling at him, wiping the annoyance from her face. No sense riling the boss, at least not this way. "Thank you. I accept."

"That was hard work," he grumbled. "Are you this tough on all the men in your life?"

"There are no men in my life."

A satisfied gleam entered his dark eyes. He pulled her up against him, his hands wrapping around her waist as he leaned in, his mouth inches from hers. "I'd like to change that."

Good heavens, Brock knew how to kiss. His lips brushed hers gently, giving her a tantalizing taste of what was to come. He held her loosely at first, but as he deepened the kiss, he pulled her closer, enveloping her in his fresh, sandalwood scent. Then he released her for a moment, looking into her eyes. "I like you, Vanessa."

"One would hope, by the way you just kissed me."

Warmth sparkled in his eyes and an infectious smile widened his luscious mouth. "You're not like other women," he seemed to puzzle out loud.

"Why not? What's wrong with me?"

He took her back into his arms, crushing his lips to hers again, her willpower waning, her mission all but forgotten. "Nothing at all," he whispered.

Brock leaned in and once again Vanessa fell into his kiss, her mind checking out for a moment. She hadn't been kissed this passionately since…she couldn't recall a time when she'd been so wrapped up in a man that she'd forgotten all good sense.

Suddenly, all the other men in her life paled in comparison to Brock Tyler. For the next few moments, Vanessa enjoyed being in his arms, enjoyed the heady taste of him and his male scent blending with the salty sea breeze. She enjoyed his expert mouth and his firm tight body pressed to her.

Then reality set in.

What's wrong with you, Vanessa? He's your nemesis, the man you came here to ruin.

As if she'd willed it, her stomach growled and she pushed Brock away slightly, pasting on her most charming smile. "I guess I'm really hungry…for breakfast that is."

Brock inhaled a sharp breath. "Right, breakfast."

"Right," she repeated, stepping even farther from

him, "You know, the reason you hijacked me from my run."

"Got it," he said, casting her a hungry look that had nothing to do with veggie omelets. "Have a seat. I'll talk to the chef. Pour us some pineapple juice while you're waiting."

Vanessa rose from her seat the moment Brock headed inside and chastised herself for letting him get to her. She'd wanted him to kiss her, and now that she knew what it was like, she sympathized with Melody all the more.

She could see how an innocent, less experienced girl could fall victim to Brock in a heartbeat. He was smooth and charming and sexy as hell.

She fanned herself and then steadied her wayward nerves. When Brock came back, she looked cool as a cucumber, sitting at the table, sipping juice from a hundred-dollar Waterford Crystal.

A feast of food was served from the galley by the chef and Brock thanked him as way of dismissal. When he disappeared out of view, she dug into her food, ignoring the fact that she and Brock locked lips pretty hot and heavily just a few minutes ago.

"This is so good," she confessed, relishing every bite of the meal. "More than I usually eat for breakfast." She gobbled up the veggie omelet covered with mango sauce, fresh fruit and with a measure of guilt, popped a tiny pastry into her mouth then washed it down with a cup of Kona coffee. She doubted she'd be able to jog back to the hotel after this.

"I'll confess, it's more than I eat every morning, too."

She didn't doubt it. He'd never keep such a muscular physique if he ate like this every day.

"But, I will admit to having an enormous appetite." He glanced at her mouth, then leaned over and kissed her quickly. "You had some mango at the corner of your lip."

Darn he was fast and…charming. She swiped at her mouth with her napkin and looked over the rest of her body for food remnants, for fear he'd take her to bed to cleanse her of them. "You could have just told me."

He rubbed his nose, trying to hide a smile. "I like my way better."

"Do you always get your way?" she asked quietly, her question pointless. They both knew he was a man who got whatever he wanted.

He glanced at her in a knowing way, looking her over from head to toe, his gaze hot with sexual promise. "Not today, I won't."

She stared into his eyes, captivated for a moment, her breath catching in her throat. "You won't?"

"Vanessa, I don't play games. I want you, but it's too soon. C'mon," he said, rising and reaching for her hand. "I'll walk you back to the hotel."

It was too soon? Vanessa worked in her office through most of the day repeating Brock's words in her mind, her anger rising as each hour passed.

He wanted her, but it was too soon.

His comment meant that she hadn't a choice in the matter. Did he bother to ask if she were interested? No, he just assumed that one day, he'd get what he wanted.

Her.

His arrogance knew no bounds.

Vanessa thought of Melody and wondered if he'd given her sister fair warning. Or had he just showered her with charm and sex appeal and taken what he wanted, then dumped her for the next female challenge that had come along.

Every time she thought of Melody's heartbreak over Brock Tyler, she silently vowed to make him pay with the one thing that seemed to really matter to him—his hotel.

"Focus on that, Vanessa," she muttered, while going over the files for the Everett wedding. *And stop thinking about how Brock's lips worked magic over yours and how his strong muscular arms wrapped you up in a cocoon of safety and warmth.*

"What's the frown about?" Lucy walked into her office with a beautiful arrangement of island flowers and set them down on her desk.

"Lucy! These are beautiful. But you didn't have to—"

Lucy put up a stopping hand. "Whoa! Don't get ahead of yourself. I wish these were in my budget, but I'm afraid all I can offer for curing me is a drink or two at Joe's Tiki Torch on the beach. When Akamu saw me headed this way, he handed me the flowers and asked if I could bring them to you."

"From Akamu? Is it tradition for new employees to receive these?"

"Not that I know of," she said, narrowing her eyes. "I've never gotten flowers like these from anyone around here." She pointed. "There's a card."

Vanessa plucked the card out of the envelope, her suspicions aroused. She read it silently.

I've never enjoyed breakfast more.
Brock

Vanessa's knees went weak. Without elaborate words, the simple sweet sentiment touched her. Images replayed in her mind of Brock's calling to her from the dock, seeking her out and inviting her to breakfast. He'd said all the right things and she'd found him easy to be with, until he'd kissed her with so much passion, he stole her breath. Instant awareness sparked between them and Vanessa had had to back off. For her own sanity.

He'd known exactly how to push her buttons. He was smooth—she'd give him that. But a few kisses and gorgeous flowers wouldn't change anything.

"Well?" Lucy stood impatiently by, trying to peek at the card. "Who sent them to you?"

"Oh, uh," she stumbled and hated fibbing to her friend. "My sister sent them from the mainland." Vanessa blinked away her guilt at lying and shoved the card back into its envelope. "Wasn't that sweet of her?"

Deflated, Lucy nodded. "Yeah, that's some nice generous sister you have."

Vanessa avoided making eye contact with Lucy. The woman was too astute. "Thanks for bringing them to me."

"I was on my way to your office anyway. So what do you say? Want to go to the Torch tomorrow night for a drink? We'll celebrate your two-week anniversary working at Tempest Maui. My treat."

Vanessa didn't have to think about it. She'd need a night out right after the afternoon wedding fiasco she hoped to create tomorrow. A case of jitters quaked her stomach, but she forged on, noting that besides needing a night out, she could also use a friend. "Sure, I'd love to."

Lucy headed for the door. "I'll pick you up at eight Saturday night. Oh, and don't worry, I won't tell anyone you got flowers from the boss."

Vanessa's jaw dropped open. "How did you—"

"I saw him in the flower shop this morning, hand-picking the orchids he wanted in the arrangement."

Contrite, Vanessa slumped her shoulders. "I'm sorry I lied. I didn't want you to get the wrong idea."

"Wrong idea? Are you nuts? Do you know how many women would trade places with you right now?" Lucy winked with a big smile. "You lucky girl."

After she walked out, Vanessa fingered a golden hibiscus, shaking her head. "If Lucy only knew the truth," she whispered to the bird of paradise jutting up from the bouquet. "She wouldn't think I'm lucky. She'd think I'm…insane for going up against the boss."

* * *

"You're drinking white wine?" Lucy said, over the blasting music of the three-piece band at Joe's Tiki Torch. The crowded beachside bar lent itself to loud chatter and laughter amid the patrons. "You should be more adventurous, Vanny. Try an Amaretto Sour or a Mojito or the cliché Blue Hawaiian."

She *had* been adventurous that afternoon when she sabotaged Brock Tyler's reputation. She'd witnessed the chaos during the wedding and had done her part to rectify the problems making sure it had been too little, too late. She'd accomplished what she'd aimed for and thought she'd feel some sense of wicked satisfaction today. Instead, her nerves went raw and the white wine wasn't doing a thing to calm her queasiness. "Maybe you're right. I'll have a strawberry margarita," she said to the bartender.

Lucy's laughter filled the tiny space they occupied at the bamboo bar. "Oh, that's better. You're getting wild and crazy now."

Lucy's playful sarcasm made her smile. Vanessa wasn't a good companion tonight. She had a good deal on her mind. She'd spoken with her sister today, maybe as a means of justification for what she'd done during the wedding. Melody had answered the phone cheerfully, which brightened Vanessa's mood a bit, though she knew her sister was covering up her heartache. Melody was still devastated and Vanessa loved her all the more for trying to pretend she wasn't, for her sake.

Miles separated them now and Melody didn't know that Vanessa had taken a job working at Tempest Maui. She'd deliberately not divulged that information, offering up a different scenario to her sister. As far as Melody knew, Vanessa had taken a temporary transfer to Hawaii and was still working for her previous employer.

"What's the matter, aren't you having a good time? You refuse to dance and you're moping around like you've lost your best friend."

Vanessa stared into Lucy's dark brown concerned eyes. In just a few weeks, they'd become close and Vanessa wished she didn't have to deceive her along with everyone else she'd met since coming to work for Brock Tyler. But to confide in anyone right now could spell disaster.

"I'm just a little tired. It's been a long week."

Lucy took her hand in hers. "That's why we're here, Vanny. You need to unwind. You know, let your hair down. Why don't you dance?"

"Yes, why don't you?"

Vanessa whirled around and found Akamu standing behind her. The hotel manager had a big smile on his face and she couldn't refuse those beckoning eyes.

"Okay," she said, taking his hand. "Mahalo."

His friend Tony asked Lucy to dance and together the four of them took the dance floor. If Akamu knew anything about what happened at the wedding, he wasn't letting on, so Vanessa didn't bring up the subject.

She wound up having a nice time with Akamu, his friend Tony and Lucy. The foursome had Bono, running and a love of healthy foods in common. When Lucy parked her car outside of her condo, Vanessa was in a much better frame of mind than when the evening had begun.

"Thanks, Lucy. I really had fun tonight. Just what I needed."

"Yeah, it took you a while, but you finally lightened up."

"I even tried a Mojito. It was pretty good, though the mint surprised me."

"Who could go wrong with rum, mint and sugar?"

They exited the car and Lucy met her by the passenger door. "I didn't want to bring it up earlier, but I heard what happened at the wedding today."

"Oh, yeah. How did you hear about it?"

"Word travels fast around here. Akamu knew all about it, but his policy is to keep work separate from playtime. I couldn't get much out of him."

"Gosh, he didn't say anything to me." Vanessa sighed. "The wedding wasn't a major disaster or anything." Well, she surmised, it could have been much worse. "But can we talk about it another time? I don't want to spoil my good mood."

Lucy smiled wide and hugged her. "Sure. As long as you're okay."

"I will be. I was feeling a bit homesick today...I miss my sister. Going out was just what I needed tonight."

"You'll get used to being on the island," Lucy said with compassion.

"Thank you. I'll see you on Monday."

"Right, Monday it begins all over again." Lucy rolled her eyes, making Vanessa laugh as they parted.

She strolled leisurely into the garden area of the development with a lingering smile on her face, a bright gleam of moonlight reflecting off the almond-shaped pool. She'd almost made it to her condo, when a man stepped out of the shadows.

"Oh," she gasped in fear, seeing anger on his face. He must know the truth. *She'd been caught.* "Brock, what are you doing here? You scared me half to death."

Three

Brock paced in front of her, ignoring the fact that she'd nearly jumped out of her skin when he'd come out of the shadows. "I was called back from a meeting I had in Kapalua. Apparently, we had quite a few complaints about the wedding today. Are you aware of what happened?" A frown settled on Brock's face.

Vanessa had dreaded this conversation, but she'd mentally prepared herself. In her preparations, though, she never dreamed he'd come to her home to reprimand her. She walked past him to her door and unlocked it. "Come in. We don't have to discuss this outside in the dark."

Vanessa entered, allowing Brock to follow her

inside and moved about the room, turning lights on and tossing her purse on the sofa.

Brock stood stock-still, a tick working his jaw. "I called your cell phone half a dozen times tonight."

"I turned it off after work." She cast him a quick smile. "I wouldn't have heard it where I went tonight anyway."

"Joe's Tiki Torch?"

"How did you know that?"

"It's the local hangout." He rubbed the back of his neck and added, "I spoke with Akamu tonight."

From his stance, it didn't appear that Brock would leave anytime soon, so she resigned herself to this confrontation. "Have a seat." She turned toward the kitchen. "I'll make a pot of coffee."

"Not for me," he said, following her. "Do you have something to drink?"

"Wine, beer and I think there's a bottle of rum in the cabinet."

"Rum," he said. "And Coke?"

"That, I have." Vanessa opened the kitchen cupboard and reached for the bottle sensing Brock standing right behind her. "Coke's in the fridge."

He moved away to open her refrigerator while she brought down a glass tumbler and poured him a few fingers of rum. He moved in close and filled the rest of the glass with the soda. Their shoulders brushed and his close proximity curled her toes. The male earthy scent of sandalwood filled the air and tension crackled with *his* anger and *her* awareness of him. "None for you?"

She shook her head. "No, I'd better not. I've had enough tonight. Would you like some des—"

"Sit down, Vanessa." He pointed to her kitchen chair and she thought for sure her goose was cooked.

She sat and he did, too, facing her across the small glass table. "What the hell happened today?"

Maybe she should have poured herself a drink after all. Her throat dry, she steadied her nerves. "Well, a lot of things *happened.* Although there were some minor inconveniences, the wedding went off without a hitch."

"Minor inconveniences? You call construction noises during the ceremony a minor inconvenience? That construction wasn't supposed to start until next month."

"I know, but their invoice had a typo on it. They got the date wrong. They started work on the west wing, by mistake."

"I'm told the buzz saw alone drowned out the wedding march music, just as the bride walked down the aisle. She got rattled and started crying. It took thirty minutes to finally find the entire crew and convince them to stop working."

"You're telling me?" Vanessa said, quite adamantly. "I was the one tracking down the supervisor and ordering the stoppage. It was an unfortunate error and we did our best to accommodate the bride and groom after that. Let me tell you that supervisor was not happy.

He had to pay those men regardless, even after I sent them all packing. I'm truly sorry that the bride was distraught, Brock. We did the best we could, under the circumstances."

Brock scratched his jaw and sighed deeply. "I suppose. But that wasn't all. The Garden Pavilion restrooms were stopped up. All the guests were inconvenienced by having to use the restrooms at the far end of the hotel lobby."

"Plumbing problems are the worst." Vanessa nodded her agreement. "We had a team working on it and finally got it all fixed before the reception ended."

"A little late, wouldn't you say?"

Vanessa bit down on her lip. She had to watch her step with Brock. He wasn't a fool. Far from it. "I can assure you, I was on top of all the problems from the moment they occurred."

"It's your job to see that they don't occur." Brock sipped his drink, eyeing her over the glass rim.

"Were there any more complaints?" she asked.

"Weren't those enough? The wedding ceremony nearly ruined and plumbing problems during the entire affair makes for a bad first impression."

"For me? Surely, I couldn't have controlled those things, not even if I were a mind reader." She defended quite convincingly, she thought.

Brock looked deep into her eyes. "No, I didn't say that. It makes for a bad impression for the hotel. Word of mouth is worth a bundle on the island. I only hope comping their honeymoon stay will make it up to them."

"That's a nice gesture."

"Costly." He shrugged. "It's expected when things go wrong."

"I'm sorry there were problems. But I don't think the hotel will suffer too much. Tempest has a good reputation." That much was true and Vanessa aimed to make sure Brock's hotel would become the black sheep of the Tempest flock.

"I'd like to keep it that way." He rose and when she thought he was ready to leave, he walked over to the kitchen counter and poured another drink, mixing rum with Coke again. Then he leaned against the corner of the counter and folded his arms, his gaze focusing directly on her. "Did you enjoy your night out?"

Vanessa rose from her seat, irritated by her vulnerability. She mustered her courage, commending herself on her bravado thus far. Brock made her nervous, especially when his eyes followed her every movement. "Yes, it was a nice evening."

"Did you dance?"

She nodded and leaned opposite him against the counter. "A little. It was nice to unwind."

Brock's gaze flowed over her leisurely, taking in her silvery dress and high-heeled sandals. "I'd like to see that, too. You…unwinding."

Her throat went as dry as tropical wind.

"Truth is, I was in a devil of a mood when I got here, Vanessa."

"Ready to take my head off?" she asked, squeamishly.

"Ready to take something off," he said quietly.

Goose bumps prickled her skin and she remained silent. Even as he set his glass down on the counter. Even as he walked toward her. Even as he stood toe-to-toe with her, her back to the granite countertop, she remained silent.

"My mood is improving," he said, touching a curling strand of her hair and looking down at her mouth.

Her heart raced. She didn't know what to do. She'd been successful in sabotaging him today and now, as he bent his head, oh Lord, she wanted to feel his lips claim hers again. A bizarre, uncanny and...*thrilling* sensation swept clear through her.

"What are—"

His mouth bore down, tasting from her lips again, obliterating her question. He clamped his hands on her hips and pulled her closer, drugging her with his kiss and demanding a response. She couldn't deny his demand, and when he moved closer yet, she wrapped her arms around his neck. "This is crazy," she whispered, the words slipping out.

"Why?" he asked, tugging on her lower lip gently, his sexy sandalwood scent surrounding her senses.

Because I'm doing my best to ruin you.

He nipped at her lip again and she sucked oxygen into her lungs, her body reacting to him on every level. The kitchen grew hotter and hotter and when he pressed her mouth open and drove his tongue inside, that heat quickly escalated to sizzling. "I'm not your boss now," he murmured between sweeping kisses.

"What are you then?" she whispered as his tongue explored and tantalized.

"A man completely drawn to you."

"You don't know me, Brock," she said, the conversation taking place between hot, hungry, wet kisses.

"I'm a good judge of character, honey," he said, moving from her mouth to nibble on her throat. "And I know what I want." His hot breath warmed her and she arched her neck, allowing him complete access. Goodness. Pressed against him, she felt the full measure of what he wanted. His erection stymied her next thoughts. Brock's charm, elegance and raw sexuality enveloped her. She couldn't fight back. His weapons were too powerful.

He moistened her shoulder with his tongue, planting little biting kisses there, his hands on either side of her shoulders now, slipping the straps of her dress down, releasing the material.

Her slinky dress betrayed her and fell down around her breasts. Brock's intake of oxygen thrilled her as his gaze swooped down. "Perfect," he offered, admiring her with open lust.

He reached up and circled her breast, outlining it

gently, his thumb flicking the erect tip, causing rapid, potent and instant desire to flare below her waist.

"Brock," she pleaded, and spoke her thoughts aloud. "We can't do this."

"We're doing it," he said softly, "don't fight it."

He cupped one breast and bent his head, his tongue moist on her nipple.

She moaned with pleasure and dug her fingers into his hair. He continued his lusty assault and Vanessa threw caution to the wind, leaning back and relishing each heated caress with total abandon.

Then the phone rang.

Vanessa blinked her eyes. She didn't get too many calls here. What if it was Melody? The answering machine would give Vanessa away. Melody's voice was earthy, with a little Louisiana accent that couldn't be missed. If she said her name into the answering machine…

Vanessa wasn't ready to give up her quest yet. She didn't want to be discovered by Brock.

The phone rang a second time. She pushed at Brock's chest. "I have to get that."

He looked into her eyes. "Let it ring. Your machine will get it."

Two rings to go and all would be lost.

"No, I'm sorry," she said, sliding along the counter and out of his grasp. "I'm expecting an important call."

She dashed into her bedroom and picked up the

bedside phone, looking at a framed photo of Melody and her, arms wrapped around each other, back in Louisiana. She grabbed the frame and tossed it into her dresser drawer, getting rid of the evidence.

Slamming the drawer closed, she answered out of breath, "Hello."

"Hi! Have you recovered from our little excursion tonight?"

"Oh…hi, Lucy," she stammered, surprised it was her friend who'd called.

"I can't find my wallet. Have you seen it by any chance?"

"Uh, no. I haven't. Maybe you left it at the Torch."

"That's my next call. But I had it when I paid the bill. I can't remember what I did with it after that. Just thought maybe it dropped out of my car when I let you off at your place tonight."

"Gosh, I'm sorry," she said, finally focusing on her friend's dilemma. "I'll look around the complex and call you right back."

"Thanks, you're a doll."

Vanessa hung up the phone and straightened her dress, setting the spaghetti straps back in place. She imagined she looked pretty disheveled, but didn't dare glance in the dresser mirror. She didn't want to see the sex-starved expression on her face.

That's what she attributed her attraction to Brock as—her lack of sex. She hadn't been in a relationship for over a year.

"Was that your important call?" Brock startled her, leaning against the doorjam, his gaze intent.

"Uh, no. But it was something important. Lucy lost her wallet. I have to try to find it outside where she dropped me off."

He eyed her for a minute. Glanced at her bed with a lingering look. Then nodded. "I'll help."

"Oh, you don't have to do that. I'm sure I can—"

"Vanessa, I said I'll help."

His tone held no irritation, thankfully. This evening was confusing enough for her. "Okay. Thank you."

When she brushed past him, he took her hand and drew her up against his body. "We're not through yet." He kissed her quickly and released her. "Not by a long shot. Just thought I'd give you fair warning."

Vanessa considered herself duly warned and walked out of her condo with Brock, realizing how close she'd come to being exposed. She'd been lucky this time.

She couldn't afford any more close calls.

But what worried her more was the close call she'd had in Brock's arms.

They'd come very close to making love.

And Vanessa hadn't the willpower to stop him.

"Just turn those car keys over to me now, Brock, and save yourself the grief." Trent's amused laughter came through loud and clear over the cell phone.

Brock winced, and leaned back in his desk chair, mentally shaking off his brother's gibe, but he couldn't banish the image of Trent's gloating face popping into his mind. "Not on your life, bro. In fact, I don't have a clue what you're talking about."

Trent laughed again, grating on Brock's nerves. "Right. Hell, the Everett wedding even made our Arizona papers. I've got the exact words here, 'Jack-hammers drowned out the wedding march and brought tears to the hopeful bride's face, the Everett marriage getting off to a dismal start at Tempest Maui's plush, but chaotic, Garden Pavilion.'"

Brock ran his hand down his jaw and heaved a sigh. "Must have been a slow news day at Crimson Canyon. What, you don't have enough going on with your fiancée, you have to call and harass me?"

"Julia says hello, by the way," Trent said good-naturedly. "She told me not to torment you, so I'm letting you off the hook. Just try to do better. You're making this too easy for me."

"Funny, Trent." Brock liked a good challenge, and winning ownership of his late father's classic Thunder-bird was part of the deal. He'd bet Trent his newly reno-vated hotel would make more money in the first year of operation than Trent's western-themed Tempest West. Now, the competition was in full swing. And his pride and reputation were on the line. "Give Julia a kiss for me."

"That, I'll be darn happy to do."

After he hung up the phone, Brock tried concentrating on work, but he couldn't get his mind off Trent's annoying phone call. Brock had worked extremely hard on renovating the hotel, trying to take a failing enterprise and make it a success. He'd hired a new staff and had faith in their abilities. He knew his management team was top-notch. He couldn't afford any more mistakes to be made.

Vanessa entered his mind and he shook his head.

She was competent, hard-working and gorgeous.

She'd been on his mind a lot lately, breaking into his thoughts at the oddest moments. He'd seen her around the offices but they hadn't spoken in two days, since that night when he'd nearly undressed her and taken her to bed. Intoxicating thoughts of what would have happened had they not been interrupted came to mind frequently. He couldn't remember a time he'd enjoyed being with a woman more.

He leaned forward at his desk and buzzed his secretary. "Rosalind, I need a meeting with Vanessa Dupree. Have her come up at noon."

"Okay, Mr. Tyler."

Brock glanced at his watch. Then concentrated on the contracts on his desk, filling the time with work until he'd confront Vanessa.

Hoping to finish what they'd started the other night.

"You wanted to see me?" Vanessa said, entering Brock's office, her mind reeling. She hadn't spoken with him since the night of the wedding fiasco. The night she'd managed to ward off his advances. Con-

sidering that entire day had been a lose-lose situation
for him, she'd steered clear of him in every way
possible. But she couldn't ignore a meeting at the
boss's request.

He stood by the window, with his back to her,
gazing out at the deep aqua-colored waters of the
Pacific, the office view the best in the hotel. His hands
thrust in the pockets of his casual tan trousers, he
turned around slowly and they made eye contact.

Jarred by the jolting impact of coming face-to-face
with him again, Vanessa stood rooted to the spot. She
fought her crazy, unwarranted attraction to him, and
ignored the dark intensity of his eyes and the ease of his
stance.

"Close the door, Vanessa."

She turned and resisted the urge to flee, shutting the
door as asked.

"Did you want to talk about the fashion show gala?"
She stepped farther into his office.

"Do you have it under control?"

She nodded. "Yes, I'm confident it'll go off as
planned." As *she'd* planned, she didn't add. She had
more work to do to ensure failure for that event as well.

"Then, no. I have every confidence that you'll make
the hotel look good."

"Thank you."

He came forward and sat on the edge of his desk,
his long legs crossed at the ankle and smiled. "You're
welcome."

They spoke civilly as if their last encounter hadn't been hot and heavy and sexually charged. As if Brock hadn't worked magic on her mouth and hadn't stripped down her clothes and her defenses, nearly making her succumb to his desire.

Thank heaven Lucy had good timing. That phone call had saved her. Vanessa hadn't counted on Brock's attraction to her or the unnerving, completely unwelcome attraction she had for him.

She steeled her resolve. Brock was, in fact, the enemy and she wasn't nearly through with him yet. This was one time the tycoon wouldn't get what he wanted. But with his gaze steady on hers, she couldn't think straight much less breathe.

"Did you need me for something else then?" she asked, fully aware of his close proximity, the scent of sandalwood an unsettling reminder of the other night.

His gaze flicked over her, taking in her aqua-blue knit tank top and white pants and she wondered if her clothes were *too* casual now. The turquoise gemstone necklace draped on her chest seemed to catch his attention, but after a "duh" moment, she realized it wasn't the stone that he admired.

"Yes, I need you. Can you clear your calendar this Saturday night?"

She gulped and blurted, "Why? Are you asking me out on a date?"

One side of his mouth quirked up. "No."

Confused and embarrassed, she blinked, feeling

heat burn its way up her throat. "Oh," she said, shaking her head, befuddled. "What do you need then?"

"I've been invited to the Hawaiian Hotel Association's annual dinner. There'll be good opportunity for networking and as my event planner, I think you should join me. Are you free that evening?"

"No. Yes. I mean I'd planned on working on the Fashion Show Gala all day and into the night."

Brock assessed her with discerning eyes. "You'll get it done in enough time. The dinner's at seven and I'll make sure to have you tucked into bed early."

Vanessa's blood ran cold. She needed that time to work on unraveling Sunday's fashion show. But she really couldn't refuse Brock's invitation. She was being squeezed tight between the proverbial rock and the hard place and needed to come up for air. Her mind worked quickly and finally she figured out a Plan B for her sabotage.

Brock stared at her. "Vanessa?"

She hadn't missed the "I'll make sure to have you tucked into bed early" comment either. Lurid images popped into her reckless mind.

"It's just that the other night, things got a little out of control at my place."

"No, they didn't." He lifted up from his perch on the desk to stand straight, arms folded, and surveyed her. "If you were being honest with yourself, you'd say they were right on track."

She snapped her head up and thought of Melody

and all he'd put her through. She wouldn't qualify his statement with an answer. "This is only a business dinner, right?"

He nodded, making no apologies for the other night. "Absolutely. And it's important."

"Okay, I'll clear my calendar."

"Thank you. And, Vanessa, this is one time it's *not* casual attire."

She granted him a reluctant smile. "I'll make sure to leave my jogging suit at home." Then she walked out the door.

Four

Brock exited his sterling silver Mercedes and walked up the steps to Vanessa's condo, reflecting on his choice to drive tonight rather than use his limousine. He wanted to be completely alone with Vanessa before and after the dinner with no interruptions. He wanted her all to himself.

She was resistant to his charms and posed a challenge that excited him. Not that other women hadn't turned him down, but with due modesty, those women had been few and far between. Women flocked to Brock and he'd known it was his charm, decent good looks and his pocketbook that impressed them. It was different with Vanessa Dupree. None of that seemed to matter to her.

In fact, more often than not, she seemed completely unimpressed with him. He found himself less irritated at that and more amused and mystified.

Brock straightened his ink-black Armani jacket, tightened the knot of his tie and knocked on her door.

She made him wait. He knocked again and she called out, "Just a sec."

It was worth the wait. Vanessa opened the door and the sight of her made his groin twitch. He lifted his brows and assessed her for a few moments. Her rich platinum hair was full, away from her lovely face and touched her shoulders in soft barrel-like curls. She wore a red strapless dress that hugged her torso and fell along the curves of her hips, draping down her legs with one side riding midthigh in a slit that would catch every male eye in the room.

And Brock would be the man bringing her home.

"You look beautiful," he said.

"It's not too much?" she asked with modesty. "I wasn't sure how 'not casual' you meant."

He glanced at her tempting cherry-red glossy lips and wished there was time to suck the gloss off and kiss her senseless. "You're a perceptive woman, Vanessa. You got it just right. Actually, perfect."

"Hardly that, but thanks for the compliment. You look very nice," she said, her gaze flowing over him for a moment. "Would you like to come in?"

He winced. "With the way you look tonight, it'd be

better if we left right now or I doubt we'd get out of your place until midnight."

She chuckled, thinking he was teasing, no doubt, until she gazed deep into his eyes and saw the truth. Then she nodded, a somber look crossing her features. "I'll get my purse."

She looked just as enticing from the backside and when she grabbed her beaded red purse and turned toward the door, it was all Brock could do from sweeping her off her feet and carrying her into the bedroom.

"Ready?" she asked when she reached him.

"Yeah." He was ready. For her. But he'd have to resign himself to a business dinner for now.

They walked through the flowered gardens and passed the pool in silence, Brock leading her with a hand to the small of her back. His fingers itched to touch more of her and he was glad he'd made the decision to drive his car, rather than be chauffeured. He needed to do something with his hands.

"Did Lucy ever find her wallet?" he asked, making idle conversation. Vanessa's soft fragrant perfume was like an erotic elixir. He needed the distraction of a conversation.

"Yes, she'd left it at the Torch. Lucky for her. I once lost my wallet and it was weeks before I got all my records and credit cards straightened out. I had to cancel everything and start from scratch. What a pain. It's a good thing my sister…uh…never mind. I'm boring you."

Brock chuckled. "No, you're not. I didn't know you had a sister. Younger? Older?"

"Um, younger."

"With pretty platinum hair just like yours?"

"No, my sister looks nothing like me." Brock couldn't miss the way her body stiffened at the mention of her sister.

"Are you close to her?" he asked, drawing her out. He found himself enthralled with all aspects of Vanessa's life. Maybe because she offered so little about herself and that intrigued him.

"Not really. No. She and I have nothing in common." Vanessa clutched her tiny purse tight and she seemed very uncomfortable with the subject. "It's sort of a sore subject right now. We, uh, we don't really get along."

"Okay, fair enough." Brock opened the door for her and watched her glide into her seat, the slit in her dress showing a fair amount of gorgeous leg. "No more questions about your sister."

He shut her door and inhaled deeply, tamping down his lust. He reminded himself once again that this was a business dinner and not a date, though the lower half of him was having trouble remembering that.

He got into the car and started the engine, looking over at Vanessa struggling to put her seatbelt on. "Let me. It can be tricky."

He reached across her body, his arm brushing up against her soft bare shoulder, pulled the belt taut and clamped it into the lock.

"Thank you," she breathed out.

He was close enough to hear the quiet intake of her breath. Satisfied that he affected her to some degree, he returned to his position and drove away with a smug smile tipping the corners of his mouth. "My pleasure, Vanessa."

The dinner couldn't be over soon enough. Brock had plans for Vanessa that included pleasure for both of them.

Clearly, Brock Tyler was the most handsome man at the dinner, if Vanessa were to make a judgment call. Female heads turned when he walked into a room and she noted more than a few envious stares from the women she passed as they made their way to the luxurious circular bar in the corner of the anteroom.

Hundreds of elegantly dressed guests milled about, their laughter and chatter rising above the soft melodic music playing. Crystal chandeliers lit the room and island flowers were displayed in stunning exotic arrangements. The pleasing subtle scent of plumeria graced the air and for the first time all day, Vanessa relaxed.

She sipped a sour apple martini as Brock introduced her to the owners, regional managers and corporate heads of major hotels on the islands. Brock included her in all his conversations, asking her opinion and making her feel on the same level with the moguls who ran the hotel industry. They spent the next forty-five minutes in the upscale bar, but Vanessa could tell Brock was getting impatient.

They slipped away from a small group, Brock's hand warm to her back as he led her to an outer hallway. "Enough networking for a while," he said, sipping his gin and tonic while focusing his attention on her.

He'd gotten her a second sour apple martini, which she carefully nursed. She couldn't afford to lose her inhibitions or her nerve. The big fashion show gala would need her undivided attention tomorrow.

"You don't like schmoozing? You do it so well." And that was the truth. Brock knew how to charm people and make them laugh with his wit and intelligence.

"So I've been told," he said with a chuckle. "But I thought you'd had enough. These dinners can be boring, but necessary."

"Me? Do I look bored?" She didn't want to give off a bad impression and arouse suspicion.

"No, you look…gorgeous."

"I wasn't—"

"I know, you weren't fishing for compliments." He leaned in and placed a delicious kiss on her mouth. When he backed away, his beautiful dark eyes held undeniable promise. "I've wanted to do that all night."

Her stomach went queasy. If Brock bottled his sex appeal, he wouldn't have to run a major hotel chain. He'd make millions in another way entirely.

"You do that so well, too," she muttered.

"Thank you. Coming from you, it's a big compliment."

She tilted her head to the side. "Why do you say that?"

Brock ran his finger along her cheek, tracing the line of her jaw ever so gently, causing prickly goose bumps to rise up on her arms.

"Because you're resisting me."

"And women don't ever resist you?" she asked, keeping her tone light and flirtatious. She couldn't reveal what she really thought about him.

Amused, he grinned and that smile stole her breath. "Now that's a question I'm smart enough not to answer."

"You're my boss," she said quietly.

"You keep saying that, Vanessa. We're both adults and I'm interested in you…more than I've been in a woman in the past decade."

Her queasy stomach clenched. Her heart raced. If it was a line, he'd delivered it convincingly. Vanessa quelled the jarring jolt his admission had to her system. She told herself not to be immensely flattered. She told herself not to believe him. He'd left Melody hurt and alone to pursue another woman.

Yet, there was something in his expression that begged to differ with her innermost thoughts.

She remained silent so long that Brock glanced at his watch. "It's time for dinner."

She smiled weakly and when he took her arm, she walked beside him into the main dining room.

Two hours later, Vanessa found herself in Brock's capable arms on the dance floor. The ballroom's lights dimmed, they danced to a smooth soft ballad that set a mood for romance.

She'd endured dinner and an awards presentation where honors were given out to hotels of excellence in service and guest relations. She'd seen Brock's eyes alight with determination watching the presenters give high honors to his competitors. He wanted his hotel not only to succeed, but to be ranked highest on the islands.

Brock Tyler always had to have the best.

It was a noble ambition for a man who loved his profession. She couldn't fault him there, Brock was diligent, hard-working and fully in command. His employees respected him. They thought him fair and forthright. Being an insider now, she'd heard plenty around the hotel about Brock. Unfortunately, she'd had to listen to female employees spout off about how "hot" Brock was and how they'd love to be one of his overnight guests on his yacht. They'd seen that yacht take off plenty of nights and all had surmised without a doubt that he hadn't been alone.

Vanessa had always kept quiet when the conversation turned to Brock, but she'd taken it all in and was reminded that Brock wasn't to be trusted no matter how charming he could be.

"You're quiet tonight," he said, holding her at a respectable distance.

"Just being a good listener."

Brock brought her slightly closer. "That's a good quality in a woman," he said quite seriously.

She lifted her head up to meet his eyes and saw a mischievous grin surface on his face. She shook her head. "There's a few feminist organizations who'd tar and feather you for saying that."

"Hmmm, I think I've met some of those women already. They don't like me."

"I don't doubt it," she said, feeling justified.

Brock brought her closer yet and whispered in her ear. "I only care about one woman liking me."

A shocking thrill coursed through her body. As much as she wanted to be immune to him, there was something so incredibly charismatic about him. "I...like you, Brock."

He nodded, satisfied. When the music ended, he guided her to the table and they took their seats. Coffee was served and Vanessa was glad that the evening was coming to an end.

Someone tapped Brock on the shoulder and a sultry voice whispered behind him. "Have you been hiding from me all night?"

Vanessa turned her head to find a stunning dark-haired woman with bright green lust-filled eyes, devouring Brock. He rose from his seat to greet her. "Hello, Larissa."

"Hello? Is that all you can say?"

She lifted up and kissed Brock gently on the lips. "There, that's better."

Something powerful tightened in Vanessa's stomach. She turned away for a second, to smile at the other eight people seated at the table. Had she imagined it, or did they all look at her with sympathetic eyes?

"Why haven't you called?" Vanessa heard the woman question him as if no one existed at the table but Brock.

Brock hesitated to answer for a second. "Vanessa," he said, and she closed her eyes briefly before turning around to glance at him. "Will you excuse me? I'll be right back."

"Of course. Take your time."

Brock nodded and excused himself to the others seated at their table. Vanessa watched him walk away with Larissa on his arm.

Fiona Davis, the older woman seated next to her, laid a gentle hand on her arm. "She's the Association president's daughter. I wouldn't worry too much. She's engaged, though she is a bit of a flirt."

"Oh, I'm not worried," Vanessa blurted. "I mean to say, this isn't what it looks like. Mr. Tyler is my employer. We're here on business."

Fiona sent her a motherly smile and said quietly, "Maybe you are, but he hasn't taken his eyes off you all evening. He's eligible, handsome as the devil and rich.

I wouldn't dismiss his interest in you so easily." Fiona sighed longingly. "Dare I say the old cliché, he's a catch?"

Vanessa stared into Fiona's soft brown eyes. "What if I'm not fishing?"

She smiled knowingly. "Ah, you don't want to get involved. Someone hurt you?"

"Yes," Vanessa admitted. She'd been hurt in the past. She'd been dumped for another woman when she was younger more than once. She'd lost her high school sweetheart to a girl with an IQ of a snail. Later on, she figured they deserved what they'd gotten since they'd cheated on each other and wound up hating one another. And in college, she'd almost gotten engaged, until she found her would-be fiancé in bed with her roommate. The shock had crippled her for a time and made her wary of men, but she'd gotten over the hurt long ago. This time, it wasn't about her. She was doing this for Melody—standing up for her sister, who'd been devastated by Brock Tyler's hurtful dismissal of her. "I've been hurt before. And it's too soon for another involvement."

She'd transposed Melody's hurt onto herself for Fiona's benefit. It made her feel less like a liar to the kindhearted woman. Lord knows she'd lied to enough people since she'd come to the island.

"I understand. Before I met my late husband, I had a crushing experience."

For fifteen minutes, Vanessa listened to Fiona speak

about her past hurts and how she'd managed to recuperate from them. They were the last ones left at the table and when Fiona also had to leave, Vanessa bid her farewell and got up to use the ladies' room.

She headed past the anteroom and down the hallway, clutching her purse in her hand, her anger at Brock over his abandonment of her in the ballroom building. When she spotted him outside on the plush grounds, standing arm in arm with the black-haired what's-her-name, she came to a halt, pivoted around abruptly and headed for the lobby where she promptly summoned a cab to take her home.

"Let him look for me," she muttered, then thought better of it. She couldn't afford to get fired. She wrote a quick note and handed it to the valet before getting into the cab. "Give this to Mr. Brock Tyler. He's the one with the silver Mercedes."

She had things to do early in the morning. She didn't want to rush him away from the event. She needed her rest.

That's what she'd written on the note and what she'd tell him tomorrow if asked.

Vanessa ignored the pangs of jealousy she felt seeing him with that woman and hated Brock all the more for making her feel that way.

She rested her head on the back of the cab's seat and closed her eyes, going over her plan for the Fashion Institute's Valentine's Day Gala. "Brock Tyler, you'll get yours tomorrow."

* * *

The doorbell rang three times in succession, the incessant chimes rattling her eardrums. "Just a minute," she called out, tossing her arms through her silk robe and tying the sash. She padded to the door and peeked out the peephole.

Oh, God.

Brock.

"Open the door, Vanessa."

Judging from the tone of his voice and the hard look in his eyes, he wasn't a happy man.

Vanessa filled her lungs with oxygen and opened the door.

"What the hell were you thinking?" Brock didn't wait for an invitation. He entered her humble condo then whirled around on her.

"I don't know what you mean," she answered calmly.

"I mean when I take a woman out, I fully expect to be the one to deposit her back home safely. You walked out on me. I don't think any woman has done that before."

The mystified expression on his face stymied her for a second. Then on impulse, she laughed at the absurdity. "I'm sorry." She covered her hand to her mouth, yet she couldn't hide her amusement. "It's not funny, but you should see the look on your face."

A tick worked his jaw. Obviously, he wasn't amused. "Vanessa, answer my question. Why in hell did you leave?"

"Did you get my note?"

"After searching for you for ten minutes."

Vanessa smiled to herself. He'd been dumped, if even for ten minutes, and he hadn't liked how it felt. Payback could be sheer pleasure at times. "I'm sorry if you were inconvenienced," she said sincerely.

He frowned.

"I told you in the note that I didn't want to hold you up. You were busy with whatever her name was, and I needed to get to bed early tonight."

"Damn it. I was talking business with Larissa Montrayne. She's getting married and wanted to ask me some questions. Do you know what it would mean if she decided to have her wedding at Tempest?"

"It'd be huge?"

"Right. It would be huge."

"But shouldn't those questions have been asked of your event planner? I thought that's the whole reason you brought me with you tonight."

"Larissa needs personal attention. She's...temperamental."

"You mean she's spoiled."

A corner of his mouth cocked up. "Maybe."

"And she wanted *your* undivided attention."

"If you hadn't hightailed it out of Dodge so quickly, you might have had a chance to talk with her. I brought her back to the table and you were gone."

"That must have been awkward." Vanessa pictured that scenario, relishing the images drifting into her mind.

"I was concerned."

"For me?"

"Like I said, no one has ever walked out on me like that."

"So you thought maybe someone kidnapped me? Or maybe I fell and hit my head in the ladies' room?"

Brock drew his brows together. "When I got your note, I was furious."

"You'd rather I'd hit my head and was lying unconscious somewhere?"

He stared at her.

"Are you going to fire me?"

"Fire you?" Again his brows furrowed and he shook his head. "Vanessa, I'm just trying to figure you out."

She shrugged and walked toward the front door, a gesture to let him know it was time to leave. "There's nothing much to figure out. I told you the reason I left."

"Couldn't be that you were jealous?"

Vanessa wrapped her arms tight around her middle and shook her head. "Of course not."

Brock made a move toward the door and she thought he'd finally taken the hint. When he gently closed the door and turned to her, she realized she'd been mistaken. "Larissa thought you were. She apologized for monopolizing my time."

"I bet she did," Vanessa mumbled. That woman's eyes sparkled with glee when she'd successfully orchestrated Brock's sole attention.

He shot her a knowing look. "I was hopping mad

when you took off." His tone mellowed and his gaze flowed over her softly.

"And now?" Vanessa feared his answer.

"Now, I'm flattered."

"Brock, don't tell me your ego needs stroking."

"No, not my ego." He sent her a sinful smile, one filled with so much hunger, her knees buckled.

She turned away from him and tried to block out the tempting look on his face and the way his strong voice had taken on a softer edge.

This was crazy. *She* was crazy. She couldn't let him get to her this way. She had been jealous, which was ridiculous. She'd come to Maui for the sole purpose of ruining his reputation. She'd wanted to hit him where it hurt the most.

"I think you should leave." She whirled around to face him only to find him directly in front of her now, his jacket and tie tossed aside. His shirt unbuttoned at the throat. How had he done that so fast?

Her pulse reeling, she swallowed and blinked her eyes away from the bronzed skin peeking out from his shirt.

Brock laid his hands on her waist and drew her closer, his voice a whisper near her ear. "I'm dying to know what's under this robe."

She wanted to say he'd never find out, but his mouth descended on hers and obliterated all thought. His hands slid from her waist to her derriere and he cupped her, pressing gently and bringing her up against his hips. Her thin silky robe did little to protect her from the strength of his body.

She savored the taste of whiskey and desire on his lips, burning her with his hunger. She met his greedy demand and roped her arms around his neck. His kisses urgent and needy, both of them were wrapped up in a moment of ecstasy.

Brock brought her with him as he stepped backward until he met with the wall. Then he pivoted, taking her with him, until she replaced his position. She arched her head back, and he drizzled hot wet kisses from her lips to her chin, her throat and down to the V of her robe.

She felt a tug and her sash released from the tie. Her robe parted, leaving the center of her body uncovered. Brock glanced at her red lace bra and thong panties and a guttural groan escaped the depths of his throat.

"Vanessa," he whispered with warm breath. "You don't disappoint."

He kissed the valley between her breasts then fingered the lace of her bra, teasing her with light butterfly caresses. She ached for him to touch more of her, to bend his head and mouth her breasts until her nipples pebbled hard.

But instead, he reached down lower, his hand skimming her torso and traveling below her navel. He dipped under her panties and cupped her between the thighs.

"Oh," she sighed softly, the tingling shock and pleasure of his touch creating tremors.

He brought his lips to hers again, claiming her with his tongue and driving deep inside, while he stroked her womanhood slowly, exquisitely.

She closed her eyes and allowed him full access. She grew moist instantly and he stroked her harder, with more demand. She surrendered to his caresses and the tremors built. She moved on him now, her body in rhythm to his delicious mouth and his expert hand. She swayed and rocked back and sighed out her pleasure.

"Brock," she pleaded, her pleasure heightened to the limit.

He continued to stroke her most sensitive spot. "Come for me, honey. Now."

His words threw her over the edge. She splintered into a thousand tiny fragments, her release fast and hard. Breathing heavy, her breasts full and her nerves quaking, she moaned with frenzied delight.

The climax left her boneless. With heavy lids, she opened her eyes to find Brock watching her with a hot steamy gleam in his eyes.

He smiled and kissed her lightly on the lips. "You should see the look on *your* face."

He tossed her comment back at her, and she bit her lip, ready to react, until he added, "It'll haunt my dreams tonight."

He picked up his suit jacket and tie and walked out of her condo.

Leaving her satisfied and wanton, and more than slightly confused.

Five

Timing was everything in this world but this time it didn't work in Brock's favor. He'd left a willing woman in the throes of passion and walked out on her.

To catch a plane to Los Angeles.

If it had been business instead of a family matter, Brock would have postponed the flight without blinking an eye. He'd be in bed with Vanessa Dupree right now, instead of sitting on the Tempest jet, traveling in the dead of night to make an engagement luncheon in Beverly Hills for his mother and her fiancé, Matthew Lowell.

Vanessa posed a challenge and Brock couldn't remember when he'd had a harder time trying to get a lady interested. She'd been on his mind a lot lately. And tonight he'd planned on a romantic evening and afterward, making sweet love to her.

Damn her for pulling that stunt at the dinner and throwing his well-planned evening into a confused, frustrating mess. If she were anyone else, he'd dismiss her as being more trouble than she was worth. Completely high maintenance, but not in a demanding, spoiled rich-bitch way. No, Vanessa had qualities that unnerved him. She was smart, charming, capable and adept at everything she did. Now that he knew her, now that he'd seen the glint of sizzling passion in her eyes, the way her body rocked sensually to his ministrations, the way little moans of ecstasy escaped her lips, Brock had to know more. He had to have her. Possess her. In every way.

Hell, he *liked* her.

More than he had liked a woman in a very long time.

There was something unique and mystifying about Vanessa Dupree. She'd been hot and ready and seeing her face when she'd combusted in his arms pulled at him in a dozen different ways. He'd been in awe. He'd been shaken.

The thought of making love to her quickly then running to catch a plane didn't appeal to him. He wanted time with her. Enough time to explore every inch of her and drive them both into oblivion. So Brock had left her, never to forget the look of lust on her pretty face, the melting softness in her eyes and the feel of her dewy damp skin under his fingertips, just before he'd walked out the door.

"Go to sleep, Brock," he mumbled as he stretched out on the sofa. As the jet's engine purred, he closed his eyes, banishing any more thoughts of Vanessa and hoping that his prediction tonight wouldn't come true—she wouldn't haunt his dreams.

The following morning, Brock exited his hotel room at Tempest Beverly Hills and met his family precisely at noon in a small private elegant dining room.

He came up behind his mother and pulled her into his arms. "Hi, Mom."

Rebecca turned around and smiled. "Brock, you made it."

The warm glow in her eyes and the happiness on her face told Brock all he needed to know—Matthew Lowell was a fine man. He couldn't replace his father, but he'd make his mother happy and that's what mattered the most. "I wouldn't miss it. Flew all night to get here."

Matthew stepped up and shook his hand. "Brock, glad to see you again."

"Same here." Brock assessed Matthew, who was his brother Trent's soon-to-be father-in-law. The older man had a contented gleam in his eyes. "Congratulations, you're getting a great woman." Brock wrapped his arm around his mother's shoulder and squeezed.

"I know," Matthew said. "I'm a lucky man. I have a

new grandson and when I thought life couldn't get any better, I fell in love."

"He's marrying a grandmother," Rebecca added. "Goodness, I can hardly believe it."

His mother couldn't be more pleased that Evan and Laney had a son and that more grandchildren were probably on the way. Trent and Julia wanted a family, too. Once again, Brock was the black sheep in the Tyler family. Heck, even his best friend, Code, was married and going to be a father. Sarah was halfway through her pregnancy.

Brock wasn't the marrying kind and he'd never thought of himself as father material. It was a good thing that his brothers had picked up the slack.

When Laney and Evan walked in, all focus went to the little boy named after their deceased father, John Charles Tyler.

Rebecca got to the baby first, snuggling him in her arms and bestowing countless kisses. Little Johnny was passed around to all the females in the family first, then Trent took a turn at holding him. He looked good with a child in his arms. *Better him than me,* Brock thought.

"Your turn, bro." Trent walked over to Brock.

"No, thanks. I can see Johnny just fine standing right next to you."

Laney walked over to him. "Now, Brock. Johnny needs to bond with all of his uncles." She took Johnny out of Trent's arms with all the instincts of a confident mother and set the baby in his arms. "There. You're a natural."

"She's right," Evan said, staring down at his son with pride. "You look good with a baby in your arms."

Trent slapped him on the back and grinned like a circus clown. "I couldn't agree more."

Brock made the mistake of glancing at his mother. Her eyes softened on him and little Johnny, and her expression filled with hope. He cleared his throat, quietly so as not to startle the baby who seemed to be studying him with curious blue eyes. "I'm not going down that road."

Evan roped his arms around Laney. "It sort of creeps up on you, Brock. Right, Laney?"

"Right," she agreed.

Julia chimed right in. "I can't wait until we have children."

"You aren't married yet."

"We will be," Trent said. "That's one reason we all gathered here today. To celebrate Mom and Matthew's engagement and to see if you wouldn't mind hosting our wedding?"

Brock handed the baby back to Laney. He needed to focus on this request. "You want to get married in Maui?"

"We do." Four voices chimed in at the same time.

Brock drew his brows together. "All four of you?"

"That's right," his mother said. "Julia and Trent and Matthew and I thought we'd marry in a double ceremony."

"It's fitting," Matthew said with a bob of his head.

"That's if you think you can keep the bathrooms from overflowing and the noise level down on the beach, bro." Trent's amusement met with a warning stare from Rebecca.

"We have discussed it, dear. We think it's the perfect location," she said.

"I thought you'd want to marry at Crimson Canyon," he said to Julia and Trent.

"Mom wants a tropical wedding on the beach. And Julia and I are fine with it," Trent said. Julia gazed adoringly at her fiancé. "We have our whole lives in the canyon to look forward to."

Trent bent to kiss her lips.

Brock nodded. "Okay, we'll have your wedding at Tempest Maui." Brock realized he didn't sound enthusiastic so he put on a big smile. "It'll be my pleasure and an honor."

If it wasn't a disaster.

The pressure was on. Brock would never live it down if something fouled up the double ceremony. Not that he had any reason to believe so. The first wedding at his Hawaiian resort had been flawed, but they'd since ironed out all the problems. The Fashion Institute's gala should go smoothly today and they'd be on the right track again.

"I'll check with Vanessa, my event planner, when I get back and we'll discuss wedding dates that work for everyone."

An image of Vanessa as he left her last night, half-naked, her eyes a soft glaze of blue and her gorgeous body glistening with the afterglow of her powerful climax stuck in his mind. His groin tightened with a need so dire it shocked him. He pictured her here, with all that platinum hair flowing, laughing beside him as she charmed his family.

The mental picture gave him pause.

"Lunch is ready," Evan said, to Brock's relief. He was grateful for the distraction.

Evan ushered them to their places in the dining room. "Let's discuss the weddings as we celebrate Mom and Matthew's engagement."

"But first, a toast," Brock said, picking up a champagne flute and looking at his family members, their numbers increasing with wives and babies. He was the outsider, the man alone, the sole bachelor in the family and Brock didn't mind at all.

He was in his comfort zone.

Brock wouldn't think of Vanessa Dupree as the woman who would settle him down and have his children.

And that was the biggest comfort of all.

Vanessa rubbed sunscreen on her legs and arms, then lowered herself down on a beach towel and let the Hawaiian rays warm her. It wasn't an overly hot day, but she wouldn't complain. It was February, and back on the mainland where she grew up near Baton Rouge, the temps were in the middle sixties. Here on Maui, the sun shone warm and soaked into her skin with a pleasant heat.

Instead of doing laundry at her condo on her afternoon off, she decided to treat herself to some R & R on the sands of Tranquility Bay. It was a celebration of sorts. She'd gotten really lucky, managing to foul up the fashion gala three days ago while Brock was out of town. Everything had gone as she'd anticipated. The lighting, the slideshow in the background, the seating arrangements, had all mysteriously gone awry, making Tempest Maui look like an amateur high school production rather than the five-star resort that it claimed to be.

She closed her eyes, commending herself on a job well done. If she managed to hold on to her employ long enough, she'd ruin Brock Tyler's business.

At least temporarily. Men like Brock didn't fail. He'd come back strong, she was certain. But as long as she tossed stumbling blocks on his path to success, making his road harder to navigate, she'd be satisfied. It might make him stand up and take notice that people weren't put on this earth for his sole pleasure and entertainment.

The way Melody described how he'd courted her, lavishing her with expensive gifts, treating her like royalty, focusing all his attention on her, thus making her fall head over heels for him, had disgusted her. He'd dumped her sister like a hot potato when he'd met another woman who'd intrigued him more. Vanessa's blood boiled, and the reminder cemented her resolve. She wouldn't allow guilty feelings to intervene. Akamu wouldn't take the heat from this last foul-up. Lucy hadn't been involved. Her new friends were in the clear.

It was all on her. She was the Tempest event planner. The buck stopped here.

She'd lucked out that Brock had been gone these past few days. She hadn't seen or spoken with him since he'd left her rather stunned in her condo on Saturday night. She'd melted into a puddle from his kisses and allowed him liberties far beyond what she'd ever expected to allow.

She squeezed her eyes tight, attempting to block out the memory. Brock had shattered her. He'd made her come alive. She'd splintered before his eyes and she'd come up panting and shamelessly wanting more. The only thing stopping her from dire mortification that night had been the hungry, appreciative look on Brock's face.

He hadn't been proving a point. He hadn't resorted to revenge for her walking out on him after the dinner. No, he'd been fully, deeply involved. He had regret in his eyes when he'd left her. He had wanted to stay. Later, she found out why he'd taken that midnight flight. He wouldn't miss his mother's engagement celebration.

Vanessa rolled onto her stomach and picked up her

cell phone. She punched in Melody's auto-dial number. The phone rang and rang. "Where are you, Melly?" she mumbled, right before her answering machine clicked on.

"Hi! You've reached Melody. You know the drill. I'll get to ya when I can." Melody's beaming voice brought a quick smile to Vanessa's face, before she frowned.

"Hi, Mel, where are you? I've been trying to reach you today. Call your big sister as soon as you can."

Vanessa worried about her sister's state of mind. Melody had been distraught and depressed when she'd left for Maui, but Melody assured her she'd manage. She'd encouraged her to go.

An hour later, sunbathed and more relaxed than she'd been in weeks, Vanessa packed up her beach gear. She bent to pick up her striped beach towel. As she turned around she came face-to-face with Brock. "Oh!"

Where had he come from? With his chest bare, wearing tan shorts and running shoes, she noted he was out of breath. He'd been running on the beach.

He watched her fidget with the items she held in her hand, keeping the towel close to her bikini-clad body. Her face flamed and she decided it was a good thing the sun shone bright today. She'd blame her flush on the heat.

"Hello, Vanessa."

"Um, hi." She gazed out at the aqua waters unnerved

by the way he looked at her. A thought struck. "It's my afternoon off. I wasn't—"

He took the towel from her hands and raked his eyes over her black bikini, or rather the parts of her body the bikini didn't cover. "I know."

They stared at each other for a long moment.

Her traitorous heart flipped over itself. She'd expected fear, loathing or something akin to dismay, seeing him again. But what she felt was…thrilling.

She filled her gaze with him. Why did he have this effect on her?

"Sit down for a minute, Vanessa."

She nibbled on her lower lip. This wasn't a request, but a command.

He set the beach blanket out onto the sand and gestured. She sat, then he sat. Both gazed at the waves rippling to the shore in white froth.

"It's good to see you," he said.

It was the last thing she'd expected him to say. "Thank…you."

Oh, Lord, Vanessa. Get a grip.

His shoulder brushed hers. A golden sheen coated his muscled chest. Vanessa was fully aware of him, the faint scent of sandalwood and man oozing from his body.

"I've been gone for three days and frankly, I wasn't happy with how we left things the other night."

"How was that?" she blurted. She wasn't sure what he was getting at and *frankly,* she didn't want this conversation. The irony astounded her. With miles of clear blue seas and pristine sand surrounding her, she felt trapped and couldn't find a way out of this exchange.

"Unfinished."

Vanessa blinked and her nerves jangled. "Maybe," she began, nibbling once again on her lower lip, "it was a good thing that you left when you did."

"I had to go. I didn't want to, Vanessa. I had a midnight flight to catch to the mainland. I don't think you wanted me to go either. I'm usually not a love 'em and leave 'em kind of man."

Liar. Melody's tearful face flashed in her mind.

"Okay." She had to play along. She wasn't finished with Brock yet.

"As long as we're clear about that."

"All clear." She feigned a big smile.

"Now, maybe you can tell me what happened at the fashion gala. I didn't get a glowing report. Quite the contrary, actually."

Vanessa spent the next ten minutes bluffing her way through an explanation. Brock listened intently, nodded his head and asked a few key questions. She'd expected these questions and had rehearsed the answers.

Brock glanced at her lips on several occasions. He lowered his gaze many times, too, his gorgeous dark eyes roaming over her skin.

When she was through explaining her way out of the gala catastrophe, Brock leaned back on his elbows and took a deep breath. "Spend the night with me, Vanessa."

Just like that, he'd voiced his innermost desires and expected her to comply. For a brief moment, the temptation to spend the night in Brock's arms carried in her thoughts. "When?"

"Tonight." She felt the heat of his penetrating gaze on her back.

"I can't. I have plans with…Lucy."

Brock sat up again and gazed into her eyes as if searching her for the truth. "Okay."

She sent him a regretful smile.

Brock's expression changed and he became thoughtful. "I need to take a more active role in the hotel. I've been absent each time we had an important event. Next time, I won't be gone. I expect you to accompany me to the luau on Saturday night. Between the both of us, we'll make sure there are no missteps."

Now, her goose *was* cooked. "That's a good idea."

Brock stood and looked at her. Then he reached down, his hand outstretched. She slid her hand in his and he drew her upright and into his arms smoothly. His hands splayed over her waist. "Just so we're clear," he repeated, before dipping his head and slanting his lips over hers. Their bodies brushed, her breasts covered in the slightest cotton material, pressed his chest.

The kiss nearly buckled her knees. When he broke off the kiss and gazed into her eyes, she nodded and managed, "Very clear."

Six

Vanessa adjusted her pareo around her body in the most flattering way possible. She tied the black material garnished with printed white gardenias slightly above her breasts into a bow the way Lucy had shown her. The sarong fell to just below her knees in an elegant angle.

"There," she said, looking at her reflection in the mirror. "Not bad for a mainlander."

Once satisfied with the dress, Vanessa swept her hair up in a twist and placed a fresh orchid behind her right ear, pinning it in place. She applied pink lip gloss, slanted a mascara wand over her lashes a few times and slipped her feet into a pair of strapless sandals.

"All set for the luau?" Lucy walked into the room, sipping on a fruit smoothie.

Vanessa turned away from the mirror to face her friend. "How do I look?"

"The pareo was made for you," Lucy said, coming to stand beside her. "You look like an island princess, Waneka."

Vanessa smiled as the phonetic Hawaiian name rolled off Lucy's lips. With Lucy's long raven hair and her dark natural skin tone, she was the true island beauty. "You fit the part better, Luana."

Lucy shrugged. "I bet Mr. Tyler doesn't think so. You're the one he's always watching."

Because he's suspicious of me, Vanessa thought wryly. Or maybe her guilty conscience was in overdrive tonight. Because, this evening her friends would be *involved.* Tonight, Akamu would oversee the food preparations and Lucy was in charge of the entertainment.

Brock was getting what he deserved, but her friends might take the heat when things got chaotic during the luau and Vanessa cringed at that thought.

She and Lucy drove separately to the hotel, Lucy giving her a knowing look when she explained that Brock insisted that she accompany him to the event for business reasons.

Once she arrived, she headed for his office and knocked on Brock's door.

"Come in," he said, and she found him at his desk, flipping through a batch of papers.

When he looked up, his eyes took on a warm glow. "Wow." He rose from his seat and walked around his desk. She wanted to exclaim "wow," too, but held her tongue. He looked like the millions she knew he had, casual but classy in tan slacks and a black silk shirt. He'd combed his dark hair back, accentuating strong bone structure and those knockout deep brown eyes.

Vanessa's blood surged in her veins. Her boss was sexy and she wasn't immune. The air sizzled around them, the sweetly fragrant Hawaiian scents adding allure to a room filled with tension.

"You look…*almost* perfect." He stood before her and reached for the orchid in her hair, removing it from her right ear. He placed it behind her left ear and nodded his approval. "Now, it's perfect."

Vanessa touched her hair, questioning him silently.

"Wearing it on the left side means the woman is taken."

"Oh." The explanation stunned her for a moment. His implication was clear.

He smiled and toyed with the bow around her breasts. One manly tug and her dress would be a gossamer puddle around her feet. "Do you know the restraint I'm managing, not to unravel you out of this dress."

Vanessa swallowed. "It's called a pareo."

Brock grinned. "You're learning." Then his eyes darkened to an even deeper brown. "But that's not my point."

For a fleeting moment, she wanted to be unraveled out of her sarong and tossed onto his desk caveman-style, disregarding all sense of reason.

He lowered his voice. "It would be so easy, Vanessa." He tugged on the sash beneath the bow gently. "Would you like that?"

Vanessa blinked and then closed her eyes. Oh, God. She would *love* it.

His lips brushed hers tenderly and she snapped her eyes open. But the kiss was so breathtakingly good she closed her eyes again, wrapped her arms around his neck and simply enjoyed the taste of Brock and his subtle sandalwood scent that made her heart beat like crazy.

His hands caressed her derriere and he deepened the kiss, applying pressure to her lips. Bringing her up close, he rubbed her against his rising manhood and she moaned longingly, the sound escaping before she could stop it.

"Damn, Vanessa," he whispered, breaking off his kiss and the hold he had on her. "Don't make plans for later tonight. We're going to finish this."

He took her hand and led her out of his office, heading outside as the sun set in orange hues over Tranquility Bay.

Ten minutes later disaster struck…right on cue. Brock stood beside her and Akamu on the hotel's private beach lit by tiki torches when all hell broke loose. He glanced at the reservation book. "There's at least one hundred extra people waiting in line, all claiming to have made reservations. Their names are not on our list." He yanked off the orchid lei from his neck and stared at Vanessa.

She heard the buzz of irate conversations from the people waiting in line and her stomach churned. Brock waited for her response.

"I don't get it. We've verified all the names on the guest list. We only signed up two hundred. We're not equipped for this many people. I'll turn them away with our deepest apologies."

That had been her plan. Turn them away disgruntled. Word of mouth would spread like wildfire.

"They're not going to like that. Those people are hungry and cranky, boss." Akamu shook his head and gazed at the line, his eyes wide with horror.

"What's your solution then?" Brock glanced from Akamu to Vanessa. "Well?"

"I'm sorry, I have no idea how this happened." Vanessa's apology met with deaf ears. "Maybe a computer glitch?" She'd managed to sabotage the guest book, deleting names and adding to the list all week long. It hadn't been difficult. "We could invite them back tomorrow night."

Brock's jaw tightened. "No. We're going to accommodate them tonight."

Vanessa's brows shot up in surprise. "How?"

He turned to Akamu. "Get into the kitchen. Have the chefs prepare one hundred more servings of side dishes. Make some calls to local restaurants. Beg and borrow, steal if necessary, fifty pounds of Kalua pig. Vanessa, you get housekeeping out here and have them set up any tables they can get their hands on. We won't turn these guests away. I'll make the rounds and speak with them myself. Let them know they'll be my guests for a complimentary breakfast on the beach tomorrow."

Akamu and Vanessa nodded.

"Go," he ordered and Vanessa saw the look of disdain on his face. She suspected Brock Tyler didn't like apologizing to anyone about anything.

Her insides knotted with tension. She'd never been a witness to Brock's wrath, but he was certainly not happy with her right now.

This may very well be her last night on the job.

Brock settled the mess at the luau and sat down more than an hour later, finally grabbing a bite to eat. Vanessa had been quiet though diligent in getting the extra guests seated and fed. It had taken nearly an entire hour, delaying the meal and the performances, to appease one hundred grumpy guests. Many were still not happy with their seats or the situation.

A strange wary feeling stormed his gut and he looked at Vanessa, seated across from him, eating mochiko chicken. She looked so beautiful and so...aloof. When she glanced at him, he couldn't read those deep sea-blue eyes.

The disaster had been averted somewhat. Brock had seen to it, but the damage had been done. Those additional guests had gotten a raw deal and Brock wasn't happy about that. The fact that his first important hotel events had been faulty, churned in his stomach.

His pride and ego were on the line.

Trent would never let him live it down if he didn't come out the winner.

And Brock hated losing.

Had he let his desire for Vanessa cloud his judgment? She'd come with impeccable references. He knew she was sharp as a whip. So what was up? How had these three hotel events become minidisasters?

They sat at a back table watching the hula performers mesmerize the crowd, and every so often two pairs of male eyes glanced at Vanessa, darting her interested looks when they thought no one was watching. Brock couldn't *blame* the men seated at their table. Vanessa wasn't just another pretty face, she had something unique—a Marilyn Monroe appeal with pouty lips and luminous platinum hair that begged to be touched.

He couldn't *blame* the men for looking her way, but he didn't like it.

Nor did he like the rush of possessiveness he felt about her. Hell, they hadn't slept together yet and he was casting innocent men cold, hard, she's-mine looks.

Had he let his lust for Vanessa mar his good instincts?

As much as he didn't want to believe it he had strong suspicions about Vanessa Dupree's actions of late.

"I think we averted the disaster," she said, licking chicken drippings off her fingers. Brock watched her tongue wrap around her index finger, then shot a narrow-eyed warning at the bald-headed father of four, who found Vanessa's mouth a little too fascinating.

"You think?" Brock shook his head. "I'm not sure."

"Well, at least we provided seats and food for everyone."

"Cost the hotel a bundle. Our competitors soaked us for the pork dishes they provided. Can't host a luau without Kalua pig and they took advantage."

"I'm sorry, Brock."

She did sound sincere. "How sorry?"

She tilted her head and glanced at him directly. "How sorry do you want me to be?"

He may have a reputation as being a playboy, but Brock wasn't the kind of man who exchanged sexual favors for anything other than pleasure. He wanted Vanessa, but not that way. Not that he thought for a second she was offering. She hadn't made his pursuit easy and he'd backed off enough to give her time to decide what she wanted.

Now, trust was an issue. He didn't know why, but he had a bad feeling about this. He rose from his seat. "I've got to go over receipts with Akamu. I'll leave you in charge here."

"Okay. I've got it under control."

Brock stared at her for a moment, then made sure the wandering eyes at the table met with his stony gaze. "I'll be back soon."

Hell, he thought. *She's got me acting like a love-struck teenager.*

Yet Brock had to put his suspicions to rest. He spent a minute speaking with Akamu, then headed straight for his office. Once inside, he closed the door and called his friend Code Landon.

"I need a favor, Code. That's if you can tear yourself away from Sarah long enough to help a friend."

"Sarah's busy in the studio working on an album."

"I thought she retired from show business. What's up? You can't keep your wife home these days?"

Code laughed. "Not in this lifetime, buddy. I built her an in-home studio. She's making a record of lullabies for the baby. Pouring her heart and soul into it. I've never heard anything so beautiful."

The change in Code's demeanor since he fell for Sarah Rose was almost tangible. The onetime bitter, confirmed bachelor was now a happily married man with a child on the way. Brock had been his friend since childhood. There wasn't anyone he trusted more, outside of his own brothers. "You hit the jackpot, Code."

"I know. You should try it sometime."

Brock flinched. The woman who entered his mind first and foremost was the one he had undeniable suspicions about. The one he would beseech his best friend to investigate. "Hey, someone has to represent the bachelors of the world."

"Man, you don't know. You just don't know. Now, about that favor, lay it on me. Sarah's gonna want my undivided attention as soon as she's through."

"Vanessa Dupree. I need to know everything there is to know about her. And I need it, yesterday."

"Okay. Give me what you've got already and I'll take it from there."

Brock told Code what he knew about her personally then faxed him her résumé. When he hung up the phone, the image of Vanessa in that easy-to-undo sarong stayed on his mind.

Code wouldn't have anything to tell him until the morning at the very earliest, and Brock's patience had worn thin.

He stared at the phone for a second, then rose and headed back to the luau that was winding down. He had unfinished business with Vanessa that couldn't wait a second longer.

Vanessa stood at the shore watching the crushing waves die down to creep along the sand. Distant noise from the housekeeping crew taking tables and chairs away drifted in the air. With the tiki torches extinguished now, only a wide beam of moonlight lit the beach.

Vanessa rubbed her forehead, smoothing out throbbing tension that pounded in her skull. Sabotage had its drawbacks. She had worried herself sick over the luau and wondered how much longer Brock would tolerate her alleged mistakes. And she worried about Melody whom she hadn't spoken with in days. Her sister sent her vague text messages saying she's keeping busy trying to forget her heartache.

"Poor Melody," she whispered and another protective wave of motherly concern swept through her.

Brock's strong arms wrapped around her from behind and drew her back onto his chest. "Talking to yourself?"

Alarmed, Vanessa froze. Had he heard her call out Melody's name? He was too smart to fool much longer and she wasn't nearly through ruining him yet. She turned around and smiled, trying to read his expression. "Not really, just waiting for you."

Brock's brows rose, surprised. "The wait is over, baby."

Vanessa backed up a step. "I'm sorry about the luau."

Brock shook his head. "I'm not Brock, your boss, right now. It's after hours."

Vanessa was so relieved she thought she'd faint. She'd escaped her fate one more time. "Oh?"

"Take a walk with me."

Vanessa nodded and bent to remove her sandals. The minute she did, cool soft sand slipped between her toes. Brock entwined their fingers and they walked away from the luau area at Tranquility Bay.

"Being originally from Texas, I never had an appreciation for the ocean. But now, I can't imagine living anywhere else."

"Hawaii is a magical place," Vanessa agreed. She'd never seen such lush gardens or beautiful exotic flowers. The moment she stepped off the plane, she'd been pleasantly overtaken by the fragrant tropical scents that filled the air.

The night air grew cooler and she trembled. Brock noticed and put his arm around her, his large hand warming her bare shoulder. "Cold?"

"A little."

"How about a drink to warm you up?"

That sounded safe enough. They'd go to Joe's Tiki Torch just down the beach and be surrounded by people. Brock's sensuous touch always confused her. She had trouble remembering how much the cliché playboy millionaire had hurt her sister.

"That sounds nice. I could use a drink." That much wasn't a lie.

As they walked farther along the beach they passed the bar. Rock and roll music blasted out the doors. "Aren't we going in?" she asked, coming to a halt. She gestured toward the bar with her finger.

Brock shook his head, grabbed her pointed finger and tugged her along. "I have someplace better in mind. Where it's quiet."

When they reached the marina, Brock led her up the dock steps toward his yacht. Warning bells rang in her head. "On second thought, maybe I should just go home." She faked a yawn. "I'm tired."

Brock kept walking. "One drink, then I'll take you home if you want. I have something to discuss with you."

Uh-oh. Vanessa slammed her eyes shut. He would lower the boom now and maybe toss her overboard.

When she hesitated on the dock, he added, "It's important. Something personal." Then he smiled and she felt a wave of relief. Whatever Brock Tyler was, he wouldn't hurt her physically. He was a lady-killer in an entirely different fashion.

When they reached the *Rebecca,* Brock helped her board his boat and led her down the steps to a cozy sitting room. "It's warmer down here," he said. "Make yourself comfortable. I'll get you a drink."

Vanessa glanced at the large cushy sofa and opted to follow Brock to the bar. One drink. That's all she'd promised him. She watched him pour her a glass of plum wine while he poured himself something more toxic, whiskey straight up.

"So what did you want to discuss with me?" she asked, leaning on the bar. She held her breath hoping he wouldn't bring up the chaos at the luau.

Brock grimaced. "My mother's and brother's wedding. They're both getting married and want a double ceremony."

"How nice," she replied, thinking of mother and son sharing a wedding day. She'd bet that didn't happen too often.

"They want the wedding here, at Tempest Maui."

"Oh, well...that will be—"

"A nightmare if all doesn't go well. We can't have any mix-ups. I'm going to have to discuss the details with you tomorrow." He sipped his whiskey and a thoughtful expression crossed his features. "I want it to be perfect for them. We'll need to find a suitable date. They don't want to wait too long."

Vanessa kept silent.

He brought both of their drinks with him around the bar and handed her the plum wine. He touched his glass to hers in a toast. "Here's to things running smoothly from now on."

She forced a little smile and brought the glass up to her lips. "Of course." The sweet fruity wine slid down her throat, calming her fragile nerves a bit. She strolled over to the sliding glass door and looked out to the bay.

"Still cold?" he asked.

She shook her head. "The wine's warming me up. I'm fine now."

Brock opened the slider and sea air freshened the room. He faced her as a breeze blew a few strands of her hair onto her cheeks. She made a move to tuck those strands behind her ears. Brock gently took her wrist and lowered her hand down. "You look good windblown."

A chuckle escaped. "Really? Most women wouldn't consider that a compliment."

"You're not like most women."

She set her hands on her hips. "Now, I'm not sure that's a compliment either."

"Trust me. As a man who knows a lot about women, saying you're one of a kind is a compliment."

Vanessa sipped her drink and stared out the sliding door to the stars above. She felt things for Brock she had no business feeling. He drew her in and made her feel special. She hadn't had any luck with the opposite sex. She'd only known men who'd taken advantage of her. Brock was no different, she told herself over and over.

Until she looked deep into his eyes and saw someone quite *different*. Someone whose eyes gleamed with love when he spoke of his family. Someone who wanted to make his mother's and brother's wedding day special. Someone who was respected and considered a fair man by his employees.

Guilt set in. She was too close to the situation. She hadn't planned on getting personally involved with him. How could she? She was out to destroy him. For Melody and for herself.

Yes, she had to admit that she'd transferred some of her anger at the men who'd hurt her in the past onto Brock. She'd wanted him to pay, maybe not only for what he'd done to Melly, but for all the smug confident guys who'd disillusioned her in the past.

"I can't do this," she blurted. Surprised that she'd voiced her sentiments aloud, her eyes went wide and she took a step back.

"Don't go," Brock said, reaching for her. His hand slipped to the bow on her sarong. "Don't go," he said more softly, looking deeply into her eyes.

She moved her hand to his to halt him. The touch sparked electric currents that sizzled between them. She looked down at his strong capable hand, then gazed into his eyes again.

"Stay with me tonight."

It wasn't a command, but a request. His soft tone and the promise in his eyes tore away every shred of resistance she had inside.

Oh, wow.

She wanted to stay. More than she would have ever imagined. She dropped her hand to her side.

Brock blinked and slowly, effortlessly pulled the sash of her bow. She felt the material give and loosen, just like the clamp around her heart.

The material slid down her body, unraveling and dropping past her hips to puddle at her feet.

Brock gazed at her body, covered now with only a tiny black pair of panties. "My God," he said, blowing out a slow breath of appreciation. He shook his head, swallowed and continued to stare at her. "Come here, baby."

Vanessa hesitated a moment, recognizing the impact of what she was about to do. Unable to stop herself, she walked straight into Brock's arms.

Seven

Brock brought his lips to hers and kissed her tenderly, reverently, taking his time. He caressed every inch of her he could reach and whispered his intent to drive her absolutely crazy tonight. Heat built quickly and she responded with little sounds of pleasure. She kissed him back fervently, locking her lips to his and then opening for more potent kisses. His tongue met with hers and the instant sensual connection heightened every sensation tenfold.

He took his time and drew out the pleasure, making her moan and sigh. Her nipples pebbled to tight buds. Moisture pooled at her pulsing core.

Still, Brock moved slowly, his hands working

magic, prickling her skin with jolt after jolt of dire intensity.

"I've wanted you. Be patient, Vanessa."

She'd never experienced anything so powerful in her life. She wanted him inside her, claiming her, making her feel like a desired woman. It'd been so long since she'd felt anything remotely like this. Her heart pounded in her ears. Her entire body shook with need. She gave in to Brock, surrendering her body and soul to him.

It felt right.

And honest.

That was a joke, since she'd lied to him over and over. Nothing about the two of them was honest. But this…*this,* was something she'd dreamed about only in her secret, most private fantasies.

He moved down to suckle her breast with his mouth, the palm of one hand rubbing the tip of her nipple, the other teasing the dampest spot between her legs. She moaned softly, the pleasure about to burst her wide open. "Please, Brock," she breathed out.

"I know, baby. I know." He broke off his kisses and looked into her eyes.

Raw desire, a potent hunger she'd never seen before, reflected back at her. Her heart beat feverishly and her desire for him escalated even more.

He lifted her in one smooth move and she clung to him. He walked briskly past the galley to the master suite. There, he set her down on the big masculine-looking bed and instead of joining her he took a step back. "I've pictured you here a dozen times. But the real thing," he said, with true awe in his voice, "the real thing is staggering, Vanessa."

Vanessa closed her eyes. She couldn't believe where she was. She couldn't believe who she was with. But it didn't matter. None of it. Not anymore. She wanted Brock Tyler and tonight her mind and body focused on only one thing.

She smiled as she watched him take off his shoes. A real man knew that's where you started to undress for a lady. Next, he tore at the buttons of his shirt. She took a deep breath, fully inspired by his broad chest, the ripples of muscles that weren't overkill, but just perfect. The zipper came down slowly and she witnessed him in full form finally, his silky manhood erect.

Her throat constricted. If it were humanly possible she was even more aroused than before.

He covered himself with protection and instead of coming down to her, he reached for her hand and lifted her off the bed. When she stood, he kissed her, crushing his mouth to hers in a lusty display of heated passion. Then he lifted her slight form up, holding her buttocks. "Hang on to me," he rasped out and she draped her arms around his neck tight and wrapped her legs around his waist.

"Oh, wow," she whispered, breathless. Then the tip of his manhood nudged inside her, teasing her with his full erection.

"Okay, baby?"

She bit her lip from screaming yes, yes, yes and nodded.

Holding her carefully, he drove himself deep, filling her full, guiding her with his hands until she learned his pace. Then she moved on him, gyrating her body, the grind and drawback inching her closer and closer to ecstasy.

Brock kissed her hard on the lips, moving with her as she took him inside deeper and deeper.

When they were both on the edge of completion, Brock lowered her down onto his bed and struck the last potent chord, arching up and groaning along with her raspy moans of intense pleasure.

She came first, her explosion stunning her. She bent her body upwards and took all Brock had to give. She shattered completely, Brock only seconds behind.

He dropped onto her and kissed her soundly before rolling next to her, his arm wrapped tightly around her shoulder.

"Wow," she said, curling up to him.

He hugged her close and kissed the top of her head. "You could say that."

"I do keep saying that, don't I?" She was blissfully happy.

"I plan to keep you saying that."

She nibbled on her lower lip, hardly containing her joy. "Really?"

Brock turned onto his side to look into her eyes. God how he hoped his suspicions about her were unfounded. He had good instincts, but he'd been mistaken before. This was one time he hoped he'd been paranoid and dead wrong. This was one time he hoped his instincts failed him.

Vanessa was the woman he wanted in his life right now. No other woman had intrigued him like this. He'd fallen deeply in lust with her.

He glanced at her pillow and noticed the lavender orchid that had adorned her hair. He picked it up and twirled it around in his fingers, staring at it. The flower reminded him of her—soft and delicate but firm to the touch and more resilient than it looked. He positioned the flower behind her left ear then gazed into her blue eyes. "Consider yourself *taken* from now on, Vanessa."

She brought her chin up. "Don't I have a say in this?" she asked, but her soft sweet tone belied the sincerity of her question.

He caressed her arm, sliding his hand up to her shoulder. "Of course. You can agree," he said. "Or I can spend the rest of the night convincing you."

There was no doubt in his mind he'd make love to her again tonight.

Vanessa blinked and then roped her arms around him. "I'm not easily convinced."

Brock smiled and kissed her lips gently. "I was hoping you'd say that."

Brock was an insatiable lover. After an hour of soft whispers and tempting foreplay, he made love to her again. With patience this time, he explored her body and made her aware of her femininity as no man had ever before. Vanessa relished the night hours she spent in his arms. She relished the way he kissed her and touched her, making sure she was completely satisfied before taking his pleasure. She drifted in and out of sleep, waking every few hours to find herself beside him, cradled in his strong arms.

In the morning, sunlight reflected onto the blue marina waters and beamed brightly into the bedroom, waking her. She savored the warmth a second and squinted her eyes open. She found Brock watching her, his body turned her way, his head propped on his hand.

"Morning," he said with a quick smile.

"Hi." She felt suddenly shy, remembering the night they'd shared together. She'd been almost as insatiable as Brock. Images of erotic positions and lusty words spoken stirred in her mind. "Am I really here with you?"

Brock caressed her arm, then lowered his hand to fondle her breast. "You're here, baby. Making all my fantasies come true."

"All?" His touch sent her mind spinning again.

He leaned forward and kissed her gently. "Maybe not *all*. I have a few left in store for you."

"Such as?"

When had she gotten so brazen? Maybe it all started when she'd found Melody crying hysterically about the man who'd broken her heart. Maybe that's when

Vanessa had become this bold, gutsy woman who'd flown halfway across the world to get revenge.

Brock yanked their sheets off. He clasped her hand and lifted her from the bed. "Want to find out?"

She did. She really wasn't ready for this to end. She'd admonish herself later for sleeping with the enemy. And wouldn't think of the complications last night would impose on her plans. Right now she'd entertain her own fantasies and deal with the consequences later. Right now she'd be selfish and take what she wanted from this man.

"Yes. Show me."

Without hesitation, Brock led her to the small enclave in the room that housed the yacht's shower. He turned the water on. "Ready to get wet and wild?"

She roped her arms around him and pressed every inch of her body to his. "Maybe I already am."

He growled, low and deep in his throat and stepped in, pulling her with him. The brass faucet spit out bursts of hot spray that hit their bodies with prickling force. Stimulating rain aroused as much as it refreshed.

Brock picked up a bar of soap and rubbed it between his palms, creating a handful of rich bubbly lather. He coated her shoulders with the lather and worked his magic, rubbing her skin and smoothing his hands over her with strong capable strokes. Next, his hands rounded over her breasts, circling and cupping them, his fingertips dragging across her nipples, teasing, tempting.

"Brock," she pleaded. She was already consumed with enough heat to explode.

She thought she'd hate herself in the morning for the sexual indulgence she allowed herself last night. But it *was* morning now and she didn't hate herself at all. No, she only wanted more from Brock.

Was something wrong with her?

Had she been so sexually deprived these last few years that she'd had to resort to making love with the one man on earth she shouldn't? Or, was Brock so damned good in bed that he made her lose her head last night?

And quite possibly her heart.

Don't fall for him, Vanessa.

The thought was obliterated when he crushed his lips to hers. His potent kiss fueled a fire in her belly and brought her back into the moment. He continued to lather her body, turning her around, running his fingers along her spine and then palming her cheeks.

She felt his powerful erection nudge her and she whipped around, smiling. "Not yet."

He looked at her quizzically when she took up the bar of soap and built up lather. Next, she lathered him up, running her hands down his chest and below his navel. She heard his soft intake of breath, which gave her the courage to go on. Splaying her fingers wide, she cupped his shaft and stroked over him sliding her hand around his male organ.

He grinned. "I like the way you think."

But his smile was short-lived when her stroking became more intense. He closed his eyes and leaned back against the shower stall, enjoying the pleasure she created. It did her heart good to hear his stirring groans of enjoyment.

When she stopped, he snapped his eyes open.

"Can you guess what I'm thinking now?" she asked.

He drew in oxygen. "I can only hope, baby."

She maneuvered herself onto her knees and sat back across her legs. Next, she cupped his manhood and drew him deep into her mouth.

He held his breath, and when she moved on him he cursed explicitly, giving up all control and power. She accepted the role as aggressor and enjoyed every second of making love to him this way. When she brought him to the height of pleasure, he halted her and lifted her up. "Can't take another second," he admitted, his expression one of fierce restraint.

He kissed her with open-mouthed frenzy and things got wild after that. Brock parted her legs and palmed her womanhood until she thought she'd go mad. Her body hummed, her skin prickled, steamy water showered her and she thought she'd burn up inside.

He brought his mouth to her parted thighs and stroked her with his tongue until she nearly cried out her climax, but she held back. "Now, Brock. Now."

He rose quickly, wrapped her legs around his waist and entered her, both were fiery hot and ready to climb to the ultimate peak together. His thrusts were sure and hard and fast. The pleasure erotic, Vanessa had never in her life been loved so thoroughly.

They climaxed together, making pleas and grunts in unison until both exploded with earth-shattering potency.

Brock shut the shower off. He wrapped his arms around her and held her there for long minutes, kissing her hair, murmuring soft exquisite words, tucking her into the safety of his body. They stood that way until a chill overtook their sated wet bodies.

Then Brock wrapped her in a big lush towel and carried her to the bed. He set her down and laid down next to her, cradling her tight. "Sleep now, baby. We both need it."

She drifted off in his arms, praying to God she hadn't just made the biggest mistake of her life.

"Melly, calm down, honey. Please stop crying." As she sat on her sofa, kicking her sandals off, Vanessa's stomach tightened with a sick ache as she listened to Melody's sad disheartened sobs. Vanessa had hoped that her sister had moved on somewhat from her heartache. But Melody had always been impetuous and spirited. Her emotions ran high. When she was up, no one on earth was happier, but when she was down, unfortunately, she felt keen despair.

"Okay, Vanny," she said, stifling her sobs. "I'll...try to stop. Sorry, I didn't mean to break down like that. It's good to hear your voice." She sounded more composed now, to Vanessa's relief. "It's just been a hard week for me."

"Still thinking of...*him?*"

"Oh, yes," Melody rushed out. *"Always."*

Vanessa snapped her eyes shut. Dear Lord. She felt like Benedict Arnold. Why had she allowed Brock Tyler to charm and seduce her last night? "Would it do any good to say that he's not worth it?"

"Oh, Vanny. He is. He is *so* worth it. You just don't know."

She did know. That was the problem. She'd just spent an entire night with him. And for a few hours, Vanessa had been caught up in a whirlwind of desire. Her mind had clouded, fogged up completely by a handsome face, a commanding male body and just the right words spoken. She'd forgotten who Brock Tyler really was and had been foolish enough to believe she'd been wrong about him. Secretly, she'd wanted out of her self-imposed mission to cause him pain and ruin his reputation.

Vanessa knocked herself upside the head mentally and pounded some sense into her brain. She told herself the last twenty-four hours were a bad dream.

The reality hit her hard.

She'd slept with the man responsible for causing her baby sister's terrible grief and heartache.

"Vanessa, you're a dope," she whispered.

"What?" Melody asked on a shaky breath.

"Nothing, honey. I'm sorry. I wish I could give you a big hug."

"Me, too. I could use it."

"Really? I mean, I can quit my job and come home, Melly. I would. I'd do that."

"Don't be silly, Van," she said on a sniffle. "You *can't* quit your job."

Oh, but Vanessa wanted to. She wanted out of this place, away from Brock Tyler, who'd done nothing but confuse and confound her. She was certain he was a master at seduction. A true devil in disguise.

"I'll be fine…really," Melody said on a shaky breath.

"You're sure?"

"Yes, I've just had a hard, stressful week. Tanya is taking me to see a movie tonight. It'll get my mind off…things."

Vanessa sucked oxygen into her lungs, grateful her sister had her best friend there to hold her hand and keep her company. If Vanessa couldn't be there, then Tanya was surely a great replacement. "That's good, honey. And work is going okay?"

"Work? Sure. The shop's picking up and I'm doing decent business."

Melody ran the gift shop in the hotel that was independently owned from Tempest New Orleans. She'd started her own business and had an eye for unique items that couldn't be found in local Louisiana venues. Melly was good with people, friendly, outgoing and genuine. Those traits probably caught Brock's eye and he'd taken advantage of her without so much as a drop of remorse.

"Well, I'm glad I reached you. You've been hard to track down," Vanessa said. "I guess I worry too much about my baby sister."

"I'm sorry. I've been, uh, like I said, it's been a stressful week."

"Just try not to think about Brock anymore, Melly."

"Brock?" Melody paused and Vanessa cursed silently. She shouldn't have brought up his name. "Oh…um, I'll try not to."

"Okay. That's a start. Give Mom a kiss for me. You *are* visiting her, aren't you?"

"I haven't missed a Sunday."

Sweeping sadness washed over her. Ten years ago, their mother had been a victim of a hit and run accident. She'd never really recovered from the physical trauma and the doctors believed it had caused her early-onset Alzheimer's disease. Luckily, their mom still knew them, but she couldn't function as a parent. While Vanessa's father had died recently, Melody's father had walked out after the accident, unable to deal with the drastic changes in their lives. Vanessa had taken over the role as parent and had mothered Melody ever since.

She couldn't help the fierce protectiveness she felt for her sister. Melody had always needed nurturing. She'd always needed to feel loved. Brock's sudden and coldhearted dismissal of her had broken her heart in the same way her father's abandonment had.

How could she have forgotten that? How had she allowed her attraction to him sway her resolve?

Vanessa said goodbye to Melody then clicked off the phone, admonishing herself for being vulnerable. She'd allowed herself one blissful night with a dangerously tempting man and now self-loathing and guilt consumed her. She'd made a slip, a false move by sleeping with Brock, but now she was back on track.

She wouldn't falter again.

Nothing would deter her.

Vanessa dressed for work quickly, her mind spinning, her thoughts keyed in on the best way to accomplish her goal.

She left her condo with a plan in mind to sabotage the next big hotel event and it was nothing short of genius.

Brock slammed down his office phone and stared at it for a long drawn-out minute, as if the damn thing would rectify the words he'd just heard come across the wire from Code Landon.

Her sister runs the gift shop at Tempest New Orleans. You dated her a while back. Melody Applegate. The two are very close.

Brock couldn't believe it. Though he'd suspected something was up, he hadn't wanted to believe it. He hadn't wanted to believe the most exciting woman he'd met since he'd stolen a kiss from luscious Serena Barton in high school, wasn't whom he thought she was.

No, he'd thought Vanessa Dupree was one of a kind.

Hell, he sure got that right.

"Damn you, Vanessa."

Brock pushed away from his desk and rose from his chair. He paced the floor glaring at the phone, going over and over every memory he had of Melody Applegate. Sure, they'd dated. For about a month. She was a sweet kid. Too sweet and young for him, he'd determined.

There hadn't been any sparks at all. He'd let her down gently once he realized that they hadn't a thing in common.

And then he remembered one other important thing about Melody Applegate.

His mind turned to Vanessa. She'd known all along. She had to. She wouldn't speak of her sister, only letting it slip once that she even had a sibling.

Brock turned black with anger. He fisted and unfisted his hands. His gut clenched and his mind ran rampant. Vanessa had been behind the disasters at the hotel. It had to be. She held some sort of depraved vendetta against him. That had to be the reason she'd been so hard to seduce. She'd been out to ruin his hotel and she'd been clever, covering her tracks so that nothing she did could be proven.

Brock strode to the wet bar and hastily poured himself a drink of whiskey straight up. The liquid splashed out the tumbler and he cursed. At the mess.

At Vanessa Dupree. At her lies and her deception. At her clever taunts and the way she'd suckered him in.

No one made a fool of Brock Tyler.

No one.

Brock gulped a swig of whiskey and strode to the balcony. Outside, all looked peaceful. The sun shone bright against the crystal aqua ocean waters. He thought of Vanessa, her eyes matching the hues of the Pacific. Just last night she'd fulfilled his fantasies. She'd been a willing, eager participant and they'd rocked that boat until sunrise. Sexy, gorgeous, erotic, she'd been everything he'd imagined and more. They had heat together and combusted into flames like two sticks of dynamite.

She'd been the one woman he'd wanted above all else.

Anger, raw and fresh, registered in what she'd just thrown away.

He gulped whiskey with a solemn vow. "I'm going to fire your ass, Vanessa Dupree."

Then a thought struck. Firing her wasn't good enough. She deserved more than that for trying to take him down. She deserved much worse.

Brock contemplated for twenty minutes, tamping down bitter disappointment and anger. He finished his drink. When his nerves calmed, he buzzed his secretary. "Send for Akamu. I need a meeting with him right away."

His hotel manager walked in a few minutes later and Brock looked him dead in the eye. "What I'm about to tell you can't go any farther than this room."

Akamu nodded, his usual big smile tucked away. He knew when Brock meant business. Yet he couldn't conceal a wide-eyed look of astonishment when Brock laid out all the facts.

"You're sure it's Vanessa?" he asked.

Brock drew in a breath, then sighed. "I'm sure. Do I have your loyalty?"

"Always."

"I'll expect daily reports from you."

Akamu nodded.

Brock went on. "I know she's your friend. This can't be easy for you, but I need to know you're looking out for the best interests of the hotel."

A thoughtful look crossed his expression and his dark eyes narrowed. "The hotel is my top priority. It's a good plan, boss. I'll do my best."

Brock smiled at the Hawaiian. "Good." Then Brock added curiously, "I thought you liked Vanessa?"

"Everyone likes Vanessa." Then he shrugged and shook his head contemplating. "I keep my business separate from my personal life."

Brock set his stance and looked out at the tranquil bay, crushing down regret that threatened to tear him up. "That's probably wise, Akamu."

He should have done that. Kept his business separate from his pleasure. But Vanessa had turned his head. And the most skeptical part of him wondered if she'd deliberately set out to keep him distracted by tempting and teasing him. She'd managed to blindside him. But never again.

The woman couldn't be trusted.

Brock resigned himself to what he had to do. At least playing cat and mouse with the wily woman would keep him entertained while he served up his retaliation. He wasn't through with Vanessa Dupree.

Not by a long shot.

There wasn't much Vanessa could do about Sunday evening's luau. After the fiasco on Saturday night with Brock in attendance patching up the chaos she'd caused, she couldn't chance another misstep so soon. She'd gotten away with it and forged forward to do more damage.

Besides, she hadn't the mind for it on Sunday. No, she'd been too busy with Brock that morning. On his boat. Making love to him.

Oh, man.

She'd really blown it.

Vanessa shook off thoughts of his stunning ripped body. His handsome face. His erotic words while he made love to her.

She turned her thoughts to her next plan of action. It was brilliant even if she did say so herself. After all, she couldn't confide in anyone, not a soul, so she commended herself with a mental pat on the back for her clever plan.

The midweek miniconferences held in spacious

ballrooms were big moneymakers for the hotel. The rooms were rented out for lectures and workshops. The hotel made money on guest charges, rental space and meals served. Hundreds of paid guests spent their money in the gift shops, bars and poolside as well.

Vanessa made the last and final phone call to secure all was right on track and sat back at her desk with smug satisfaction.

"A.R.M. meets Lily's Designs," she whispered with a smile. "It's better than Frankenstein meets the Wolfman."

"Talking to yourself again, Vanessa?" Brock stood at the threshold of her office.

"Uh, a bad habit of mine," she said. Then gulped. She hadn't seen Brock in the office, or anywhere for that matter, for three days.

He'd called her house and left a sweet message every day apologizing for his busy schedule. She'd been home, listening, screening the calls and staring at the phone, debating whether to pick it up. What would she say to him? How would she react? The coward in her won out and she'd let her answering machine accept all of her calls, avoiding him. Which was ridiculous since she knew they'd have to come face-to-face eventually.

"Did you get the flowers I sent?"

Vanessa rose from her desk and straightened out her black-and-white-print dress. Mustering bravado, she smiled. "Yes, they were lovely. Thank you."

Brock walked into her office and closed the door behind him.

Vanessa worried her lip, sucking in oxygen.

Brock looked good. He wore white trousers and a russet shirt that set off his tanned skin. Her heart dipped a little. But she picked it right back up, determined to stay the course. The gleam she witnessed in his eyes told her he had other plans.

"I've missed you," he said, coming to stand before her.

She blinked. "You missed me?"

"In my bed, Vanessa. You do remember how it was between us," he rasped in a low voice, his gaze leveled on hers.

Staggered by his bluntness, she fumbled for the right words. "Oh…yes," she said breathlessly, not at all how she'd intended to respond.

Brock grinned, his eyes darkened with intensity. "I don't think I've had a better night in my life." He moved closer. "How about you?"

She backed up. "Me?"

He came forward and lifted a strand of her hair, studying it. "I think I counted four orgasms, Vanessa." His gaze found hers again. Rapid heat sizzled between them. "Does that qualify for a great night with you?"

Vanessa squeezed her eyes shut momentarily, reminded of her wanton behavior and her intense physical enjoyment that night. "It was wonderful." She couldn't lie about that. She wasn't that much of a fraud.

"Good, I hope you aren't the kind of woman who'd say it was a mistake. That nonsense doesn't fly after spending the entire night naked together, doing the things we did to each other."

"Oh, um." What did he expect her to say to that?

It had been a mistake. *A big mistake.* And more importantly, there would be no repeat performances. But a tiny part of her wondered what Brock would do for an encore if they were to get together again.

Brock leaned in. Vanessa backed up again. This time the back of her legs hit the edge of her desk. She was as far as she could go, in many ways.

Brock closed the gap between them. His stance spread wide, encasing her body. He took hold of her waist and tugged her to him, splaying his hands on her backside. The second he touched her, sensations swept through her with shocking force. Her body reacted. She hated that it did. She stared at his shirt, opened at the throat and remembered gliding her tongue over that very spot.

"What's the matter, Vanessa?" he asked.

"I'm swamped. Feeling distracted at the moment," she said. "You caught me by surprise."

"I caught you talking to yourself. You didn't look busy."

"Trust me. I'm busy."

Brock hesitated a moment, then released her. He glanced at the papers on her desk. Walking around the desk, he picked up a manila folder and studied the cover. "Working on the A.R.M. account?"

Vanessa reached for the file and tugged it out of his hand. "Yes. It's coming up in less than a week." Without looking at the folder, she tucked it away quickly in her drawer, her heart hammering, worried she might have made some notes that were for her eyes only.

Brock walked over to the window in her office and looked out. "I'm fond of animals myself. What about you?"

She nodded. "Love them."

He turned. "So, you're an advocate for the Animal Rights March?"

She tilted her head and became thoughtful. "They can be a little extreme at times. But I'm all for kindness to animals."

"You should see my brother Trent's place in Crimson Canyon. He's got a herd of wild horses on his property. It's a sight to behold."

Vanessa remained silent. Brock seemed reflective at the moment and she was grateful he'd focused his attention on something other than her.

"That's why I'm here, Vanessa. To talk about Trent's wedding. And my mother's. We need to find a date that's doable for everyone."

"Oh, I'll be happy to do that."

Brock nodded and studied her a moment. "The luau went smoothly on Sunday. I'm pleased with the results. I think we may have ironed out all of our problems."

The luau went well only because she'd been in bed with him when she should have been plotting another minicatastrophe. She returned the nod. "Me, too."

Brock walked over to her and cupped her face in his hands. Before she could react, he brushed his lips over hers gently, kissing her with tenderness. "Check your calendar and get back to me with those dates."

He left her, staggered by the impact of that kiss.

And wishing he was anyone but Brock Elliot Tyler, her sworn enemy.

Eight

The next day, Akamu walked into Brock's office, a file folder tucked under his right arm. Brock gestured for the hotel manager to sit down across from him. "I take it you have some information for me?"

"Boy, do I. Starting Monday we have five scheduled conferences booked for the week. One that's an all-day event, three that are two-day events and," he said, opening his file and checking, "one that goes for three full days."

"Should bring the hotel revenue up. Can we accommodate that many?"

"It'll be tight, boss. We've never had so many booked in one week before. All the meeting rooms will be holding events."

Brock contemplated. "Any other news?"

Akamu grinned, then caught himself and soured his expression. "If you're asking about Vanessa, yes. I have news. I know what she's up to."

Brock took a deep breath. A small part of him held some hope that he'd been wrong about the blond bombshell with brains. Akamu's admission now slashed that hope. "What news?"

Again, Akamu's mouth quirked up before he spoke and his expression took on a look of respect. "She planned the Long A.R.M. for Justice meeting in the Melia Room. And Lily's Designs sales meeting in the Loke Lau Room."

"Those rooms face each other. Now explain." Brock leaned against the back of his chair and steepled his fingers, waiting.

Akamu didn't attempt to hide his admiration. "You know what A.R.M. stands for, right?"

"Only a hermit living in the Sahara Desert wouldn't know A.R.M. They're a very vocal group."

"Animal activists," Akamu said.

"Go on."

"Lily's Designs specializes in selling designer handbags and accessories made exclusively with fur and leather. Seems our event planner has made a deal with Lily herself to showcase some of her top-selling designs in glass cases just outside the ballroom where her sales meeting takes place."

"Hell! Vanessa will rub A.R.M.'s nose in it."

Akamu bobbed his head in acknowledgment. "It's brilliant."

Brock glared at him, frowning at Vanessa's deceit and Akamu immediately cleared his throat and shifted in his seat nervously.

"Brilliant," Brock droned between tight lips. "They'll have a volcanic shouting match at best."

"Or, they might come to blows. I've seen it a few times on late-night news. One of these activists sees a fur coat and they go *pupule*." He circled his index finger around his temple a few times.

Brock rubbed his forehead. He'd seen the craziness, too. Red wine splashed across a fur coat. Riots in the streets. Celebrities rising up to the A.R.M. cause. "Is she planning anything else?"

Akamu shook his head. "I don't think so. I've been over everything a dozen times."

"No, she probably thought this would be enough. There's no need for icing on the cake. She's probably thinking this was a sweet enough deal."

Akamu remained silent.

Brock thought on this awhile and then leaned in, lowering his voice. "Okay, I have a plan. Here's what will happen next."

Twenty minutes later, satisfied that his plan would work and his reputation would be salvaged, at least this week, Brock walked the distance to Vanessa's office.

* * *

"Darn it, Melody. Why don't you answer your phone?" She stared at the screen for a second, wondering why her sister was so hard to contact. She'd been checking in with her every other day leaving voice mail messages. Most of the time Vanessa only got brief text messages back from her.

Vanessa slipped her cell phone back into her little pink leather purse she'd bought at a discount, a knockoff of one of Lily's classic designs. She couldn't afford the real thing. Those designer handbags went for a small fortune. Her mind clicked forward to the little fiasco waiting to happen on Monday. What a way to kick off the week.

"I need a word with you." Brock Tyler appeared at her door. His eyes, deep, dark and deliciously brown, honed in on her.

She gasped. She had to be more careful. Brock was one to simply show up unannounced. Not that he hadn't a perfect right—he was the owner of the hotel and her employer. She did answer to him, on one level.

"Hi!" She sounded a little too glad to see him. Overcompensating had always been a flaw of hers.

She must have given him the wrong impression because he closed the door behind him and strode over to her desk. She kept her eyes on him as he bent down and kissed her soundly on the lips until her nipples puckered under her blouse. He nuzzled her neck a second and she drank in his familiar scent. "Hi, back at you, baby."

Vanessa chewed on her lip. "You wanted to see me?"

Brock's grin was pure sin. "Always."

Heat crawled up her throat. With just a look he could make her squirm. She hated that about him. He was like a force of nature, a windstorm that pulled you in the wrong direction.

Lucy opened the door and popped her head in. "Hey, how about lunch today," she blurted before realizing Vanessa had company. "Oops! Sorry, Mr. Tyler."

Brock backed away from Vanessa and smiled at Lucy. "Not a problem."

"I'll come back later."

Thank God for Lucy. She had good timing, Vanessa thought. "Lunch sounds good, Lucy," she managed to call out before Lucy shut the door, her footsteps fading down the hallway.

Vanessa gathered up files on her desk and set them in neat little piles. She inhaled, aware of Brock's eyes on her.

"I won't keep you from lunch," he said. "Just wanted to get back to you about the date."

"The *date?*" Vanessa's mind raced. Had she made a date with him?

"For the double wedding."

"Oh." Was that disappointment she felt? She'd spent one erotic night with Brock and he'd only made half-hearted attempts to see her again. Her ego was bruised in one respect but in another she was grateful that she didn't have to come up with excuses to refuse him.

He pointed to the calendar on her desk. "This day works good for everyone."

Vanessa glanced down at the calendar to where his finger had landed. "That's less than three weeks away!"

"Are you saying it's not doable?" He pinned her down with a curious look.

"Well, um." She'd given him dates that were available last night, but she'd never dreamed that they'd take the earliest possible one. Vanessa didn't want to be working at Tempest when his family arrived. She didn't want any part of their wedding. "It's gonna be a push to get everything perfect."

"I have faith in you. You're more than capable of pulling this off."

Vanessa looked away momentarily, chewing a little harder on her lip. He trusted her to make his mother's and brother's joint wedding perfect. Vanessa's resolve dipped to a new low. Ruining his family's wedding would put her in a reptilian class of creatures. "Sure, I can pull it off. But maybe *they* need a little more time."

"Mom's been alone most of her life. She and Matthew don't want to wait any longer. And Trent doesn't have a patient bone in his body."

"Well, okay. I'll see what I can do."

She caught Brock's quick frown before he nodded. "Consider it a personal favor to me."

Vanessa didn't want to do Brock any favors.

"Lucy will help you with anything you need."

Oh, great. Now Lucy was involved. "Wonderful."

"Thank you." Brock braced his hands on her desk and leaned in. He smiled and touched a finger to her cheek, the soft caress gliding down to her mouth. He traced her lips tenderly and she caught the potent yet subtle hint of his sandalwood scent. He brought his mouth down gently. The sweetness of his slow kiss rippled through her heart.

"Have a nice lunch, Vanessa."

She snapped her eyes open and found him staring at her with an odd expression. Just a glimpse, a second in time, she noticed vulnerability on Brock's face before he turned and walked out of her office.

He left her shattered and confused. Vanessa crossed her hands over her chest and slumped in her seat fighting the question that had begun to plague her constantly. Was it possible to hate someone and love them at the same time?

She feared she knew the answer, because a heart didn't lie.

It was worth the cost of Tempest Maui itself, to see the bewildered look on Vanessa's face Monday morning when she walked down the hallway to the bank of meeting rooms that in no way resembled the chaos she'd originally planned. Her gaze darted from one meeting room to the other and finally settled on the construction blockades in front of the Melia Room.

"What happened to the Animal Rights March group?" she probed Akamu.

Brock stood in an alcove, out of sight, listening and sneaking a peek at her discourse with his hotel manager.

"I had them scheduled in the Melia Room. The room should've been set up by now."

Akamu replied, "A pipe burst in that room last night. Water soaked the carpets. The whole place reeks. Mold. Yuck." Akamu pinched his nose. "You wouldn't want to go in there."

"Why wasn't I notified?" Vanessa asked. Brock smiled hearing her ire rise.

"Oh, no need to wake you up. It happened very very late last night."

Vanessa paced and narrowed her eyes as a crew set up the Loke Lau Room for Lily's Designs. Lily's employees worked diligently, placing handbags and accessories on display tables, the smell of new leather strong.

"What on earth did you do with the animal group?"

"A brainstorm," Akamu answered. "The Atrium Restaurant is available today on the top floor. It's being set up as we speak and I'm sure the president of the group will be glad to hear they'll have such a beautiful room for their conference."

"They don't know?"

"No, I thought you should call him. You're good with smoothing things out. Here," he said, punching in the number and handing her his cell phone. "Be sure to tell them we have natural exhibits up there and a waterfall. They'll have no complaints. The room is ready for them."

Vanessa's lips curved down as she took the phone from his hand. "Right. But you should have called me about this."

Akamu shrugged, ignoring her irritation.

Brock waited until she finished her phone conversation to walk up to them, enjoying every second of Vanessa's discomfort. He glanced around the bank of meeting rooms, making a point to note the construction blockades. "Problems?" he asked.

Akamu launched into the story, finishing with, "And Vanessa just called the president of A.R.M. to tell them they'll have their conference today in the Atrium Restaurant. She set it all up."

"Is that true? They're okay with it?"

Vanessa nodded. "Yes, they seemed pleased when I explained the amenities in the Atrium. They won't have a moment of delay. Their conference will start as scheduled."

"Good thinking, Vanessa," Brock said. "You averted a disaster."

"But it was Akamu's idea," she blurted.

Akamu nudged her. "Vanessa is too modest. She's the charmer. She could sell sand to a beach bum."

"Good job." Brock glanced at Vanessa, whose smile was reluctant at best. "Both of you."

Akamu looked at his watch, then excused himself.

Vanessa started to retreat as well. "I'd better get back to—"

"Just a minute, Vanessa," he said, reaching for her arm. He slipped his hand down to her slight wrist then took her hand. "I want to talk to you."

The beautiful deceiver stiffened and fear entered her eyes. Brock enjoyed her moment of guilt. He led her to the alcove he'd ducked into minutes ago. With her back to the wall, she blinked and refused to look him in the eyes. "What?"

He tipped her chin up and forced her to meet his gaze. "This."

He met with the softness of her mouth and kissed her until her tension faded. He wanted her still, even though he knew she was out to destroy him. Even through all the deceit. Brock wasn't going to forgive her. He wouldn't let her off the hook. But he wasn't immune to her charms.

She was an addiction.

And a challenge.

Now that Brock knew what he was dealing with, he'd watch his back, cover his bases, but wouldn't deny himself the pleasurable benefits Vanessa could provide.

No way would he let her have anything to do with his mother's and brother's wedding. He didn't trust her. But she didn't know that and he had to keep her thinking that he was clueless.

Until he tired of the game.

"Brock," she huffed out, breathless.

He searched her deviously gorgeous blue eyes. "What?" he whispered, trailing kisses along her throat. She arched her back instinctively; the erotic move jarred him and he groaned. "Damn it, Vanessa."

She had him hot and ready in a flash. He had to control his animal instincts or he'd be dropping her to the floor, right there in the middle of his hotel. He backed away from her and she opened eyes filled with the same hunger as his.

"Brock," she murmured, repeating his name. Her voice sounded small and vulnerable this time. Tears filled her eyes. Confusion marred her expression. She shook her head and brushed past him in a flurry, her high heels scraping the marble floor as she raced to get away.

Stunned, Brock watched her leave, his stomach knotting up and gutted inside.

She deserves this, he told himself.

But he walked back to his office without feeling one true ounce of satisfaction.

Joe's Tiki Torch was less crowded than usual for hump Wednesday, yet the music blared as if people were packed in wall to wall. Vanessa sat at a small corner table facing her piña colada and her friend Lucy.

"You didn't eat much at dinner, now you're not drinking. What's up?" Lucy asked, with kindness in her eyes.

She really was a dear friend, not the frivolous kind that would dump you at the first of sign of trouble, or worse yet, relish your particular anguish. No, Lucy was true blue.

Which made Vanessa feel terrible about what she'd been trying to do. Pangs of guilt plagued her lately. She'd set out to destroy Brock in his newly renovated hotel, but she'd never contemplated making friends here, ones she cared about dearly.

Lucy was a gem.

Akamu had come through like a trooper and a loyal friend on Monday. He'd covered for her and taken care of the conference fiasco on his own—then generously gave her full credit for fixing the very problem she'd tried to create.

She sighed, plucked out the yellow flowered umbrella from the tall colada glass and took a sip. She couldn't believe her rotten luck. Who would think a water pipe bursting would actually save Brock's butt?

"I'm a little down tonight. Sorry if I'm bad company," she said to Lucy.

"That's why we're here. To cheer you up! You've been like this since Monday."

Lucy had asked her several times in the past few days what was wrong and Vanessa had made up one excuse after another. What could she say? *I'm falling in love with the man I'm planning on destroying? If I succeed, your job might be in jeopardy.*

She reminded herself to think of all the Melodys in

the world who'd been hurt badly by men like Brock. She reminded herself how hard she'd tried to be both mother and father to Melly these past years. She'd protected her from fickle girlfriends, teachers who'd been unfair and cagey young men who weren't good enough for her. She'd taught her how to drive defensively and how to dance. She'd helped her with her high school prom and college sorority events. She'd always been there for Melody, her baby sister.

"I'll lighten up." She smiled for Lucy and sipped her drink again. The pineapple, coconut and rum slid down her throat like an alcoholic milk shake. "This isn't half bad."

Lucy narrowed her dark eyes and nodded. "You can tell me anything, you know."

"I know." But she couldn't tell her *this*.

Vanessa was asked to dance a few times and each time, with Lucy's prodding, she got up and danced. Lucy was a free spirit. She lost herself in dance, laughing and moving around the dance floor with her partners without a care in the world.

Vanessa really tried to lighten up. She wanted to have fun, but lately she felt like a stick in the mud. She'd refused an offer to go outside and get some air and another blatant offer to see her dance partner's own *tiki torch*.

She sat down, winded, looking at her watch and wishing she'd driven her own car to the bar. Those thoughts were quadrupled when Brock walked into the

Torch with Larissa Montrayne, the woman who'd monopolized all of Brock's time the other night. Supposedly, she was engaged to be married, but one wouldn't know it by the way she clung to Brock's arm. They strode up to the bar, their backs to her.

Vanessa turned away from them, wishing she could escape out the back door. She met with Lucy's questioning stare instead. "You look like a tiger ready to pounce."

Vanessa clenched her teeth. "No, I don't. I'm fine." She plastered on a fake smile.

"You don't look fine." Lucy looked around the entire room and stopped when she spotted Brock with Larissa at the bar. She cast Vanessa a sympathetic look. "Oh, I get it now."

"I don't think so," Vanessa said, keeping her voice down. "But I can't talk about it here."

"Do you want to leave?"

The question was music to her ears. She grabbed her purse. "Let's not stop to say hello."

Lucy nodded and rose from the table. "I wouldn't dream of it."

They slipped out the front door without Brock noticing them. He was oblivious to anything but what he wanted, when he wanted it.

He'd made love to Vanessa days ago, then kissed her with enough passion to make her toes curl and her heart ache every time they'd been together since. He'd made her doubt herself, her intentions and her life.

But she was glad she'd come here tonight.

Seeing him with another woman firmed up her resolve. Seeing him with Larissa reminded her what kind of man he really was. She'd been a fool. She wouldn't allow herself warm feelings for him. She certainly wouldn't fall in love with him now. Her course was set. She wasn't finished with Brock yet. She owed him for the pain he'd caused her sister. She had three major events coming up and the plans to disrupt each one were solidly planted in her head.

There was no turning back.

Brock would get exactly what was coming to him.

Nine

"I want to give you what you've got coming, Vanessa," Brock said, standing behind his desk wearing a devastating smile. She'd been summoned to his office just a few minutes ago and hadn't a clue what he'd wanted.

He paced now, hands clasped behind his back. In an uncharacteristic business tone, one he almost never took with Vanessa, he began, "You've been here about six weeks now."

Vanessa nodded, estimating in her head that he was correct give or take a day.

"And in that time, you've worked hard. I've seen the hours you put in. Your efforts haven't gone unnoticed."

His sensuous mouth curled up in another smile. "I'm speaking as your employer now, Vanessa."

She gulped. What was Brock up to?

"Let me get to the point, I'm giving you a bonus."

Vanessa flinched inwardly. How had she botched up her plan so much that Brock offered up a bonus? The news crushed her, but she maintained her outward composure.

"Since you've been here, working on events, the hotel has thrived."

"Oh." More bad news.

Vanessa kept disappointment from her voice the best she could. Her last three attempted foul-ups had become hugely successful events. "I'm happy to hear that."

"I'm sure you are." Brock's tone sharpened for a second. "It's why I hired you. I knew you were the only one for the job."

She nodded with a feigned smile, swallowing a lump that lodged in the pit of her stomach. It was still a mystery to her how she'd deliberately underbooked last weekend's luau only to have the event sell out at the last minute.

The amateur Surf and Turf BBQ on the beach had gone off without a hitch, even though she'd *misplaced* the surfboards and made sure the propane tanks were empty in the gas grills. But no panic ensued. Somehow, everything had come together and the guests wound up having a marvelous time.

Even the one hundred geckos released around the

pool during the new innovative Water Massage Demonstration hadn't caused the uproar she'd hoped. Hotel security had rounded up the tiny green lizards within seconds. There'd been no scrambling, no wild screams from the guests, no chaos. In fact, the slight disturbance only proved how well the water massage worked. The guest going through the demonstration hadn't even flinched, displaying uncanny evidence how effective the relaxing technique worked.

Vanessa had failed miserably and now, adding insult to injury, Brock handed her a bonus envelope. "You deserve this more than I can say."

She gazed down at the envelope, biting her lip. "Thank you."

"You're welcome. Open it."

"No, I, uh…I'll open it later."

Goodness, she didn't want to see the monetary extent of her failure. She didn't know if she could pull off a grateful smile. Tears threatened and she banked them down.

"If that's what you want. You'll find it generous. Personal feelings aside, you've done a bang-up job here at Tempest Maui."

Botched was the better term. "Thank you, Brock. Anything else?"

Brock relaxed his stance and came around his desk. Leaning on the corner, he folded his arms over his chest. "How are the wedding plans going?"

She blinked. "Smoothly."

"Great. Is there anything you need from me?"

Vanessa shook her head. "Not at the moment." She'd hoped she'd have ruined him by now. Instead, she'd helped his hotel make money hand over fist. How had that happened?

Baffled, Vanessa debated about whether or not to sabotage the double wedding. It would be lower than low on her part. Brock's mother had finally found happiness after years of being a widow. But, how better to ruin the hotel's reputation if the owner's very own family wedding turned out as a nightmarish fiasco?

Her face fell at the prospect.

"Anything wrong, Vanessa?"

"What?" Vanessa peered into Brock's concerned eyes. "Oh, no." She waved the unopened bonus envelope in the air. "What could be wrong? I'm glad you're happy with my work."

Brock slanted her a look. "Thrilled is more like it. I'll probably win my bet with Trent. And I have *you* to thank for that."

Her heart sunk to her feet. "Right, the bet that your hotel will outperform his hotel in Arizona."

"Then there's the matter of winning my father's classic Thunderbird." Brock's voice quieted and he gazed deep into her eyes. "I can't wait to show you that car."

The moment Brock lifted up and approached her with a hot gleam in his eyes, Vanessa spotted trouble with a capital *T*. She backed up instantly, almost stumbling. "I'd better get back to work."

Brock pursed his lips, disappointed, but he let her go without stopping her and she made a clumsy escape. She had big decisions to make regarding the Tyler double wedding coming up next week.

Could she destroy two innocent Tyler weddings just to prove a point?

At the end of the day she walked out of her office, the Tempest envelope stuck between her checkbooks and her wallet in her purse, still unopened. She hated that it was in there, hated what it represented.

When she reached her condo, she stripped out of her clothes, ran bathwater scented with plumeria and stepped in. Warm water surrounded her weary bones and she melted into the sweetly fragranced bath until she finally relaxed.

When Plan A doesn't work, you go to Plan B, she told herself. But Vanessa didn't have another plan. Certain that her sabotage would work and she'd be free of Brock Tyler by now, Vanessa had only this one vision.

"Now what?" she whispered, cupping water over her bare shoulders and arms.

Vanessa glanced at her new Lily's Designs alligator purse she'd tossed on the bathroom counter. Not a knockoff this time. Lily herself had given the purse to her after the conference concluded for a job well done.

Another reflection of her plan gone awry.

Her muscles tightened once again. She glared at the

purse, thought of the bonus it housed inside and mentally chastised herself all over again for failing.

"Don't open it, Vanessa. Don't cash the check. Don't even think about it."

But curiosity got the better of her. She stepped out of the tub, covered herself with a big towel and walked over to her purse. Biting her lip, she snapped it open and pulled the envelope out.

On a deep breath, she ripped open the envelope and gasped when she saw the amount on the check. Tears immediately welled up. She'd made Brock a fortune and he'd given her a percentage of that for her good work.

She found a note enfolded inside the envelope. With a flick of her fingers, the note parted.

Join me tonight on the Rebecca *at seven sharp to celebrate.*

Vanessa stared at the note. Those commanding words just added to her dismay. Brock thought he could summon her at his will, whenever he wanted. Anger bubbled up. Her nerves grew tight. Her body shook. The implication was clear. He'd given her a large amount of money and now expected her to pay up with the one *other* thing that was important to him. Sex. She whispered, "How dare you, Brock."

Vanessa dressed quickly, putting on a seductive little gown, piled her hair up with a clip and put on her best jewelry. She wanted out. And she wanted Brock to see what he'd be missing when she told him off and walked out on him.

Vanessa reached the yacht just as the sun set on the horizon. Festive twinkling lights illuminated the marina and dock, guiding her way to Brock's boat.

She found Brock easily enough, looking handsome in tan trousers and a black silk shirt on the deck, waving her aboard. He met her when she approached and helped her climb the steps. "Glad you could make it."

She nearly snorted. "Did I have a choice?"

Brock grinned and took her hand. "I have something to show you."

"I bet you do."

He guided her down the stairs leading to the main sitting room. Suddenly, bright lights flashed, cameras went off and a roomful of people called out, "Surprise!"

Startled, Vanessa backed up a step, only to fall back against Brock's willing arms. She righted herself and looked up at the sign above the wet bar. "Vanessa Dupree—Tempest Employee of the Month."

She glanced at Lucy, who couldn't keep from grinning, Akamu and two dozen coworkers she'd come to know from the Tempest offices, all welcoming her with smiles. She turned to Brock. "Are you serious?"

He smiled, a gleam in his eyes unreadable. "Dead serious."

"You throw an elaborate party for your Employees of the Month?"

"Not every month. Just when someone exceeds our expectations."

A glass of champagne was shoved into her hand and Lucy came over to give her a hug. "Congrats. This is a great honor."

"But I…um." What could she say? "Thanks."

Brock took that opportunity to give a little speech about the hotel's recent success and Vanessa's part in that. She was met with a round of applause and afterward they dined on a catered buffet outside on the deck. The night was warm for late winter, but that didn't stop Vanessa from getting chilled to the bone.

She hadn't expected this. *None of it.* She didn't deserve the friends she'd made here. She didn't deserve to have Lucy's and Akamu's support and love, either.

The yacht toured the bay, moving slowly and Vanessa found herself alone at the railing, looking out at Tranquility Bay, fully enraptured in the moment.

A wealth of emotions sought her out: guilt, joy, loyalty, deceit, allegiance, cowardice. Her head spun with confusing thoughts. And then the "if onlys" took hold.

If only all of this was real, the job and the friends she'd made here.

If only she deserved the honors bestowed upon her for a job well done.

If only she was free to fall in love with Brock Tyler without guilt or deception.

When the yacht docked, Vanessa said goodbye to

all of her friends and coworkers, thanking them for coming and sharing this special time with her.

After everyone had left, Brock walked up to her, took her hand, and she gazed deep into his eyes. She'd accused him of horrible things, but he'd been up front and honest with her. More than she'd been with him.

Except, one thing bothered her and she had to know the truth. "I saw you at the Torch with Larissa Montrayne the other night."

"I was there." He nodded quietly and sipped his champagne.

"You admit it?"

"Yes. I didn't see you."

"I left."

"If you'd have stayed longer, you would have seen her fiancé come in. I met Larissa in the parking lot. I didn't take her there. She'd been waiting for him and we decided to grab a drink inside."

"That's it?"

"That's it." He leaned in and kissed her lips. He tasted of warm alcohol, smelled like musk and looked like sin itself. "Anything else?"

Had it been that simple? Had Brock met Larissa like he'd claimed? Had it been an accidental meeting? She'd only stuck around for a minute after seeing him at the Torch before thinking the worst and running off.

Vanessa connected with his eyes. Whenever he looked at her she saw desire, a mesmerizing gleam that drew her in with magnetic force. She swallowed hard and did a mental head shake.

She'd come here so determined and now she felt herself melting, losing herself in him again. "I should go," she whispered.

Brock cupped her face with one hand. "I need you tonight, Vanessa."

It wasn't a command or a demand. It was a statement of fact. The sweetly earnest tone of his voice charmed her.

"Why me, Brock?" Her question slipped out. It was a question she'd been asking herself since she arrived on the island. They'd been inexplicably drawn together and it was the last thing she'd wanted.

But here they were—a man with playboy tendencies and a woman who despised that lifestyle. She nibbled her lip. "You could have any woman—"

"That's not my style." Vanessa arched her brows, which prompted him to add, "Anymore."

Brock drew her into his strong arms. "We're wasting the night talking. I promise to answer all your questions in the morning. Stay, baby."

He took her hand and Vanessa followed him to the bedroom.

Brock loved making love to Vanessa. She was responsive and sensitive to his every touch, every caress. She liked sex and he didn't think many women really did. They'd go through the motions to please a man, but they didn't enjoy the act itself.

Vanessa enjoyed the connection, the physicality of making love. She threw caution to the wind, knew no inhibition and lost herself in the pleasure.

Just seeing her laying on his bed, her platinum tresses spread out on the pillow, waiting for him, made him crazy for her. She was as hot for him as he was for her, and that turned him on more than anything else.

Naked and fully aroused, Brock laid down next to her on the bed. He took her into his arms and made powerful, deliberate, desperate love to her like there was no tomorrow.

Because there *was* no tomorrow.

Brock was through playing games with Vanessa. She'd gotten under his skin and when she was breathless and panting beneath him, he could almost forget her deceit. But he wouldn't allow himself that luxury. She was the enemy of her own making.

Yet everything inside him wanted to forget what she'd done and who she was. He wanted her. Period.

After tomorrow she'd be out of his life for good. He'd see to it. All they had was tonight.

And Brock planned on using his time wisely.

After their first climax together, Brock rolled onto his back, his body coated with a thin sheen of perspiration from the heat they'd created. He glanced at Vanessa, whose skin glowed with the aftermath of lovemaking.

She was so beautiful. At times he thought her vulnerable and innocent. He shook his head at the ridiculous notion that Vanessa could be either.

She lifted her head from the bed and charmed him with a pretty smile. "What are you shaking your head at?"

Brock inhaled. He'd tell her half the truth. "You. You're not what I expected."

She answered quietly, tracing a finger around his mouth. "Neither are you, sweetheart."

Brock stared at her. It was the first time she'd used an endearment with him. Her tone was sweet and sincere, which destroyed him inside.

She'd tried to make a fool of him, yet Brock couldn't think past the melodic softness of her voice when she called him *sweetheart.*

"Ready for round two?" he asked, fully aroused again.

Vanessa grinned and stroked his thick erection. "Ready. But one of us is bound to get knocked out sooner or later."

Brock groaned. "Later. Much later."

She climbed on top of him and straddled his thighs. Without hesitation, she lowered herself down and he jammed his eyes shut briefly from the exquisite sensation of Vanessa taking him in and riding him with purposeful thrusts.

He held her at the beautiful arch of her back and watched her make love to him, her head thrown back, her silvery tresses flowing.

He knew when her body couldn't take another second. He felt her tighten, the constriction pulsing around him and witnessed the look of sheer tortured pleasure on her face when her body released.

Brock let her ride it out until she was sated and damp. Then he held her hips and thrust into her once, twice. It was all he'd needed, her mind-blowing climax enough of a rush to satisfy his own.

She rested against him, her breasts crushing against his chest and Brock didn't think life got any better than this.

Sex surely didn't.

He held her until she fell asleep, then he succumbed, banishing any disturbing thoughts from entering his mind.

There was a chill in the room when Vanessa woke up. She rolled over to find Brock gone from the bed. Flashes of last night entered her sleep-induced mind. They'd made love three times during the night and each time had been more thrilling, more intimate than the time before. She smiled, remembering. Her body ached from Brock's thorough lovemaking.

Vanessa knew she was a goner.

She'd fallen head over heels in love.

She nibbled on her lower lip, more confused than ever.

What now?

She rose and tossed on her panties and bra, then

went in search of Brock. She found him standing by the window in the main parlor looking out at the bay, sipping whiskey.

Whiskey at seven in the morning?

Bone-chilling fear swept over her. "Brock?"

He turned and his face was an unreadable mask. For a moment, when his eyes flickered over her body, she noted a quick flash of the man who'd made love to her last night. Then as quickly as it had come, it was gone.

"You like sex, don't you, Vanessa?"

"Sex?" What kind of question was that? "Yes, with the right man. Of course."

He nodded and finished the tumbler full of whiskey in one gulp. "The right man? Hell, I'd hate to see what you'd do if you were with the *wrong* man."

Confused, Vanessa shook her head several times. "What are you talking about?"

Brock slammed his glass tumbler down and she jumped. "I know who you are, Vanessa. I know how you set out to sabotage my hotel. I know everything."

Vanessa blinked. Then gasped and took a step back, suddenly feeling vulnerable in her half-naked state.

She saw a man's dinner jacket lying over the sofa and put it on, her heart racing like mad.

Brock knew? How had he found out?

Her stomach squeezed tight.

Before she could formulate her thoughts, he approached her. "Was having sex with me your way of distracting me from the truth?" he asked, his jaw tight, his lips even tighter.

She couldn't believe the accusation. "Me? You're accusing *me* of using *you* for sex?" Suddenly, Vanessa's temper flared. "That's rich, Brock. You're the one who charms innocent young girls then drops them like hot potatoes, breaking their hearts!"

Brock's face evened to a placid expression. "You're confusing me with someone else, babe."

"No, you broke my sister's heart. You hurt her badly, Brock. You didn't give a damn about it either. She told me all about how you dumped her for another woman. *Melody Applegate?* Or do you even remember her?"

"I remember her."

"So you admit it!"

"I dated her for half a minute. I don't know what she told you, but she was a sweet kid and we parted as friends."

"You nearly destroyed her! She's been crying and distraught ever since."

"Wrong. Take it up with her. As of right now, you'll have plenty of opportunity. You're fired, Vanessa. I want you off Tempest property before noon."

Vanessa gasped again. She should have expected this, but she'd never been fired before and it stung. Raw emotion racked her system, the pain twisting in her gut. "I hate you."

He shrugged. "I know. I've known it all along, even

when you were making love to me until I could barely take my next breath."

Vanessa slapped his face.

But it didn't affect him. He spoke with calm resolve. "You set out to destroy me, didn't you? How stupid did you think I was? After your first few attempts, I was on to you. Didn't you think it odd that all of your attempts failed after the first few? I have to admit, the geckos were a stroke of genius. You're entertaining, Vanessa. I'll give you that. Your level of deceit amazes me."

Vanessa's lips trembled. She'd been taken for a fool. And he'd been basking in her failures, enjoying every minute of it. The bonus and last night's party was a calculated ruse. Brock had secured his payback. He must be so proud of himself.

The ache of it went straight to her heart.

"Did you really think I'd stand by and let you ruin my mother's and brother's wedding? Every plan you've made on their behalf has been changed."

She shook uncontrollably. Tears stung her eyes. Brock obviously thought her lower than a snake. "No," she said, shaking her head. "I wouldn't do that. I couldn't."

His eyes narrowed. "And why should I believe that?"

Vanessa wanted to defend herself, to tell him she had limits. The problems she had with him didn't overlap into his family. She had nothing against them.

She couldn't bring herself to ruin a widow's new marriage, or a brother who had done nothing to her. But she feared her pleas would go on deaf ears. He had his mind made up about her.

Brock watched her discomfort, his gaze flowing over her as if memorizing her every move. "Go," he demanded, his voice filled with regret.

Vanessa didn't want to leave this way. She wanted to know the truth. What had gone on between Brock and her sister?

"Go," he repeated, his voice firm but quiet. "Before I bring you up on charges."

Shocked, a surprised gasp tumbled out. "Are you threatening to go to the police?"

"I have a right."

"You are a bastard, aren't you?"

"I protect what's mine, Vanessa."

Brock walked out of the room and onto the deck.

By the time she dressed and left the yacht, he was nowhere in sight.

Tears streamed down her face the whole time Vanessa packed up her clothes from the condo. She couldn't control her sobs as she returned the keys to the manager and only contained her crying long enough to turn in her leased MINI Cooper before she broke out in another pitiful bout of sobbing.

She didn't have the heart to face Lucy or Akamu, her new dear friends who had been so kind to her when she'd come to the island. Bolstering her nerve and momentarily quieting her tears, she'd placed voice mail messages on their cell phones—the coward's way out—to let them know that something had come up at home and she had to leave immediately. She fully planned on speaking with them personally, once she got this whole mess straightened out.

Her thoughts turned to Melody. Her sister hadn't answered her phone calls and she couldn't reach her on her cell either. "Melly, where are you?"

She sniffled, her eyes burning from crying as she rode in the cab to the airport. Her sister was an adult, but Vanessa still worried about her. "I'm on my way home," she whispered to the deaf walls of the taxi as she passed palms and sugarcane fields, leaving the ocean behind.

Vanessa watched the island become nothing more than a speck of sand from high above in the airplane. She stifled sobs, holding tissues to her nose, trying not to garner attention from the other passengers. Yet when she dared to peek around the cabin, she met with sympathetic eyes.

Melody will straighten this all out, she told herself. Yet Brock had been so convincing that he knew nothing about Melody's heartache. He'd lied to her before. He'd fooled her. Made love to her. She'd like to believe at least that part was honest. It had been for her. Making love to Brock hadn't been part of the plan, though he'd accused her of it. He'd accused her of many things and some were true. But the most important of his accusations about her were wrong. She hadn't used sex to throw him off track about her sabotage. And she wouldn't have ever compromised his family's wedding plans.

It hurt her deeply that he would think it. Yet she couldn't blame him entirely. She'd given him ample reason to believe the very worst about her.

A sob escaped and she sucked in oxygen, making noises that had passengers turning their heads.

Once she landed in New Orleans, she headed straight for Melody's apartment. Her tears gone, only a pitiful ache remained in her gut. Grateful they shared keys to each other's apartments, she turned the key in the lock and entered. Her shoulders slumped and her limbs went limp as every ounce of her body surrendered to exhaustion.

Melody jumped up from the sofa, wearing a smile beaming from ear to ear. "Vanny, what are you doing here?"

"I, uh…" Vanessa knew a moment of joy, seeing her sister looking healthy and fit, then glanced past her to the sofa to find Melody had company. She directed her attention back at her sister. "It's…a long story."

"Never mind. Tell me later." Melody's smile broadened and as her red hair caught the afternoon light, she positively glowed. "I have the best news!"

Vanessa blinked. The man sitting on the sofa stood to his full six-foot frame and sent her a sheepish smile.

She recognized him. She turned to her sister, curious. Warning bells rang out in her head. "What news?"

Melody stuck her left hand in Vanessa's face and wiggled her fingers. "I'm engaged!"

...

...

...

...

...

...

Ten

Vanessa stared at Melody in shock. "Excuse me. What?" It took her a full five seconds to wrap her mind around what'd she'd heard. "You're *engaged?*"

"Yes!" Melody could barely contain her joy. She bobbed up and down again like a child who'd won a big prize.

Vanessa's eye twitched. Lord, she hadn't twitched like that since she'd found her college boyfriend playing doctor with her best friend.

"You remember Ryan Gains."

Ryan stood beside Melody, wrapping an arm around her shoulder. "Hi, Vanessa. It's been a long time."

"Ryan," she said, trying to sort this out. "I remember you." Vanessa scratched her head, slanted him a look and pursed her lips. To Vanessa's knowledge, the high school football star had dated her sister briefly in their senior year. Melody had the biggest crush on him. "Didn't you marry right out of high school?"

"He's divorced now," Melody explained.

Vanessa shot Melody a stare.

"Don't look at me like that. I didn't have anything to do with the break up."

Vanessa sucked oxygen into her lungs. None of this seemed real. She felt like she'd been tossed into a nightmarish episode of the *Twilight Zone*. "Ryan, would you give me some time alone with my sister?"

Ryan glanced at Melody, then nodded. "Sure, I've got to get back to Tempest anyway." He turned to Melody. "Bye, honey." He took her into his arms and laid a thirty-second kiss on her. Melody nearly swooned watching him walk out the door.

"You didn't even congratulate us," Melody complained once she focused on Vanessa again. She flopped onto the sofa.

"Congratulate you?" Vanessa took a seat, fearful that what would come next would buckle her knees anyway. "I thought you were heartbroken! Destroyed. Devastated."

"Gosh, Vanny. You sound like you're sorry I'm not."

"Don't be ridiculous. I just want the truth. And what's this about Ryan getting back to Tempest?"

"He works there. He was promoted to hotel manager. When Brock left, the chain of command changed."

"Brock?" Vanessa's heart surged, hearing his name. "I thought you were madly in love with him. I thought Brock was the only man for you."

"Oh, that." Melody waved her off. "That was nothing."

"Nothing, you cried your heart out for days! My God, I thought you were suicidal at one point. That's all I heard from you. 'Brock destroyed me. I'll never love again. I can't go on without him.'"

Melody's gaze darted away. She avoided eye contact. Vanessa's blood ran cold. Dread coursed through her system.

"It was never about Brock," Melody confessed on a quiet whisper.

Oh, God.

"Explain, Melly. Look me in the eye and explain."

Melody made eye contact. "Well, you know how you're always babying me? Not that I don't love you too, Vanny, but I'm old enough now to make my own decisions."

"And mistakes."

"There, you see!" Melody nearly jumped out of her seat. "You've got no faith in me."

Vanessa's eye went on a twitching field day. She rubbed the corners of her temples to calm down. "We'll argue that point later. Go on."

"Well, I've been in love with Ryan for years. Ever since high school. I knew you'd never approve, so I kept quiet, but I've been pining away for him all these years. It's the real thing, Vanny. Trust me."

Vanessa made a grunting sound.

"I saw him every day at the hotel. We'd talk casually but when I found out he was getting a divorce, I'm sorry to say I was thrilled. I made up my mind I wasn't going to let him get away this time. I could tell he liked me. He'd come into the gift shop to browse around almost daily. We flirted for weeks. And, oh, Vanny, every day I'd pray he'd ask me out. And then one day he did. We dated for a few weeks, the *best* weeks of my life. Then he stopped asking me out."

Vanessa's heart landed in her stomach. Melody painted a far different picture than what she had originally been told. She feared where this confession would take her. And she was furious with Melody on so many levels right now, all she could do was sit back and listen as her nerves tightened under her skin.

"I was beside myself. I knew he had feelings for me. We connected. We enjoyed being with each other. I was totally in love with him and had to do something. Ryan needed a good nudge."

Vanessa closed her eyes. Oh, no. "That's where Brock came in."

"Yes, Brock was handsome and rich and a ladies' man. I thought going out with him would make Ryan jealous. You know how fast hotel gossip spreads. I was desperate, Vanny. I was seriously in love and, well, a girl has to do something crazy to get her man, doesn't she?"

Vanessa bit her lip so hard she was surprised blood didn't spurt out.

"I dated Brock for a few weeks. I was so crazy in love, and even more desperate now, because Ryan didn't react at all. He stopped coming by the shop. That's when I fell apart."

"Fell apart, like claiming your life was over? That you'd never love again." Vanessa's nerves were at the breaking point. But she had to hear it all from Melody before she allowed herself the luxury. "That he ruined you for all other men?"

Melody glanced away. "Yeah, but I felt all those things. I really did. I just couldn't admit to you that I'd pined away for a married man for seven years. I had enough on my plate and I didn't want to hear your lectures. I felt humiliated that he'd rejected me. Ryan's the one, Vanessa. A girl just knows those things."

The way Brock is the one for you.

Vanessa bounded up from her seat fearing that thought true. She paced the floor. "Finish, Melody. I want it all."

"Well, uh. I was devastated if you remember."

Vanessa sucked in oxygen. She'd remembered.

"Nothing worked with Ryan and I thought I'd lost him again. Forever!"

Melody was such a drama queen. Vanessa rolled her

eyes. "So what did you do to change his mind?" Then it struck her. The thought had never occurred to her before. "Are you pregnant?"

"I wish!" Then she smiled. "Someday. Ryan wants children."

"What, then?"

"I took a good piece of advice. Thanks to Brock."

"What on earth did he say?"

"He came to see me, to let me down gently, I think. It was a gentlemanly thing to do. We'd never...uh, you know, not even close. I broke down crying and confessed my story about Ryan. Anyway, he saw how devastated I was. He was very sweet and sympathetic. He told me to go to Ryan and tell him the truth. He told me men don't like women who play games. That if there's anything real there, Ryan would come around. But most importantly, a man wants a woman to be up front and honest."

Vanessa braced her hands on the back of the sofa to steady herself. "Oh, God."

"After weeks of crying and feeling hurt and rejected, I finally got up the courage to tell Ryan the truth. And just like Brock said, he appreciated my confession. He said he was gun-shy after the divorce. It all happened so fast between us that he needed more time so he backed off. But then, just a few days ago, he told me how much he loved me and that he wanted a life with me. And I knew everything would work out."

Looking at Melody's dreamy expression sparked Vanessa's anger. "You lied to me."

"I know. I had to."

"No, you didn't have to! You have no idea what you've done!"

"Vanny, calm down. It all worked out."

Tears sprung from Vanessa's eyes. "No, it didn't all work out! Your lies have cost me, Melody."

Vanessa ached inside from gnawing guilt. Brock had been innocent of any wrongdoing. Her stomach squeezed tight thinking of the accusations she'd tossed at him. The pain she'd caused him. The deception and lies she'd told that she'd justified unequivocally in her mind. All of it came crashing down on her, the weight a heavy burden to bear.

She loved Brock Tyler.

And he'd threatened to have her arrested.

Vanessa looked Melody in the eyes and launched into her story, making her foolish sister listen as she poured out what was left of her heart.

If confession was good for the soul then Vanessa's soul went through a superdeluxe cleansing. She'd called Akamu first and confessed everything she'd done, explaining her motivation without defending her position. She'd been wrong and she admitted it. Surprise registered briefly when Akamu confessed he'd known of her deception, too. She supposed Brock had to have an accomplice in his retaliation.

Vanessa apologized until the words wouldn't come anymore. Akamu said he understood and that the person she should be apologizing to was Brock. Before hanging up the phone, they decided to put the past behind them. Vanessa was certain and relieved that she and Akamu would remain friends.

Next she called Lucy, explained the situation and begged her forgiveness. Lucy surprised her most of all. "You're my hero, Vanessa."

"I don't feel like a hero at all."

"Listen, you made a mistake, but your motivation was dead-on. And you had the guts to follow through on your plan. I thought I was the gutsy one!"

Vanessa allowed herself a small smile. "You are. Only you don't make a fool of yourself when you think you have *right* on your side. I went full steam ahead, but not without guilt, Lucy. I want you to know that I never meant to deceive or hurt you. I just never thought I'd make such wonderful friends on the island."

"You're still my friend, Vanessa. And that means I can tell you a thing or two. First, you need to come back here and ask for Brock's forgiveness. It's been almost a week since you left and our boss has been immersing himself in work, not speaking to anyone but Akamu. He goes out on his yacht alone every night. Which makes our lives tough, since he's pulled a few of us in to helping with the double wedding."

"It's in a few days, right?"

"No, that's been changed."

"Oh, so he meant what he said. He's basically undone everything I did for the wedding, including changing the date."

Lucy didn't acknowledge what Vanessa knew for fact. "Did you know he threatened to have me arrested?"

"He wouldn't do that. Bad for business."

"That's what Akamu said!"

Lucy chuckled. "Sorry, but it's true. Akamu has been pressuring him to hire a new event planner. We need help around here. But the boss won't consider it. He only stares out the office window and shakes his head whenever Akamu brings it up."

"I've ruined him for event planners," Vanessa said sourly. "That's all I meant to him."

"I think you meant more than that…a lot more. Do you love him?"

Vanessa nibbled on her lip.

"Do you?"

"Yes," Vanessa said finally, with no joy. Shouldn't a person have joy in their heart when they admit to falling in love? "But I'm sure he hates me. He'd never trust me again. I know I tried some awful things, but he *believed* I'd ruin his family's double wedding. There's nothing I can do to change his mind."

"Now that's *not* the determined friend I know. You're gutsy, remember? And quite determined when you need to be."

Vanessa sighed into the phone. "Not anymore. I've learned my lesson."

"You'll always have my friendship, Vanessa, but if you want to maintain hero-status in my eyes, you need to do something. You can't just give up!"

"I treasure your friendship, Lucy. But I'm not a hero. I'm furious with Melody for lying to me, yet I did the same thing to people I cared about." Vanessa's eyes misted and she held back tears. She was through crying outwardly, but inside she bled with infinite remorse. "I played a dangerous game and I lost."

The next day, Melody barged into the guest bedroom she'd offered Vanessa for the time being. She didn't have a job or a place to stay. Her own apartment five miles away was rented out until summer. "When are you gonna stop moping?"

"I'm not moping," Vanessa defended, lying sideways on the bed. "I'm job searching." She flipped the newspaper to the want ads and pretended interest.

"I've never seen you like this," Melody said.

"I've never been in this position before. Hmmm, I can't seem to find 'saboteur' in any job description."

"Cut it out, Vanny. You're scaring me. You've always been the dependable one."

Vanessa shook her head with wry amusement. "I babied you. Mothered you until I smothered you. I was furious with you a few days ago, but now I've had time to reflect. I understand why you lied to me. I probably would have lied to me."

Melody sat down on the bed. "Oh, no, Vanessa. You didn't baby me too much. I needed you. When Mom got really bad, I was still young and you were there, showing me that you cared. You have no idea how much that meant to me. You're my big half sister but you always were my whole sister in every way. I took you for granted and I realize, now that I'm older, how much you sacrificed for me. I love you so much for being exactly who you are. A sister who'd go to battle for me, when she thinks I've been wronged."

Vanessa sat up on the bed and slanted her sister a look. "Really?"

Melody nodded. "Really and truly."

"Thank you," Vanessa said quietly.

Melody reached out and took Vanessa's hand. "I've learned not to play games with people's emotions. Honesty works. And if it doesn't, then you gave it your best shot."

"Why do I think a lecture is coming?" Vanessa asked.

Melody smiled wisely. "Because you're the expert on giving them. Now it's my turn. Be still. Be quiet and listen to me."

"Gosh, now you're repeating my words."

"Heaven knows I've heard them so many times, they're ingrained in my head. Now, about Brock Tyler..."

* * *

The view from his rental house was breathtaking.
Brock stood out on the backyard cliff overlooking the
Pacific Ocean with a vodka tonic in one hand and a cell
phone in the other. He had calls to make, business to
conduct, but today he wasn't in the mood.

Instead he stared down at the blue waters cast
somewhat murky by gray clouds overhead, lost in
thought. He hadn't really planned on business calls
when he took his phone out of his pocket. No, he'd
been tempted to call Vanessa Dupree.

But he couldn't bring himself to speak to her by
phone. He wasn't ready to forgive her. He might never
be ready. He feared he'd fumble his words and end up
arguing with her again. The anger hadn't yet faded, but
something else was there, too, and that something had
kept him from sleep every night since she'd left.

Vanessa had him fooled and not too many people
had ever accomplished that with him. He thought he
knew her. He thought, now here's a real woman, someone he wanted to know on every level. When he'd
been with her, fleeting thoughts entered his mind of
settling down, of caving in and abandoning bachelor-
hood like his brothers Evan and Trent and his best
friend, Code.

Thoughts of Vanessa tormented him since he
ordered her off his property. He couldn't shake her.
Brock slipped his phone back in his pocket, writing off
any idea of calling her, and sipped his drink. The

strong liquor, more vodka than tonic, burned his throat and dulled his senses, but nothing washed Vanessa's image from his mind. She'd tried to ruin him, and yet when he compared her to the other women he'd known in his life, she always came out on top.

Hell, he was a fool and an idiot.

Because, still with all she'd done, he had to admire her loyalty to her sister. Vanessa thought Melody had been wronged and she went full steam ahead with her plan to exact her revenge. Brock understood that in an elemental way. He'd do anything for his brothers.

The clouds drew closer to shore, marring the last burst of sunlight on the horizon and putting a chill in the air. The weather matched his mood.

Stormy.

Brock polished off his drink and sought his nightly escape on the *Rebecca*. Sailing off at sunset brought him clarity, and he needed that right now. His mind rattled with unease. Was letting Vanessa go in his best interests? Everything inside him pushed and pulled. He wanted to go after her.

He missed her like hell.

"A girl has to do something crazy to get her man, doesn't she?" Vanessa repeated her sister's words in a whisper as she secretly slipped onto the *Rebecca*.

You can't just give up. Lucy's advice rang in her head.

If this didn't work, she'd blame both of them for planting the seeds.

Of course, if she were really brave, she'd confront Brock face-to-face in his office, or at his home. Instead, she chose to stow away on his yacht where he couldn't turn her away.

He could throw her overboard, though. The image passed in her head and she immediately discounted it. Brock wouldn't do that.

That would be terrible for business.

"You love him. Tell him, Vanessa," she said, sneaking into the bedroom where they'd made love. "Tell him you're sorry you misjudged him."

Vanessa took her shoes off and waited.

It had been a horrific day. She'd been taken out of the line at the airport for a security check and if that hadn't been enough, her flight had been delayed. The airplane had been kept on the runway for thirty minutes before allowing them clearance for takeoff. When they'd finally landed, she'd discovered her luggage had been lost.

Vanessa took everything in stride. She was determined to see this through and find out, once and for all, if she'd destroyed any chance she'd had for happiness with Brock.

She glanced at her watch. She was still on Louisiana time, but she figured it was past seven here, since the sun had already set and there was a chill in the air. She hadn't seen Lucy yet. She hadn't told a soul her plan. All Melody knew was that she was heading back to Maui to talk with Brock.

Vanessa shivered as she sat in the dark on the bed. She pulled up a blanket and wrapped it around herself. She closed her eyes just to rest them a little and laid her head back.

The boat swayed and stirred restlessly and Vanessa popped her eyes open, realizing they were out to sea. She must have fallen asleep.

Which meant that if they were moving, Brock was on board. Vanessa rose and almost lost her footing. The boat rocked back and forth. Rain pelted down, the sky dark and dismal from what she could see out the window.

She made her way carefully to the deck and came face-to-face with Brock, dripping wet, helping his crew stow away equipment. He took one look at her and cursed.

"Damn it, Vanessa. What the hell are you doing here?"

He didn't give her time to answer. He grabbed her arm and led her to his room. "There's a hurricane out at sea. We're getting hit with a big storm. Stay down here. I'll be back later."

With that, he left and Vanessa shivered. Not from the cold. Not from the storm they'd encountered. But by Brock's chilling tone. It was clear to her she'd made a big mistake coming here and now there was no escape. She'd have to wait out the storm and hope she'd be left with some semblance of dignity when they made it back to shore.

She ached inside, the pain the worst she'd ever felt in her life. She'd lost a really good man, and she may never recover. Brock's fierce expression told her all she needed to know. She experienced the same hollow hurt that Melody felt when Ryan had rejected her. She understood better now the devastating loss.

Waves crashed and the boat rocked violently. Vanessa's fear intensified. She'd been thrown a few times, so she laid down again, hugged the bedpost for support, closed her eyes and waited for the storm to end.

The next time Vanessa opened her eyes, she found Brock beside her, his warmth soothing her, his arm draped around her body. She blinked and thought she was dreaming.

"Hi," he said, gazing at her softly. "We're out of danger and almost back to Tranquility Bay."

Vanessa swallowed and nodded. Cushioned by his strong capable arms and looking into his seriously gorgeous face, she could think of worse disasters. "Will you have me arrested for breaking and entering?"

Brock smiled and traced the corners of her mouth with a finger. "That depends. Why are you here?"

She turned to her side to face him fully. "To ask for your forgiveness. I've misjudged you. Melody told me everything. She lied to me, Brock, and made me think awful things about you. I know that doesn't justify what I did and I don't know how to apologize enough. I'm probably the last person you want to see right—"

"Wrong," he said firmly. "When I saw you here, my heart nearly flew out of my chest. My feelings for you were cemented when you came on deck during the storm. I thought you might get hurt. Or tossed overboard. I couldn't stand anything happening to you. Not on my watch. Remember, I protect what's mine." He rose from the bed. "Wait here."

He left her cold and curious. When he returned, he held an orchid. He laid down on the bed again and placed the light purple flower behind her left ear. "Consider yourself taken, but not just for tonight this time, Vanessa. I'm in love with you."

Hope swelled in her heart. "I'm in love with you, too."

"I want you in my life forever."

"I want that, too…so much." Then Vanessa shook her head. "But I don't understand why you would."

"For sex, why else?" A mischievous gleam entered his eyes and then he kissed her deeply before she could react. "Lucy and Akamu came to me tonight. They pleaded your case but, honey, they didn't have to. You weren't the only guilty party. I played along and I'm sorry for lying to you. I was just as deceitful as you were. I could have confronted you when I first found out what you were doing, but I chose to play your game and drag it out. I hope you can forgive me."

"I do forgive you."

Brock sighed and admitted, "I booked a trip to the mainland to see you before they spoke with me. I had to know if I was crazy falling in love with a woman who would see me ruined."

"But it was a mistake! And I'm so sorry."

"How sorry?"

"Very, very sorry."

"Sorry enough to come to the double wedding with me as my fiancée?"

"Oh, yes," she answered, breathless. "I would love to."

"And no more games?" he asked softly.

"I promise, the only games I'll play from now on will be in bed with you."

Brock grinned. "I can wrap my mind around that. You know, I'll have to thank Melody next time I see her."

"You can't possibly be glad she lied about you."

"I am. If she hadn't made up that crazy story, you wouldn't have come to the island. And we wouldn't have met."

"Even after all the trouble I caused you? I was such a—"

Brock put a finger to her mouth, stopping her sentiment. "You were just what I needed—a beautiful, smart, determined *challenge*. The hardest thing I've ever done was to throw you off Tempest property. All I wanted was to love you."

Joy warmed her heart. "Really? That's sweet."

"I'm a sweet guy, when given the chance. So it's a date. You and me, forever?"

"It's a date, sweetheart," she replied, kissing him softly. "I'm crazy in love with you."

Brock relaxed against the bed and released a big sigh. "That's a relief." He nuzzled her throat and came up over her on the bed, another teasing glint entering his eyes. "A really good event planner is hard to find."

Epilogue

"Geckos? There are geckos roaming the grounds again?"

Brock glanced around the Garden Pavilion where his mother and Matthew were speaking vows. His brother Trent and his fiancée, Julia, were standing next to them.

"Don't look at me," Vanessa whispered, innocently. "I learned my lesson."

"It's taken care of, boss," Akamu said quietly. "Willie Benton has been collecting them for a week and they got loose on the property."

"Got loose? Or were let out?" Their young hotel guest had a reputation for making mischief.

Akamu shrugged. "Don't know. There must have been about three dozen running around. Security has them all rounded up."

Brock nodded and glanced at his beautiful fiancée. Soon they'd be saying their vows and Brock couldn't wait. He took her hand and together they watched the weddings take place without a hitch.

Sarah Rose, famous country singer and now his best friend, Code's, wife sang sweet ballads throughout the ceremony, looking happily pregnant. Code stood beside her with pride.

Evan and Laney stood as best man and maid of honor, and little John Charles Tyler Junior sat in his stroller, the youngest ever Tempest Maui ring bearer.

The ceremony ended amid a round of applause from family and friends as the newly married couples made their way down the aisle.

Afterward, the Tylers got together for a brief meeting of the minds. Brock gave a toast then took Vanessa in his arms. "I'm gracefully bowing out of the competition with Trent even though I'm certain I'm the winner."

He winked at his fiancée and joy filled his heart enough to last an eternity. No more games for him either. He considered himself a winner, just by loving Vanessa.

"Wait a minute," Trent said, holding Julia's hand. "You beat me to the punch, brother. I was planning on opting out of the competition." He and Julia exchanged loving glances. "Tempest West is thriving and I'm sure *I'm* the winner, but it's not important now."

Brock squeezed Vanessa's shoulder, bringing her closer. "So I'm out and you're out."

They all turned to Evan, who held his new son with his wife Laney looking on. "You guys are no fun anymore."

Brock glanced at Trent and when he nodded, Brock stepped up. "Trent and I agree that Dad's T-Bird should go to you, Evan."

Rebecca stood with tears in her eyes, beside her new husband, Matthew. "I think that's fair."

When Evan balked, Brock went on. "For your son. He's the first Tyler heir—the beginning of a new generation. It's fitting that John Charles gets the car when he's old enough."

"Like when he's thirty," Laney said seriously and everyone laughed.

Evan peered lovingly at the son he held in his arms. "Did you hear that? You're not even one yet and you've got your first set of wheels already. Say thank-you to your uncles."

And John Charles Tyler Junior promptly cooed.

* * * * *

Desire™

FROM PLAYBOY TO PAPA! by Leanne Banks

Surprised to learn he has a son, Rafe demands the child live with him and he suggests his ex-lover's sister comes too…as his wife.

TEMPTING THE TEXAS TYCOON by Sara Orwig

Noah will receive five million dollars if he marries within the year—and a sexy business rival proves perfect…

BOSSMAN'S BABY SCANDAL by Catherine Mann

What's an executive to do when his one-night stand is pregnant and his new client hates scandal?

EXECUTIVE'S PREGNANCY ULTIMATUM by Emilie Rose

Flynn Maddox thought he was over his ex-wife until he learned they were still married—and that she was trying to have his baby!

Mini-series – Kings of the Boardroom

CLAIMING HIS BOUGHT BRIDE by Rachel Bailey

To meet the terms of his inheritance, Damon convinces Lily to marry him. But he plans to seduce her into being more than his wife on paper.

SEDUCING THE ENEMY'S DAUGHTER by Jules Bennett

She was the enemy's daughter. Business magnate Brady Stone set out to seduce corporate secrets from her, but was she worth more to him than his revenge?

On sale from 17th December 2010
Don't miss out!

"Did you say I won almost two million dollars?"

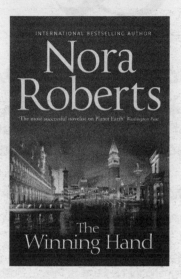

2 FREE BOOKS
AND A SURPRISE GIFT

We would like to take this opportunity to thank you for reading this Mills & Boon® book by offering you the chance to take TWO more specially selected books from the Desire™ 2-in-1 series absolutely FREE! We're also making this offer to introduce you to the benefits of the Mills & Boon® Book Club™—

- **FREE home delivery**
- **FREE gifts and competitions**
- **FREE monthly Newsletter**
- **Exclusive Mills & Boon Book Club offers**
- **Books available before they're in the shops**

Accepting these FREE books and gift places you under no obligation to buy, you may cancel at any time, even after receiving your free books. Simply complete your details below and return the entire page to the address below. You don't even need a stamp!

YES Please send me 2 free Desire stories in a 2-in-1 volume and a surprise gift. I understand that unless you hear from me, I will receive 2 superb new 2-in-1 books every month for just £5.30 each, postage and packing free. I am under no obligation to purchase any books and may cancel my subscription at any time. The free books and gift will be mine to keep in any case.

Ms/Mrs/Miss/Mr _____ Initials _____

Surname _____

Address _____

_____

_____ Postcode _____

E-mail_____

Send this whole page to: Mills & Boon Book Club, Free Book Offer, FREEPOST NAT 10298, Richmond, TW9 1BR